THINKWAVE

The Battle to Keep All Worlds Free

Book 1: The Clouds of Ecclon

R Duncan Williams

ISBN: 1500724785
ISBN 13: 9781500724788
Library of Congress Control Number: 2014913911
CreateSpace Independent Publishing Platform
North Charleston, South Carolina

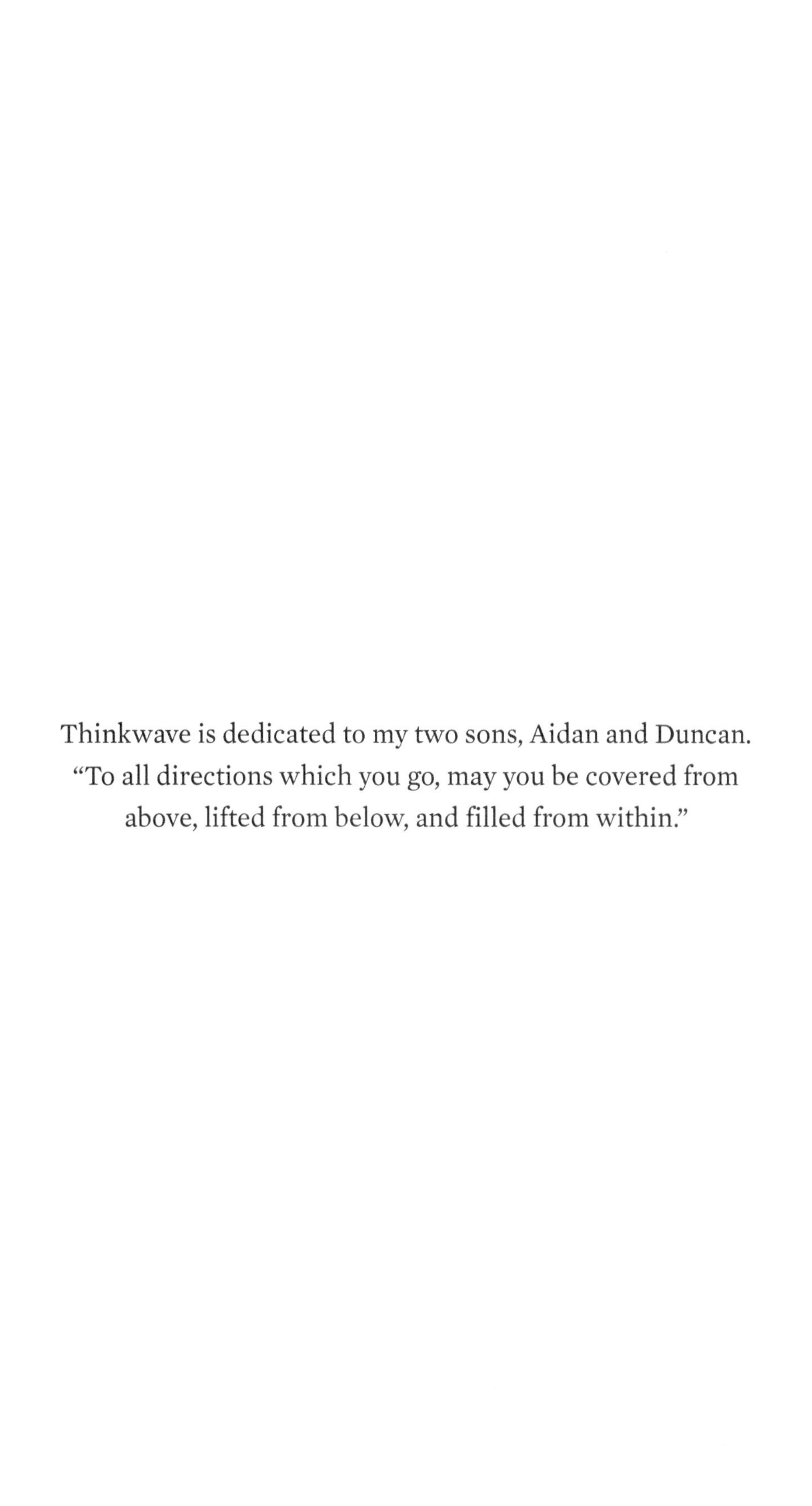

Thinkwave is dedicated to my two sons, Aidan and Duncan.
"To all directions which you go, may you be covered from above, lifted from below, and filled from within."

ACKNOWLEDGEMENTS

My idea for a book would have remained a mere idea had it not been for the effort and support of others. With deepest gratitude, I would like to thank the following individuals for their help:

Dan Peterson for his persistence in pushing me to write; Mit, Deana, Sabrina, and McKenzie Morgan, whose early support and excitement about the book meant more to me than they will ever know; My loving wife, Terri Williams, who patiently sanded, smoothed, and polished many of my words and phrases; Paul Schultz for his support and optimistic enthusiasm for the project; Scott Moneyhon, whose wisdom, counsel, and encouragement kept me writing and rewriting when I felt like giving up; Sarah Scott for her assistance in editing and wonderful suggestions; and Margie Morgan, whose hawk-like eyes caught so many of my goofs and helped me chuckle at myself.

PROLOGUE

A curious hunger dilated the animal's pupils. Frustrated energy rippled through every muscle, desperately seeking escape. He wanted to bolt, to let loose pent-up power, to run free. But not yet. He had to wait. With paper-thin patience, he readied himself to receive instruction and command.

The animal's eyes met those of his master. Engaged and locked. The mission was conveyed, not through spoken word but silent thought. The animal excitedly whined. How could he not? This was precisely what he was created for.

Words were finally spoken, but only two: "Retrieve him!"

The animal streaked forward in an indigo flash. In seconds his body was stretched and gone. Vanished.

His master looked to the failing light in the sky. There wasn't much time. He knew the plan was outlandish, but what choice did he have? He would travel to the open plains on the far side of the gorge and wait for the animal's return. If he were successful, he wouldn't be alone. The weapon would be with him. He would bring back the boy.

ECCLON

1

There is much happening in the world today that very few people notice. This has nothing to do with their eyesight, but rather the result of their hectic daily schedules. Frantically scurrying from one activity to another, they have little time to rest and reflect on their lives and the world.

But this has not always been the case. In the not-too-distant past, the young and old alike found great fulfillment in quieting themselves and experiencing the peaceful exhilaration of deep thought. It was not uncommon, in fact, for a person to let a particular thought lead to another particular thought, and this in turn lead to another particular thought, and so on for countless hours.

Harvey George was born when pondering for any length of time was losing its place as a laudable habit of the mind. Many would, no doubt, see this as a frittering away of an important commodity that could be used for something more productive, such as watching television. In Harvey's house, the only television that was still operational was in his mother's bedroom. The one in the family room hadn't functioned since Harvey's curiosity had gotten the better of him, and he had dissected it in hopes of figuring out how it worked.

At times, shades of sadness shadowed Harvey's young world. The warmth from a loving and nurturing family was cooled and grayed by days of loneliness in which Harvey had no one but his thoughts for companions.

Harvey's father was a salesman for the Meadowland Paper Company, which supplied many of the schools and businesses of the southeastern United States with paper products, primarily toilet paper. His dad always made it a point, only seconds after meeting someone new, to inform him or her of the incredible job security that was available in toilet paper sales.

"If I've said it once, I've said it a thousand times, there's just no safer job to have, especially in a shaky economy, than toilet paper. Why it's a basic necessity! I would chalk it up with air and water. And I'll tell you another thing, when times get financially tight for a family, you'll see computers and televisions go by the wayside long before toilet paper holders spin empty."

It was mortifyingly embarrassing for Harvey whenever his father began to champion the merits of the consumable waste product industry. The occasions for him to be mortified, however, were becoming less familiar with one another, as the demands of his father's sales job increased.

Being responsible for all the major accounts in his tri-state territory, his father was on the road during the week, drumming up new business and keeping his existing clients well stocked. Unfortunately, when he pulled into the driveway on Friday evenings, the weighty responsibility of his career followed him into the house like an uninvited guest, steamrolling quality time with his family with the demands of its own agenda. So even when his father was physically present at home, he was so consumed with paperwork and tying up loose ends, that the line demarcating the work week from the weekend had all but disappeared.

For the most part, Harvey's mother was bedridden. Numerous doctors had yet to determine the cause of her debilitating weakness and lack of energy. In the end, the consensus of the medical specialists was that she was chronically fatigued but with no apparent cause, a diagnosis that left her where she started, without energy and without much hope. The only way for her to make it through the day was by anchoring herself to her bed for the majority of it.

She wore away the hours primarily by sleeping. When she was awake, she watched classic black and white movies from the 1930's and 40's, a period that she referred to as "the Golden Age of Hollywood". In fact, the reason that she had named her son "Harvey" was because she considered it one of her favorite names from this cinematic age.

Unfortunately, Harvey's peers at school didn't share his mother's affection for the name. To their ears, it was peculiar and foreign. In a sense it was, a name not imported from another country, but another time. The name was so unusual sounding that they reacted in the manner that too many thirteen and fourteen year olds do when encountering something "out of their box"; they made the name the butt of endless, asinine jokes.

On a number of occasions when Harvey walked down the hall, some of the boys hiked their pants up above their bellybuttons and performed their best impression of a decrepit old man. He tried to ignore them, never even giving them a peripheral glance, but this did little to discourage their theatrics. Shuffling behind him, they would cry out in the halting voice of a ninety year-old, "Har, Har, Har, Har, Harrrrveeeey." And no matter how many times they performed their little show, it never failed to light the fire of their own hysterics.

Needless to say, Harvey hated the name. He vowed that when he was out on his own, he would change it to something that blended in so well with the culture that no one would ever give it a second thought.

The movies that his mother watched were interspersed with reruns of television detective shows that she had grown up watching. Harvey didn't particularly enjoy watching television, but spending time with his mom when she was awake meant that he had to, and inadvertently, he actually became quite a fan of classic films and the deductive reasoning powers of many of television's greatest sleuths.

Sadly, there were very few days when his mother was able to get out of bed to do any of those wonderful motherly things that children don't fully appreciate until they become adults. So much of what people solidify into as adults is dependent on what was inscribed in the wet cement of their childhood. Even at the age of thirteen, Harvey was aware of this, and it contributed to his unarticulated desire for a healthy, nurturing family, continually present, both physically and emotionally.

His father's absence, coupled with his mother's illness, made the house feel hollow. To Harvey, whenever he walked through the house, it seemed that each room resounded in a hollow echo, like the sterile crispness of a museum or library interrupted amidst its slumber.

The only consolation and comfort Harvey had were in his thoughts. His ponderings, in time, became almost tangible, his very closest friends with whom he spent hours interacting with on the porch in his backyard. Typically, he began his "Thinks", as he liked to call them, by casting his thoughts into shallow water, often imagining what it would be like to be raised in a different family. This frequently led to him going after weightier speculations which lurked in the greater depths: the meaning of it all, where he came from, where he was going, and the notion of whether there was someone directing this strange play known as life, or if it was all nothing more than a cosmic anomaly, erratically spinning through time for no apparent purpose. These are lofty, philosophical queries even for adults, much less a boy green unto his teenage years. A hardship of the heart, though, often causes one to peel away life's carefree veneer, revealing the harsher realities of existence that invite even the young to ask humanity's most perplexing questions.

Harvey could never imagine nor foresee that his Thinks would ever leave his own head and have an impact on those around him, but in this, he could not have been further from the truth. His thinking had already attracted outside attention and was about to lead Harvey down the road to a most incredible adventure.

Now those who enjoy hours of unstructured thinking know that it is imperative to have a proper perch from which to ponder. For Harvey, this was his grandfather's worn and weathered rocking chair. Long ago the wicker seat had given way to a large hole, but the absence of a seat didn't seem to bother Harvey. Every day after school, he lowered himself down into the wicker crater. He kept his body from falling through the hole by draping his gangly, thirteen-year-old legs over the wooden frame that once supported the wicker seat.

One pleasant spring afternoon, when the air was cloyingly sweet with awakening leaves and blossoms, Harvey arrived home from school to his still and lifeless house. His father was once again on the road, and when he peeked in on his mother, he observed her sleeping soundly. In the background was the dialogue from a classic film about a man who said that his best friend was a six- foot invisible rabbit.

Not wanting to disturb his mother, Harvey quietly began to make his way to the back porch for a long and productive Think in the rocker. On his way outside, he stopped in the kitchen and fished out a sizeable pickle from a large glass container.

One of the television detective shows that his mother watched featured a detective, who, regardless of the weather, always wore a trench coat and was continually puffing on a cigar. It seemed to Harvey that the manipulation of the cigar by his teeth and fingers enhanced the detective's cognitive powers, specifically his uncanny ability to deduce things from the minutest of details.

Harvey settled himself into the rocking chair and launched his mind into the atmosphere of speculative thought. Thinking of the detective, Harvey imagined that he was working a case, not trying to piece together the clues from a crime scene, but unraveling some of the tangles to questions he had about life. To enhance the effect, Harvey imitated the manipulation of the cigar with his pickle.

He gazed at the elderly moss-covered oak trees in the back-yard, thinking of them as ancient sages, gnarled and bent in body, but nimble and brilliant in mind, longing to reveal their deepest secrets to a patient and quiet observer.

2

Harvey's thought on this particular spring day had to do with color inversion. Staring at the azure sky, he began wondering what the world would look like if the blues of the sky above were interchanged with the greens of the plants below. He concluded that it would only appear strange to him if the colors suddenly switched with one another, but if all he had ever known were green skies and blue leaves, then it would be perfectly normal to him, and the notion of there being a blue sky and green leaves would strike him as bizarre and alien.

This thought opened the door to the idea that so much of what humans consider normal is a consequence of the environment into which they are born, and he was about to use this thought as a machete to bushwhack his way into the jungle of undiscovered ponderings, when his pickle fell from his mouth. He bent over to pick it up, remaining hunched over for a few seconds so that he might brush off a pine needle and a few ants that had become stuck to the pickle.

When he sat up again, he was startled to see a huge dog sitting in the middle of his backyard, intently staring at him. It had the size and appearance of a Great Dane, with an enormous, boxy snout, but had the pointy, erect ears of a German Shepherd. Its fur was short-haired, the color of indigo with a silver iridescence, speckled with tiny flecks of white, as if someone had used the animal for a drop cloth while painting. Attached to its hindquarters was a tail, equal in length to that of its body.

The sight of the animal, sitting on his haunches only twenty feet from the deck, startled Harvey so much that he jolted backwards, causing him to fall through the hole in the rocking chair. The edges of the hole were painfully poking into his leg, but he was unable to move, paralyzed by the fear that moving might induce the animal to attack. However, as Harvey continued to stare at the dog, the animal's behavior did little to indicate any malicious intent. Instead, it seemed to be quizzically studying Harvey, curiously tilting its enormous head to the right and left.

Harvey had no idea where the dog had come from. One moment there was nothing but trees and grass in the yard, and three seconds later, the largest dog he had ever seen was casually sitting only twenty feet away.

The dog and the human continued their stare-down for a protracted minute, after which the animal lay down on its stomach and began to pant. Harvey no longer felt like he was being studied; in fact, it seemed that the dog was now satisfied, and was waiting for Harvey to make a move.

Grabbing the arms of the rocking chair, he heaved himself up and out. There was no reaction from the dog. He thought briefly about making a dash for the house, throwing open the door and then locking it shut, but against all logical reasoning, he decided to do the exact opposite and tentatively walked over to where the dog lay. Somehow he knew that the animal posed no threat whatsoever, and was, therefore, safe to approach

When he was six feet from the dog, it suddenly stood up on its four lion-like paws and approached him. The animal's nose, which was level with that of Harvey's chin, was only inches away when the dog stopped walking. A large pink tongue emerged from its mouth and slathered salvia across Harvey's face. And then, for no apparent reason, the animal turned away. A sense of relief trickled down his nerves. He had faced the enormous whatever-it-was, from who-knew-where, and was still in one piece.

He mistakenly thought the animal was done with him, and then without warning, its lengthy tail jutted out towards him like the tentacle of a squid and wrapped itself tightly around his waist. The animal's head turned back and looked at Harvey, its large brown eyes meeting his. The faintest glimmer of a smile appeared on its face, and with incredible strength, the animal's tail lifted Harvey three feet off the ground.

Like a puppy chasing its tail, the animal began to spin with ever increasing speed. At the end of its tail was Harvey, being whipped about as if he were riding in the last seat of a roller-coaster. Faster and faster the creature raced. Soon, neither Harvey nor the dog could be distinguished from one another. A vortex of blurred, wild colors swirled. And then with a whoosh, both Harvey and the animal were gone, vanishing into thin air, leaving behind nothing more than a cloud of rotating leaves and grass.

3

If you have ever spun yourself around and around for no other reason than to render yourself utterly disoriented and dizzy, then you know exactly how Harvey felt when the cyclonic motion finally stopped, and he found himself flat on his back. Though his body had ceased rotating, he still felt as if he was moving.

From his supine perspective, it appeared as if the branches of the tree directly above him were caught in a whirlpool. The sight made his stomach warm, not in a pleasant way as you would feel after finishing a delicious supper, but in a queasy way when your food rebels and reverses direction. He thought it best to remain motionless until his head stopped swimming and his stomach cooled. He shut his eyes tightly, hoping that the darkness would act like a bicycle brake and bring the rotary motion in his head to an end.

When the illusion of movement finally disappeared, Harvey opened his eyes. Initially he thought that he was still in his backyard. There was a tree above him that looked similar to the oaks surrounding his house. But as he looked up at the tree and the backdrop of sky, he realized two things. First, the sky was no longer blue, but had become dark grey, punctuated with splotches of gold. Second, the tree directly above him appeared to be moving, not as a tree would in response to a breeze, but as a person would if he was bending over to closely examine something on the ground.

This notion that Harvey had of being examined, was, in fact, true. The tree, which Harvey was beginning to believe wasn't a tree at all, was closely observing him as a doctor might do to a patient who had just been wheeled in on a stretcher. Something that was tree-like was peering down at him!

As Harvey gazed up at the tree, he realized that something was amiss. To begin with, the trunk was all wrong. Trunks are typically wider at their bases and progressively narrow with height, but with this tree, the pattern had been completely reversed: its trunk was narrower at the base and wider at the top. It was as if someone had cut a tree down, inverted the trunk, and stuck it back in the ground. The base was about three feet in diameter but increased to over six feet by the time the top of its eight foot trunk was reached.

From the top of the trunk, branch-like growths emerged. Two of these were quite large and grew downward along the sides of the trunk like arms. Smaller and greener branches grew out of a large nob in the middle top of the trunk. These branches curved over the back of the nob, where they loosely dangled like locks of human hair. Its skin-bark was dark red, streaked with colors of earthen brown and burnt orange.

The thing, whatever it was, continued to bend down until the nob on top of its trunk was less than a foot from Harvey's nose.

From this distance, Harvey, to his horror, could clearly see the distinct features of a wooden face.

The creature suddenly stood upright and turned its attention to something to its left. Harvey saw one of the arm-like branches move in the same direction. Soon, the sound of scratching could be heard. Harvey turned his head in the direction of the sound and was startled to see the large indigo dog standing directly under the moving arm-branch of the tree creature. There was no doubt in Harvey's mind; the animal's back was being scratched.

Sounds soon began to emerge from the tree trunk, and though Harvey couldn't understand them, he could tell by their tone that they were words of praise for the animal. After a few minutes of scratching, the tree-creature stopped and appeared to give the dog a command. The animal lay down on the ground as the tree redirected its attention back to Harvey. And then, the most terrifying event thus far occurred. The tree bent back over Harvey and began speaking to him.

"Welcome to Ecclon, Harvey. I have been anxiously awaiting your arrival. I am Bellock, Lord of the Flurn."

4

In a soothing baritone, Bellock continued, "I can see that you are a bit unsettled, but please let me assure you, you have nothing to fear neither from myself nor from Fromp, the warp-hound that retrieved you from your world."

"Harvey..." Bellock said to himself, pondering the name. "It is a wonderful and powerful name. If I am not mistaken, I believe it means 'battle worthy'".

Here he turned to Fromp and said, "How appropriate for our situation, Fromp. Someone who is battle worthy is exactly what we need if we are to repel the darkness and safeguard the worlds. Fromp, you retrieved well." As he spoke these words, he gently patted the top of the animal's head.

Apparently, Bellock knew a fair deal about Harvey's world and had "retrieved" him so that he could battle against some type of darkness. Harvey thought that there had never been a more ludicrous idea.

As if reading his mind, Bellock apologized, "Forgive me, Harvey, for it appears that I have cleared the table before anyone has eaten. I have spoken before providing you with any background. As if the trauma of being whisked here was not alarming enough, there I go discoursing about darkness and saving worlds. Where are my manners and my consideration? I am sure you have many questions. Please, tell me what would you like to know first?"

So many questions were ballooning in his head that Harvey had no idea which one to grab first. He opened his mouth, but instead of a question, a statement tumbled out.

"I'm not a warrior," Harvey mumbled without the least bit of inflection as he slowly stood to his feet.

Bellock replied, "Well of course you do not see yourself as one, but that is only because you are thinking in terms of what a warrior is like in your world. You humans are so very young. So many of your perceptions and conceptions of life are greatly distorted because they are based on your own experiences, and you humans are very shallow in regards to experiences."

"Do you not see?" Bellock continued. "If your experiences are greatly limited, then your understanding is greatly limited, and if your understanding is greatly limited, then much of what you believe to be true is greatly skewed or simply incorrect. In short, you humans find it difficult to see beyond your experiences. And this is exactly the case with your not seeing yourself as a warrior.

"The reality is that you, young Harvey, are an extremely powerful human, armed with a most formidable weapon, a weapon that very well might save Ecclon and thousands of other worlds as well."

Bellock briefly stopped speaking and chuckled softly. "But there I go again, getting ahead of myself. At times I am quite garrulous, untethering my words and letting them run wild. It would probably be best if we parted with this particular topic until tonight's gathering with the Flurn Council."

Harvey's head was swimming. No, actually at this point it was drowning. He still had no idea where he was or what had occurred, and here was an overly talkative tree-creature going on about his being a warrior and saving the world! Harvey was trying his best to grasp Bellock's words, but the task was like attempting to hold onto a flopping, slippery fish. And the thought of possibly encountering more talking trees tonight muddled his head even further.

Before Harvey had a chance to catch his breath, Bellock began again. "You must be wondering where you are and how you arrived here. As I said, this is Ecclon. It is the gateway planet to all dimensional worlds."

"Dimensional worlds?" Harvey asked.

"Why yes, there are thousands of them, existing at this exact time, but in other dimensions. When I say 'worlds', though, I am not referring merely to planets, but to universes."

"There are thousands of universes?" Harvey asked in disbelief.

"Of course. There are countless other universes, filled with orbiting planets and suns, existing at this very moment in time."

Bellock paused. He rested his chin on one of his twiggy hands, and with the patience and cadence of a seasoned teacher, he said, "I realize that this is difficult for you to grasp. Thinking beyond the three dimensions with which you are so familiar is a struggle. I have no doubt that the root of your not being able to conceive of such a notion is to be found in the difficulty of grasping something which is beyond your five senses."

Harvey nodded, still stunned and bewildered, but his state of confusion did nothing to stop Bellock from continuing on.

"Perhaps the following explanation might help. Remember what I said about one's experience limiting one's understanding?"

Harvey wasn't sure if he did.

"The same sort of idea is true in regards to the senses. If you restrict your comprehension of reality to only what you can perceive by your senses, then it follows that anything beyond your senses must not exist. But even you know that this idea is erroneous. For example, on your planet, I believe your inventors have fashioned a technological apparatus which has the capability of sending messages through your airways."

"A radio?" Harvey asked.

"Yes, the radio. Now, Harvey, can you observe with your eyes the radio waves as they course through the atmosphere? Can you hear with your ears the music and the voices that are flying through the air from the radio station to the radio receiver?"

Harvey thought about it and shook his head.

Bellock continued. "No, your human senses lack the ability to perceive the radio waves. Are you to conclude, then, that they do not exist?"

Harvey shook his head again.

"Of course not, Harvey. The idea that they do not exist because you fail to detect them with your senses is utter nonsense. It is exactly the same with the idea that there are many universes or worlds.

"Thousands upon thousands of different worlds simultaneously exist, even as I speak. Just because you cannot see, hear, or touch them, does not change this fact. Incidentally, your mere presence on Ecclon should be proof enough that what I am saying is true."

"Ecclon and Earth are not in the same universe?" Harvey gasped.

"Certainly not," Bellock retorted. "Perhaps another example from your world will help."

Harvey didn't think any number of examples from the loquacious tree creature could help him. His head was still spinning from the realization that he was no longer on Earth.

Bellock continued, "Think of a book from your world. Your poets and story tellers put their words down on paper and bind them in what you call books. Imagine, if you will, a large book that contains ten thousand different short stories, all of which are unrelated to each other. Each story, in a sense, is its own separate, fictional world, and yet they are still all bound together in one book. And though you do not have the ability to read all of them at once, all the other stories are still there.

"The fictional worlds of the other nine thousand nine hundred ninety-nine continue to exist even when you aren't reading them. It is much the same with other universes. Your traveling here to Ecclon is like flipping the page to the next story in the book."

Bellock must have observed that Harvey's eyes were beginning to glaze over, for he came to himself and exclaimed, "There I go again! A barrage of words all at once! When will I ever learn not to overwhelm new arrivals? I apologize once again. I believe I shall take a break from speaking and allow you to rest."

He then turned to Fromp and uttered a command in a language that Harvey had never heard before. Fromp immediately stood and bolted away in the direction of a spacious meadow. He returned moments later with a yellow orb in his mouth, which he dropped at Harvey's feet.

5

"It is called Kreen. It is a type of fruit that grows abundantly on Ecclon, excellent for the body and mind," Bellock explained. "Go ahead and eat."

Harvey tentatively reached down for the tennis ball-sized fruit while keeping a wary eye on Fromp. The last time he was this close, Fromp had lassoed him with his tail and whipped Harvey into some type of cross-dimensional whirlpool. This time, however, Fromp just sat on his haunches with his tongue hanging out of his mouth.

Harvey had this thing about eating food after someone had put his or her mouth on it. To him, taking a bite of someone else's food was just like kissing that person, and there were very few people, if any, at this point in Harvey's life that he desired to kiss. And now, he had some sort of alien fruit dripping with an alien dog's saliva, which a talking tree wanted him to eat. He didn't see any way out of this one, so he vigorously rubbed the fruit dry with his shirt before cautiously placing it in his mouth. With both eyes scrunched up as if expecting a jolt of electricity or the poke of a needle, Harvey took a miniscule bite.

To be shocked is to be taken by great surprise, never suspecting that the unexpected should be expected. This was exactly the case when Harvey took his first bite of Kreen. When his teeth punctured the fruit's thin skin, a sweet, delectable nectar flooded his mouth. Bursts of energy crackled on his tongue and then surged throughout his entire body. Seconds later, a thirst, he wasn't even aware of having, was quenched.

"Well?" Bellock asked with a quizzical look on his wooden face. "What do you think of Kreen? How does it taste?"

"How does it taste?" Harvey thought to himself. How can one even begin to describe the colors of a sunset to a man with no sight, or the sound of crashing waves to him who has no ears? Harvey had no words for the unique and delightful taste in his mouth. It was something completely foreign to him. He rummaged through his mental files of memories, terms, analogies, and metaphors, looking for the right one that would give words to what he was experiencing. In the end, the closest he was able to come to describing it was to relate it to a glorious "Mistaken Morning".

Mistaken Mornings don't occur all that frequently, and no doubt this is one of the reasons that make them so savory when they do. They happen when you wake up in the morning and mistakenly connect the new day with the wrong day of the week. Imagine that you wake up at 6:00 a. m., for example, and in your mind, you have the unpleasant notion that it's Monday morning, another laborious day of school.

The long day looms ahead. The shadows lengthen. But just as you have reluctantly determined to emerge from your cozy cocoon, your ears and nose perk up. You hear the hum of lawn mowers outside your window and catch a whiff of cooking pancakes and bacon. "Mowers, pancakes, and bacon..." you think. "Why would this be happening on a..." And that's when you realize you've made a wonderful mistake. A glorious mistake! It's not Monday at all. It's Saturday! No school, no work, and most importantly, no need, other than pancakes and bacon, to get out of bed. Your heart slows, your mind clears, and smiles fly free.

Now imagine being able to take this feeling and to somehow transform it into something that you could taste. If you are able to do this, then you have an idea of how pleasant and refreshing Kreen can be.

Harvey, however, didn't describe it this way to Bellock. What did Bellock know about Mondays, Saturdays, and lawnmower sounds? And so, he simply said, "Lovely. It tastes absolutely lovely." It was the first time that he had ever used this word, and it even surprised him.

Strangely, after only one small taste of Kreen, Harvey felt completely full, as though he had just eaten a large meal, and as so often happens after a large meal, he felt a bit drowsy. He would come to find out later that trans-dimensional travel is extremely wearing on one's physical body. If traveling across the ocean by plane fatigues the body in the form of jet lag, what happens when a body jumps from one universe to another?

The previous January Harvey had stayed up all night in his backyard in order to watch a meteor shower. Nature's firework show was breathtaking. He saw meteors arc across the sky leaving trailing ribbons of fire. He paid dearly for staying up all night, though, to view the spectacle. The next day he fell into a hard sleep, face down on his Spanish test.

After writing out the third word on the test, "caiman", the Spanish word for alligator, the letters began to swim, as his eyelids struggled to bear their own weight. For ten minutes, Harvey had closed and reopened his eyes dozens of times as he valiantly fought off the impending sleep.

Finally, like a weight lifter's arms giving out because he has done too many repetitions, his eyelids did the same and collapsed shut. Harvey's head slumped on the desk, and soon drool leaked out of the corners of his mouth. When his teacher, Mrs. Morales, tapped him on the shoulder, he sat up straight away. His test was stuck to his face, and the caiman had been blurred.

He had never again felt so tired, that is, until he jumped to another universe and tasted a piece of Ecclonian fruit. But unlike the Spanish test incident, this time there was soft, alien grass to lie down upon.

Harvey curled up like a cat and was soon fast asleep. One of Bellock's branch-arms reached over and gently took hold of Harvey, lifting him over to a patch of thick grass next to his trunk. Harvey continued to sleep soundly, and Bellock thought it might be a good idea if he, too, closed his eyes before the evening's gathering. Soon his leaves were lightly rustling, in time with his rhythmic snores.

6

Harvey awoke refreshed. He had only napped for a half an hour or so, but apparently slumbering next to a snoring Flurn has therapeutic and restorative effects. Bellock had already awoken and was preparing to leave for the Flurn gathering.

"Harvey, we must leave immediately so as not to be late. Flurn detest tardiness - puts them in a foul temper and what not. Shaking branches, snapping twigs, and even snarling. It really is most unpleasant." Bellock fretted in a tone that revealed to Harvey that they were already on the road to being late.

"What is the time of the council gathering?" Harvey asked.

Bellock replied a bit flustered, "What time? It is when it is and not a minute sooner or later."

Harvey didn't even bother.

"Well, let us be about it then," Bellock determined. And with those words, Harvey felt a slight rumble underground. In front of Bellock's trunk, two oblong patches of grass began to bubble and swell. It looked to Harvey as if enormous blisters were rapidly growing and would burst at any moment. Harvey took a few steps back, not wanting to be in range if the blisters did decide to blow. Instead of exploding, however, a split formed down the middle of each grassy bubble. From these splits two rather large logs – at least twelve feet in length – popped up and out, as if they had been held underwater and were suddenly released to buoyantly bounce upward. Both of the logs were notched in the middle, and from the ends of each, thick mats of crisscrossing roots grew.

Once the logs had fully surfaced, Bellock himself began to move, or more accurately, to rise. It was then that Harvey saw it clearly. They weren't just logs; they were Bellock's legs! The notches in the middle were his knees and the woven mats his feet. When he had finally unfolded and stood erect, he was over twenty feet tall.

"Ah, that feels wonderful," Bellock said. "My legs have been subterranean for many a day now, but I had to stay put, did I not? If I had not, then whom, may I ask, would have been here to welcome our young warrior from Earth?"

"Are your legs sore from being underground for so long?" Harvey asked.

"Only slightly. My legs were only under for about a week of your earth time, not long enough to do much damage. The real problems begin when they remain under for months or years. That is when Flurn legs begin to grow new rootlets into the surrounding soil, making it, when they finally do stand up, very strenuous indeed. It reminds me of Gnarl the Petrified."

"Gnarl the What?" Harvey asked.

"Gnarl the Petrified, and he is a who and not a what, although that was not originally his name. It only became his name after he was petrified of course. Before that sad occurrence, he was known far and wide as Gnarl the Deep, for his wealth of knowledge about other worlds."

"What happened?" Harvey asked.

"The story goes that one afternoon, Gnarl the Deep fell into a most intriguing line of philosophical thought. What the thought was no Flurn may ever know, but he must have become completely lost in a maze of pleasurable reasoning and questioning, because before he knew it, five Ecclonian years had flown past. That would be about seventy earth years. You can only imagine how many roots had sprouted during that time. "

"Was he ever able to get free?"

"No, and what is worse is that he had exhausted all of the nutrients in the soil surrounding his trunk."

"Did he die?" Harvey asked with genuine concern in his voice.

"No, he petrified. Remember his name? As a matter of fact, he is still standing there to this today."

"Where?"

"At the entrance to Council Gorge. Where, as matter of fact, we had better be off to at once if we are to be punctual."

Before they began walking, Bellock turned to Harvey and said, "My strides are much longer than yours. If you travel atop your own legs and under your own power, you will quickly tire, and we will never make it to the gathering on time. It would be much better for your sake and time's sake if you were to ride".

Harvey easily saw the logic in this and nodded in agreement, but when he made motions toward climbing upon Bellock, Bellock pulled back and asked, "What exactly are you doing, young one?"

"What you said. Riding."

With a tone of disbelief Bellock said, "You do not genuinely suppose I meant for you to ride upon me, did you? You humans are full of the most uncanny notions! Imagine someone, a human no less, riding on a Flurn. No, no, no, that will not do at all. I apologize for the confusion. What I meant is that you should ride on Fromp."

Bellock turned to Fromp and gave a one-word command. Fromp immediately bounded over to Harvey, his long pink tongue hanging out the side of his mouth. He stood still next to Harvey. The only thing moving was his enormous tail, which curved up and over Fromp's back where it coiled itself into a furry disk. There, hovering about three feet over the animal's back was what appeared to be a seat.

"There you are, Harvey," Bellock said. "Your own *tailored* seat." Apparently, bad puns weren't just confined to Earth.

Hesitantly, Harvey climbed onto Fromp's back and then aboard the floating tail seat. It dropped down slightly under the pressure of his weight, but then quickly recovered as if the seat was being supported by a large coil. The entire trip atop Fromp would be a bouncing and floating experience, similar to a kiddie plane ride moving about on a metal spring. Luckily, Harvey was traveling on an empty stomach.

Bellock took a large stride eastward and said something to Fromp which sent him prancing and leaping alongside his Flurn master. Harvey lurched back and nearly fell off, save for his death grip upon Fromp's coiled tail. He had barely righted himself when the entire tail seat lurched to the port side. Just as he was about to roll over and onto the ground, Fromp leaped to his right, saving Harvey from falling, but slinging him over to the starboard side. This unsettling affair continued until Harvey started to gain his "tail seat".

After a mile or so, he began acquiring some essential skills for successful tail riding. He learned how to shift his weight to one side in order to counteract a tail sway in the opposite direction and how to use his feet as stabilizers upon Fromp's back when the animal decided to leap or turn quickly. After five minutes of riding, he was, believe it or not, actually enjoying the ride.

And so they headed eastward to the gathering with Bellock striding wide and Harvey imagining that he was a royal prince in route to a meeting of the utmost importance, ushered there atop a litter.

7

Bellock, Harvey, and Fromp traveled in silence for nearly an hour. Bellock was thinking about the gathering, worried about how Harvey would be received by the Council. There were many Flurn who thought that Bellock's idea of using a human boy to combat the enemy was ludicrous and further evidence that he was no longer fit to lead them.

Harvey was worried himself, wondering why in the world he had been tail- lassoed and whipped into another universe. And what was all this nonsense about darkness and saving? He was certain that Fromp had somehow gotten confused and mistakenly retrieved him from the wrong address.

Bellock decided that his concern was gaining no good ground, and that it was all rather foolish scrap anyway. He was confident that Harvey was the right one for the task. And wasn't it all in the hands of someone else? The best thing for him to do now was to begin explaining things.

He began with a question. "Harvey, I realize that your time on Ecclon has been brief, but have you noticed anything unusual about the light?"

Harvey gazed up at the sky. "I hadn't really thought about it until now, but it looks exactly like it did when I first arrived. I mean... the light seems the same. Doesn't it ever change and get dark? When is night?"

Bellock thought for a moment before replying. "We have no night on Ecclon. To have a night would mean that Ecclon is continually spinning on its axis while orbing a nearby sun. We do spin, but as for the latter part, well, we do not have one."

"You don't have a sun? But that's impossible? Life can't survive on any planet without a sun close by to provide light and warmth. Everything would freeze solid in less than a day."

"What you said," Bellock answered, "is all very factual for life to exist on Earth, but remember, you are no longer on your planet, nor for that matter, even in your own universe. You should not suppose things on Ecclon to be the same as they are on Earth. Things here are much different."

Harvey couldn't argue with that. Since arriving, he'd spent his time with a talking tree whose faithful pet was some type of hound that seemed to enjoy fetching people from other universes. To say life was different here was like saying water was wet.

Bellock continued speaking. "Harvey, consider both the truth and the logic. Have I lied to you about anything thus far?"

"I don't think so. It's all so crazy, all these things you've told me since I arrived here. I hardly even know you, but, somehow, I don't believe you would ever tell me a lie."

"You are quite correct. A Flurn is incapable of prevarication."

"Prevari - what?"

"Prevarication. It means lying"

"Oh."

"And are we frozen solid?"

"Obviously not," Harvey said with a grin.

"Good. Now, if you put those two pieces of the puzzle together – the truth and the logic – what can you deduce?"

"You must be telling the truth because you haven't lied to me, and I don't think you ever would. So what you said about Ecclon having no sun must be true"

"Yes, and what else?"

Harvey mulled this one over for a minute before replying. "Since we're not frozen, it's only logical to conclude that there must be another source of light and heat for the planet."

"Very good, my young scholar! And what do you think that source of light and heat might be?"

"I'm not sure...uh, maybe...I don't really..." was Harvey's halting response.

"Ask yourself. Where does the light appear to be coming from?"

Harvey thought for a moment as he looked back up at the sky. "Light seems to be coming from the clouds. They seem to be glowing."

"That is correct. They are glowing. And like the clouds of your planet, which are composed of hydrogen and oxygen, the Ecclonian clouds, or what we call orbs, are also composed of gas."

"Hydrogen and oxygen?"

"No. Floreclon. It is a highly excitable and volatile gas which glows brightly and generates heat when its molecules are agitated."

Harvey tilted his gaze upward once again and scanned the atmosphere from horizon to horizon. Thousands upon thousands of dimly lit golden spheres were floating about one thousand feet above the ground. It looked to Harvey like a massive colony of jellyfish was effortlessly sailing on the ocean's currents.

The sight was beautifully mesmerizing and for many minutes Harvey continued to stare heavenward. Bellock didn't interrupt. He let Harvey absorb and enjoy the sight. He would learn soon enough of the truth. All was not well with the glowing orbs, and for this very reason, Harvey had been brought to Ecclon.

The more Harvey studied the glowing orb clouds, the more details he observed. Each of the countless orbs seemed to weakly pulse, alternating between a dull yellow and a nearly extinguished gold, as if they were dying organisms, being robbed of their life by faltering hearts. They were all about the size of hot air balloons and seemed to be underpowered. It was as though each of the large orbs was being illuminated by a single low watt light bulb, like an enormous gymnasium being lit by a solitary bedside lamp.

"You see it, do you not?" Bellock asked.

"See what?"

"The weakness of the light. The orbs are burning duller now. They are becoming dimmer and dimmer by the day, like a man withering away from malnourishment, which if truth be told, is not far off the mark. If this diminishing continues, it will not be long until all light and heat vanish from the planet, and then..."

"And then what?"

Bellock stared heavenward. His gaze seemed to reach beyond the floating orbs, beyond space, and into a bleak future. While still staring off into the distance, he continued speaking, "Then all life will perish, including the Flurn, and once the Flurn are gone, there will be none to stand sentry... none to guard. All worlds will be exposed to those bent on decimation and ruin."

Bellock paused for a moment, and then like a man coming out of a hypnotic trance, he snapped out of his morose contemplation and turned to look upon Harvey. He smiled and his voice took on a more pleasant tone as he said, "But there is a good chance that it will not come to that, especially now that you are here."

Harvey was flabbergasted. "What do you mean now that I'm here? How can I make any difference whatsoever? I'm a teenager from Earth. You called me a warrior, but I can't even fight! I have zero skills, and when it comes right down to it, I don't even know what you're talking about!"

Bellock bent down and placed his twiggy hand upon Harvey's shoulder as he soothingly said, "There are numerous ways to engage in battle and to vanquish a foe, many of which do not rely on brawn or talent with sword and axe. And you are gifted with the only thing that might turn the tide in our favor. There is no mistake, Harvey, you are the one, but to understand your strength, we must return to the orbs. Tell me, why do you think their light is weakening?"

Harvey took a deep breath to try and settle his nerves. When the emotional surge of his outburst had subsided, he looked up at the sky again and calmly said, "Maybe they're old, at the end of their life span."

"A very educated guess, but incorrect. Ecclonian orbs are similar to your clouds in that they are always forming and dissipating. New clouds appear and disappear continually. Their weakening has nothing to do with life span, but everything to do with life source."

Harvey scrunched his face into a variety of contortions and acute angles of confusion.

Bellock continued, "Consider your own star. Your sun warms, illuminates, regulates weather patterns, and sustains all organic life with its 386 billion billion megawatts of energy, generated by nuclear reactions in its core. However, on Ecclon the orbs are not powered by any such reaction. The gas molecules of the Floreclon clouds glow and generate heat when they are agitated by strong waves of energy passing through them. It is similar to how the florescent bulbs work in your classroom at school. And do you have any idea where the waves of energy that light up our orbs come from?"

"Outer space?" Harvey guessed.

"Oh no, they do not come from space, but from your very own world, Harvey. Waves of thought energy from the brain of every man, woman, and child on your planet are what power the orbs and give life to every creature on mine."

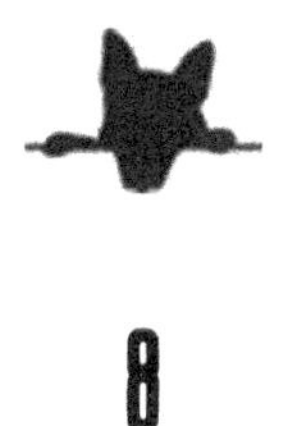

8

The idea of thoughts affecting and altering the physical world struck Harvey as so bizarre that his face took on the stupefied expression of the proverbial deer caught in the headlights.

Bellock decided that he should go ahead and mitigate the shock of his previous statement by elaborating with additional details. If Harvey remained with his mouth agape, he would soon invite a horde of Ecclonian horned flies to land on his tongue.

Bellock continued, "Like much of what you have already heard today, this must sound, not only unbelievable, but nonsensical as well. How could a thought have any effect on the physical world outside of a human's boney skull? I am confident that your experience has led you to believe that such a brain effect is impossible, for if you are like most humans, and I have no reason to think otherwise, I am certain that at one time or another you have attempted to move a physical object with nothing else but your mind. I believe your scientists call this telekinesis."

Harvey was beginning to think that Bellock knew more about humans than Harvey did because he had attempted that very thing less than a month ago.

It all began when he watched a documentary on the untapped power of the human mind in science class. Part of the documentary focused on the abilities of a young man named Benjamin who reputedly was able to move things with nothing but his mind. His most impressive feat was inserting a pencil into a pencil sharpener and turning the handle without using any of his limbs. He claimed that he did it all by a "concentrated focusing of his full mental capacities".

Although Benjamin was later proved to be a clever con artist, it was beside the point to the students. Everyone in the class was drawn in and inspired to try his or her mind at moving an object.

Harvey decided to access his "untapped" telekinetic powers by making his ham and cheese sandwich turn a 360 during Mrs. Driscoll's Language Arts class.

He pulled out the half-finished sandwich and set it on his desk. First, he visualized everything in his mind. The sandwich began to vibrate. Soon it was violently shaking and rattling like a miniature snare drum. Finally, when it appeared as if it had been electrocuted and might convulse to life like Frankenstein's monster, it began to rapidly spin, turning multiple 360's before jettisoning off to his left, directly into the head of Ella Fritz. All of this, of course, only occurred in his imagination.

Benjamin claimed that before he could move any object, the entire sequence of motion events had to first be sketched out in his imagination. Once Harvey had formulated the play of telekinetic events in his head, he began to concentrate his mind on the motionless sandwich. “Move, vibrate, spin, spin!” Harvey mentally commanded the sandwich.

The ham, cheese, and bread failed to comply and remained motionless. Harvey concentrated even harder. Being so intent on moving the sandwich with nothing but his mental prowess, he failed to blink or breathe, as if his purpling face and bulging eyes would somehow strengthen his brainwaves. But no matter how much he altered the color of his face, the food failed to change its position.

The positions of his class mates’ heads, however, did change. Believe or not, the students found Harvey’s protruding veins and increasingly blotchy face to be more captivating than Mrs. Driscoll’s elucidation on the effective use of adverbial prepositional phrases. Just as people slow down in their cars and strain their necks in order to turn and observe a traffic accident, so too did all of his classmates.

Students on Harvey’s left craned their necks to the right, while those on his right craned their necks to the left. It wasn’t long before Mrs. Driscoll realized that something was amiss. The world behind her back was too quiet. Either the students had suddenly become enraptured by the finer points of English grammar, or they had located something else in the room to relieve their boredom. Oh how she wished it was the former, just for once, but experience wouldn’t allow that possibility to exist more than a second, and therefore she knew, it must be the latter.

With a sigh of resignation and defeat, she turned from the whiteboard to the room of budding young scholars, and there, smack dab in the middle of the room was Harvey George. His eyes were bulging like a lemur’s. Assuming the worst, Mrs. Driscoll panicked. Her instinct and training took over as she sprinted toward Harvey, hurdling over Connor Jennings, who had leaned around in his chair so much to get a good look at Harvey that he had completely blocked the aisle.

Later on, students swore that Mrs. Driscoll had easily leapt five feet in the air, an impressive feat by anyone, but especially by a heavyset fifty-eight year old English teacher wearing a long, frumpy dress and kitten heels.

When she landed, she quickly pushed Harvey out of his desk and onto the floor. She then tightly wrapped her saggy-skinned arms around his stomach and violently thrust her fists inward. She had mistakenly thought that he was choking. The roughly applied Heimlich maneuver didn't remove anything from his airway, but it did propel a piece of half-digested ham and cheese sandwich from his stomach. Up and out. It landed directly atop his grammar worksheet. Needless to say, it was the last time Harvey attempted to move anything with his mind at school.

"Harvey," Bellock said, seeing that Harvey was probably lost in a memory.

"Sorry, Bellock. I was just thinking about what you said. The whole thing about trying to move objects with the mind, I've tried it before and nothing happened."

"And it never will. Not in that way. It's very difficult for a human thought to move a physical object if both are in the same dimension, but cross-dimensionally, human thoughts grow in intensity. It is much like an ocean swell. In the middle of the ocean a wave of energy moving through the water is hardly noticeable, but as it approaches shallower water, it grows in height, and when it breaks, it has tremendous power to move and even destroy objects. Think of human thoughts in the same way, a 'thinkwave' if you will. On Earth, the power of a human thought is like a swell in the middle of the ocean with very little noticeable power, but watch what that very same thought does when it travels to another dimension. It is like the ocean wave crashing on a sandbar or reef."

"Or in the case of Ecclon, generating light," Harvey interjected.

"Exactly!" Bellock said in a complimentary manner.

"But how did this happen? People's thoughts affecting another world?" Harvey asked.

"To that question I have little to reply. On Earth your plants and animals have a symbiotic relationship. Humans and animals inhale oxygen and exhale carbon dioxide, while the plants absorb carbon dioxide and release oxygen. They are dependent on each other for their survival. How did such a thing come to be? It came about in the same way as the relationship between thoughts and the lighted orbs of Ecclon. It is all part of the Unseen's master plan. He has choreographed the dance, and even though we may not understand it all, we can still recognize His handiwork."

"Are you talking about God?" Harvey asked.

Bellock replied with much reverence, "He is known in our world as the Unseen." Bellock paused for a moment before continuing.

"Considering how the worlds were formed might deepen your understanding of how it is all possible. Many of your own ancient sages maintained that the Unseen spoke everything into existence and that man himself was created in the image of the Unseen."

Harvey had a vague recollection of hearing something along those lines.

"Now, Harvey, assuming that it is true that the Unseen's spoken words brought everything you see into being, what do you suppose occurred before He spoke?"

"I don't know. How could anyone know that?"

"Well, we cannot know with complete certainty what occurred before, but I believe we can make a strong deduction. In whose image do many of your ancient sages believe man was created in?'

"The thing you call the Unseen?"

"And if we take this to be true, which I myself do, then it is logical to assume that when a man or a woman creates something, it must be similar to the way the Unseen creates as well. So what follows?"

Harvey was flipping the switch, but the light bulb just wouldn't turn on. Seeing no response from Harvey, Bellock continued.

"Think about it, Harvey, before any human paints, sculpts, composes, or builds, does not he or she first think of what is about to be created in his or her mind? Is the Unseen any different? Did He not first imagine all that He was about to create in his mind: the elements, colors, stars, animals, and plants?

"And when He was ready to bring them to life, what did He do? He expressed His thoughts in words. From one dimension, what you humans refer to as the spirit realm, He created an entire world in a completely separate dimension – your physical world.

"His thinking in one world powerfully affected and altered life in another world. And if humans are created in his image, then is it not reasonable to conclude that they might also have a similar impact with their thoughts?"

The light bulb in Harvey's mind flickered to life and light. It was many minutes before he said anything. He needed time to mentally digest Bellock's words. After riding on Fromp in silence for ten minutes, Harvey turned to Bellock and asked, "So what's wrong with our thoughts?"

"What do you mean?"

"Well, if human thoughts illuminate the orbs on Ecclon, and the orbs aren't burning very brightly, then something must be wrong with our thoughts."

"Very good, Harvey," Bellock complimented and then continued, "Let us stop here and rest while I answer your question. We have made good time and are not far from Council Gorge and the Flurn Gathering. I think it would serve you well if you knew more about the situation before arriving. Besides, it looks like Fromp could use a break from carrying you."

9

Fromp was in the process of lowering his tail-seat so that Harvey could disembark when the warp-hound detected movement. It was slight. Just a flash of color. A quick blur. Over a boulder and into a cluster of berry bushes. Harvey didn't notice anything. How could he? Only keen hound eyes could catch such a whoosh and zip.

Vigor rippled through Fromp's body. Tension gripped his muscles. Ears at rigid attention, he tilted up his snout. Nostrils flared with hunger. The scent was apprehended. Confirmed.

The tail-seat went back to its full and upright position. Fromp lifted one paw, pointing in the direction of the blur's path.

"What's he doing?" Harvey asked in a tremulous voice.

A grin emerged on Bellock's face. Knowing what was about to occur, he had time to shout only two injuctions: "Harvey, hold on tightly with everything you have! Whatever you do, do not let go!"

If Harvey knew what was about to occur, he would have immediately jumped off the tail-seat. But he didn't. He had no idea what was about to transpire. He stayed on the tail seat and followed Bellock's commands, strongly grasping the edges of the tail-seat. A hair of a second later, Fromp sprung forward with cheetah-like acceleration.

What induced Fromp to behave in such an erratic and speedy manner is the same thing that induces earth dogs: small, furry prey. On Earth, the most alluring animals for dogs to chase tend to be cats and squirrels. On Ecclon, it was the Zuit.

In order to understand the appearance of a Zuit, imagine that a squirrel, cat, otter, and chameleon collided with one another. The result would be a new creature, with key characteristics from each of its four contributors.

The head of a Zuit is cat-like: whiskers, triangular ears, and slit pupils. The body is oblong and otter-shaped, allowing the animal to slink and weave around or under most objects. Attached to the body are four compact, powerful legs, tapering down to paws and claws similar to a squirrel's. Affixed to its hindquarters is a lizardish tail which helps to balance the agile creature during climbs, sprints, and leaps. And like the defense mechanism of many earth lizards, the tail easily breaks when grasped. The Zuit is covered with long fur, which is constantly changing colors in order to blend in with its environment.

It's an elusive prey, rarely ever apprehended. And it is probably for this very reason that the highly intelligent warp-hounds, like Fromp, find the chase to be irresistible.

Fromp was soon on the scent trail of the fleeing Zuit, following its path over the boulder and into the berry bushes. His paws hardly touched the boulder before gracefully leaping off and onto the ground with bullfrog finesse. Harvey wasn't so graceful. When Fromp performed his touch-and-go, the tail-seat and Harvey swung erratically to the left, violently slamming into the side of the boulder. A dull pain clanged the bone of his left kneecap, and the pain probably would have felt more intense if his mind had not been distracted by what came next.

The Zuit's body enabled it to navigate the small gaps and tunnels of the berry bushes. Fromp, on the other hand, had neither the inclination nor the body to follow the Zuit. He bulldozed his way through, blazing his own gaps and tunnels. Harvey, unfortunately, was caught in a debris trail composed of branches, thorns, leaves, and purple berries. The berries pelted his face like hailstones. Soon his eyes were stinging from their juices. He shut them tightly to try and protect them.

Fromp twisted and turned through the bushes for another twenty seconds before breaking out into an open field covered with lime-green moss. Even though they were clear of the bushes, Harvey was surprised that the berries continued to smack his face. Tears brought about by the stinging berry juices were beginning to flush some of the sting from Harvey's eyes, allowing him to open them to a sliver. Everything he saw was blurry and indistinct.

Seconds after reaching the open field, Harvey saw a flash of pink to the right of Fromp's head.

"Is that what Fromp's chasing?" Harvey asked himself.

The indistinct pink blur disappeared, but quickly reappeared, this time to the left of the warp-hound's head.

"Whatever it is," Harvey thought to himself, "it's only inches away from his jaws. Why doesn't he just chomp down and be done with it?"

It disappeared yet again, but Harvey knew that Fromp would catch it any second and the ride would thankfully be over. But he didn't, and the chase continued. He saw the pink thing vanish and reappear three more times. Harvey was baffled. How could it remain out of the warp-hound's grasp being so close?

With every tear that flushed Harvey's eyes, his vision became clearer. The fuzzy pink blur that he had seen to the right and left of Fromp's head began to reveal itself. The reason that it seemed so close to Fromp's mouth is because it was attached to it! Fromp's long, slobbering, wet noodle of a tongue was lollygagging in the wind, flip-flopping back-and-forth. It was swinging in whatever direction the mad hound turned. And those weren't berries still splotching Harvey's face. They were foul globs of saliva!

A mere second after realizing that they weren't berries, an extra-large glob was flung from the tip of Fromp's tongue. Caught by the moving air, it arced backward. It was the worst possible moment for Harvey to open his mouth, but he couldn't help it.

A berry fragment had found its way into his left nostril. The urge to expel it had come and gone three times, the faux-sneeze. The fourth time, however, it was for real. He tilted back his head as his nasal passages cocked for firing. This pre-sneeze motion opened his mouth wide. The wrong time for the wrong object. A blob of slobber the size of a super ball entered his mouth, slipping easily by his distracted teeth and lips.

When it landed on the tarmac of Harvey's tongue, the glob exploded into hundreds of tiny distasteful spheres, each making an unpleasant impression upon his taste buds. It was repulsive. If wet dog was a flavor, Harvey swallowed a heaping helping of it.

Harvey was attempting to spit away the taste from his mouth when Fromp leapt over a small brook. As the warp-hound descended from the jump, Harvey was able to get a good look at what was in front of them. The moss-covered field continued for another quarter mile or so before ending at the trunks of what looked like a row of palm trees. And no more than twenty feet in front of them was the Zuit.

The fleeing creature was out of his element. Nearly impossible to catch in tight spaces, nooks, and crannies, out in the open, it was easy prey for something as fast as a warp-hound. The compact legs of the Zuit were designed for short spurts of speed, not for prolonged running. It was tiring quickly and would soon find rest between the jaws of its pursuer.

Fromp leapt again, this time over what looked like a turtle shell. The old humorous eyes, set on either side of a wrinkled, reptilian head, peered up at the soaring dog and boy. With a sigh, humph, and slight shaking of its head, the creature receded into its shell.

The jump again enabled Harvey to clearly see what was ahead. The row of palm-like trees was less than fifty feet away, while the Zuit was mere inches from Fromp's teeth. On the other side of the trees, the field changed in color to a blood-red orange.

The quick glance led Harvey to falsely conclude that the field was probably covered with some type of alien wild flower, and not what it really was – floating algae atop a shallow pond of grainy muck.

The Zuit, the warp-hound, and the tail-bound boy were only a few feet from the trees when Fromp lunged forward with mouth agape. Little was left in the Zuit's tank, but there was enough for it to make one more evasive move. A second before Fromp's lunge, the Zuit sprang to the right, digging all four claws into the tender flesh of the passing tree trunk.

Fromp was momentarily stupefied. He had snapped his jaws shut but trapped nothing but air. There was snickering. When Fromp heard it, he realized what had happened. He turned back at the tree, and there, firmly affixed to it like a koala bear, was the panting and cackling Zuit. A smug smile was painted across its whiskery, color-changing face.

Fromp was still looking back and running at full speed when the matter below his paws changed states: solid, spongy, and then finally, liquid. When he hit the pond, his momentum displaced an enormous plume of mucky water interlaced with tangles of blood-red algae.

The collision with the water violently halted the forward movement of Fromp's body. The motion of the tail-seat and Harvey, however, continued to move. The science of it all was evident. The law of inertia was as equally binding on Ecclon as it was on Earth: an object in motion will stay in motion unless acted upon by an unbalanced force.

When Fromp stopped, Harvey's inertia kept him moving. The tail-seat was flung forward with such force that Harvey's exhausted fingers let loose. He was catapulted skyward and kept moving until he was stopped by the unbalanced force of the algae and muck in the middle of the pond. Splash down! Harvey surfaced seconds later, drenched with a large piece of algae hanging from his left ear.

Fromp was already out of the pond, running circles around the tree and wildly barking. At the very top, resting securely on a swaying frond, was the chattering Zuit.

Harvey's feet sank down in the gunk of the pond's bottom. The motion awakened the putrid, rotting odor of the muck, which surfaced and clung to Harvey's body. He slowly trudged towards the edge. Once out of the water, he lay down on the soft, mossy shore. He closed his eyes and sighed deeply.

The barking stopped. A shadow moved across Harvey's closed eyelids. They opened. There was Fromp, tongue, teeth, snout, and all, just inches from his face.

"You stupid mutt," Harvey growled.

Fromp responded by lying down on his stomach and licking Harvey's forehead.

"No thanks, Fromp," Harvey said, "I think I've had enough of your slobber for one day."

Getting back to Bellock wasn't difficult. Fromp's trail of destruction was clearly marked.

The ordeal had lasted less than two minutes, so it took Harvey and Fromp only ten to return to where they had started. Because of his height, Bellock had watched the entire fiasco unfold.

When a muck-logged Harvey was in earshot of Bellock, the Flurn said weakly with suppressed merriment in his voice, "So I see you have encountered a Zuit."

" A what?"

"A Zuit. The creature you were pursuing."

"Pursuing? Bellock, I wasn't pursuing anything. I was a prisoner atop that insane hound of yours!"

"That is a warp-hound for you. No matter how much they age, they really are nothing but over grown houndlings that cannot resist the temptation of the chase."

"Yeah, well it seems I just learned that lesson," Harvey remarked sarcastically.

"Oh come now, Harvey. Look at it this way. You had the unique opportunity to see and even taste more of Ecclon." Bellock said this because he could see all the berry stains around Harvey's lips. And try as he might, he was failing in his attempt hold back his barky smile.

"Very funny, Bellock. I'll have you know that I got a mouthful of your dog's slobber."

"Oh, I do apologize, Harvey. Fromp truly does have the most atrocious breath and I..."

Bellock couldn't finish his sentence. The sight of the muck-covered and berry-stained boy, in addition to what he had just said about Fromp's slobber, was more than even the most dignified Flurn could handle. He placed one of his rootlet hands over his mouth in an attempt to muffle his rising laugh.

Harvey could tell Bellock was breaking into hysterics. The leaves on his head were shaking erratically. He was angry at first, but when he looked down at his scraped, drenched body, highlighted with purple berry splotches, he began to laugh as well. Before long, they were both lost in the hilarity of the moment. It was exactly what they needed.

When they were finally able to catch their breaths and string together coherent sentences without giggling interruptions, Bellock said, "Suppose I get you and Fromp cleaned up so that we can finally take that rest."

"Cleaned up? How are you going to do that? If you think I'm getting back in that pond..."

Laughing once again, Bellock reassured him, “No, no, Harvey. No more ponds. I believe on Earth you call it a shower.”

“A shower on Ecclon? And I suppose it will also have hot water?”

“Whatever you desire, my soiled and drenched young friend.”

Harvey was dubious about a shower being anywhere on Ecclon, but when Bellock brought both of his rootlet hands together and asked Harvey to stand underneath, he complied.

“Hot water you said?”

“Harvey, a tad more nervous and less sarcastic said, “Warm would actually be better.”

“Warm then it is! Coming up and out!” shouted Bellock.

Roots sprang from Bellock’s feet, burrowing into the grass and soil. With a concentrated, intentional expression on his face, Bellock said, “The choicest water is not always easy to find. Sometimes you have to search awhile and dig deeply.”

“You’re really searching for water?”

“Of course. You did not think my roots were only for stability, did you? Oh, yes, there it is,” Bellock said as if reaching out to grab something. “A pocket of cool spring water. This will do quite well. Give me a minute to bring it up.”

Harvey stood under Bellock’s interlaced rootlet fingers for five minutes before saying anything.

“Where’s the water?”

“It is here within me. I am warming it for you.”

“You’re warming it? How?”

“Photosynthesis. With light from the orb clouds. I am converting the light into energy to heat the water. Unfortunately, the dimmer orb clouds are making the process take much longer.”

"You do this a lot?"

"Yes. Warp-hounds dislike cold water. And as you have recently experienced, they often need baths. I would never be able to bathe Fromp without warm water."

Just then a shower of water rained out of Bellock's hands, completely covering Harvey. Fromp was immediately at his side, snapping at falling droplets and periodically rattling water from his body with spasmodic shaking.

Harvey reached down and scratched him under his chin.

"Sorry about what I said, boy. I didn't mean it."

Fromp responded with a yelp and a lick.

The shower lasted for fifteen minutes. When it was over, Bellock unlaced his fingers and placed one of his hands gently upon Harvey's shoulder.

"How was that?"

"Almost as good as Kreen."

"Very well stated. You know, Harvey, I am quite proud of you."

"For what? I haven't done anything."

"Oh, but you have. You were able to let go of a situation that many people would have held onto and remained angry about, and even more importantly, you were able to laugh at yourself."

"You're proud of me for laughing at myself?"

"I am. The ability to laugh at one's self is a significant part of being humble. And believe me when I tell you, in the fight you are about to enter, humility will be like armor."

Bellock's words were soothing, warm shower water on the inside, flushing through Harvey's heart.

10

After the shower ended, Harvey and Fromp found a place in the soft Ecclonian grass to rest their bottoms. Fromp shook a number of times, hastening the drying of his coat but saturating Harvey's clothes even more. It would be sometime before Harvey was completely dripped-dry.

You wouldn't think that a tree would become weary from walking, but then again, not many would think of a tree walking in the first place. As it turns out, walking trees grow tired also, and this one in particular welcomed a rest. Bellock sat down, making a baritone thump when his ponderous tree-trunk posterior hit the ground. He slowly stretched out his log legs and rootlet toes, as a guttural rumble vibrated through his barked chest.

Bellock set his gaze in the direction of Council Gorge. A flock of Ecclonian orb clouds weakly pulsed above a forest in the distance. Without breaking his gaze, he began speaking to Harvey.

"The thought power of humans is rapidly declining. For centuries the thoughts of those on Earth burned brightly, causing our orbs to burn in like fashion. But there has been a turning of late. The thinking of too many men and women has begun to dull.

"Do not misunderstand what I am saying. Your scientific discoveries and technological breakthroughs have been quite impressive. Humans, I must concede, are rather endowed with cleverness and ingenuity. What your scientists have discovered of the workings of your world and how to exploit these discoveries to advance civilization is exceedingly commendable. You are a very young race to be unfolding so many mysteries of your universe so soon."

"Then it doesn't make sense," interrupted Harvey. "Since humans are smarter than ever before, shouldn't their thoughts be powerfully energizing the orbs here on Ecclon?"

"One would think so, but what darkens the human mind, and correspondingly my world, is neither intelligence nor ingenuity. It is something deeper and more fundamental."

At this point Bellock broke his gaze and looked directly into Harvey's eyes. Harvey felt unnerved and exposed.

Bellock looked back toward the forest as he resumed speaking.

"Harvey, imagine that you live in a house which has only one large room. The room has only one window and one door. The sole source of light for the room is the window. However, the entire window frame is filled with a mirror. On the middle of each side of the mirror's frame is a swivel. This swivel is attached to the window frame, allowing the mirror to tilt up or down.

The purpose of the swiveling mirror is to catch sunlight and redirect its rays inside the room to provide light. In order for this to occur, you would have to continually adjust the mirror so as to catch and reflect the rays of the ever-moving sun. But what would happen if you refused to adjust the mirror and left it standing in the window frame completely vertical, sealing off the room from the outside?

"I suppose there would be no light," Harvey replied.

"And?"

"And?" Harvey asked, having no idea as to what thought the conjunction was intended to lead him.

"How would you function in a room of total darkness?"

"I guess it would be hard to do much of anything. I don't know how I would survive. I would always be banging up against the walls and furniture. I'm sure before long both the house and I would be damaged."

"Harvey, if you understand this, then you can understand what is occurring in the minds of many men and women on your planet. There are growing numbers of those on Earth who are no longer receiving light into their minds, and as a consequence, their thinking has darkened. It has become dull and weak, hurting human lives and providing little thought energy for the orbs of my world."

Harvey nodded slowly while mulling over Bellock's words. Bellock let Harvey feel the texture and shape of these new thoughts before asking another question.

"Tell me, Harvey, who is the source of all understanding and knowledge? Who provides the light?"

Harvey thought for a moment. "I suppose it would be the Unseen."

"Correct you are. The Unseen. Unfortunately, an ever increasing number of your human race is no longer catching His light that so that their minds and thoughts might be illuminated. They are no longer adjusting the mirror in the window. They have begun to drift into dull and dark thinking. This is not the first time that this has occurred. However, this time there is something different afoot. In times past, when a certain area of the world grew dim, another would continue to burn brightly, but I fear now that a worldwide tilting away from the Unseen is occurring."

"But why? What's different this time?"

"That, my young friend, is the topic of tonight's conversation. Let us end our talk here and once again be on the move."

And with these words, Bellock arose to his towering height while Harvey climbed aboard Fromp once again. They traveled the remainder of the way to Council Gorge in silence.

11

The group journeyed for at least an hour before reaching the entrance to Council Gorge. The distance was only four miles as the crow flies, but the terrain had become rugged and more difficult to navigate. Whereas before travel was pleasurable when they were rolling effortlessly over the rising and sinking swells of lush alien grass, now it had become more cumbersome. The path they were on was becoming steeper, and they had to zigzag around enormous boulders.

Surrounding the gorge was a forest composed of what looked like pine trees, ten stories or more in height. If you were color blind, you might erroneously conclude that you were on Earth, merely looking upon a forest, but unlike the evergreens of Harvey's planet, these trees had a plumage more in line with a flamingo. Each of the needles of these Ecclonian pine trees was bright pink in color. Whenever a breath of wind wound its way through the forest, the needles swirled and swayed like the tentacles of a sea anemone.

Harvey asked Bellock what they were called. Bellock replied with a name that was a collision of so many syllables and consonants that Harvey didn't even bother trying to pronounce it. He dubbed them "Everpinks", a name that Bellock did not appear to be overly fond of.

The trees of the forest were so close to each other that it made Harvey think that they were traveling through the faded pink carpet of his grandmother's living room. Like the eye of a hurricane, the gorge was located directly in the middle of the surrounding sea of Everpink trees.

Traversing the forest took about thirty minutes. When they finally made their exit, Harvey was startled by the appearance of an imposing Flurn who seemed to be playing the part of a sentinel, guarding the entrance to the gorge. Harvey slid off of Fromp and stood still, paralyzed by the unblinking stare of the Flurn's stoic face. Bellock didn't say anything. He wanted Harvey to make the recognition on his own.

"What is he looking at, and why doesn't he move?" thought Harvey.

Walking slowly up to the Flurn, he tentatively reached out to touch his trunk in order to confirm his suspicion. It was cold to the touch – stone cold.

"It's him, isn't it? Harvey asked. "The one you told me about, Gnarl the Petrified. This is the Flurn who turned to stone because he was chasing a thought for so long."

"It is indeed," replied Bellock. "A reminder to us all of the danger of losing oneself in oneself."

Just beyond Gnarl the Petrified, the ground dropped and opened, creating a gorge five hundred feet deep and six miles wide. The walls of the gorge were composed of rock and quartz, a variegated mosaic of greens and blues. At the bottom of the gorge the walls closed in upon one another, leaving a flat plain only two miles in width, completely covered with trees. A large piece of blue quartz, flat and level on its top, rose from the ground at the edge of the tree line.

"This gathering is perhaps the most important of them all. That is why thousands of Flurn have been called to attend, but let us make our descent with haste. It appears that they are waiting, and you, my young friend, are the main attraction. "

Bellock started down the winding path that would lead them down into the basin, but Harvey remained standing, staring into the gorge, and in a moment, understood. He wasn't seeing thousands of trees. It was a massive assemblage of Flurn who were waiting for the proceedings to commence.

On the way down the trail, Harvey made a point of keeping his distance from Fromp, who was bounding on all four paws as if his legs had been replaced with springs, erratically bouncing him in every direction. It was obvious that this wasn't the first time Fromp had been to a gathering at Council Gorge. Apparently, he was overly excited about cavorting in nips and sniffs with others of his kind, for as Harvey could clearly see now, each Flurn in attendance was accompanied by his own warp-hound.

When Harvey finally reached the bottom of the trail and his eyesight leveled off, what he observed begged for a word weightier than "pandemonium" or "chaos". Numerous Flurn were wildly waving their branch arms, accentuating their passionate conversations, or more likely, arguments, about Bellock's selection, while the warp-hounds were frolicking with one another.

Harvey didn't think that a meeting could ever be called to order, but surprisingly, just as Bellock stepped off the trail and onto the floor of the gorge, every Flurn stopped speaking and turned in his direction. They had sensed the proximity of their leader, and so too did the warp-hounds, for after a few seconds of whining, they brought their frolicking to an end and dejectedly sat down next to their Flurn.

Parting before his presence, Flurn nodded in respect as they created a path to the raised platform of blue quartz. Harvey felt that Bellock had taken on a nobler air, not arrogant, but rather stepping with ease into an earned position of honor.

It was at this point that Harvey recalled that Bellock had introduced himself when they had first met as “Lord of the Flurn”. It was a title, based on the way Bellock carried himself and the respect and deference displayed by all in attendance, that he wore exceedingly well.

Every Flurn and warp-hound watched Bellock’s movements as he climbed the chiseled steps of the quartz platform. Fromp followed on his heels, tilting his snout upward as he regally pranced across the platform, enjoying the attention from his fellow warp-hounds, which most certainly were envious that Fromp belonged to such an illustrious and well respected Flurn.

Bellock had instructed Harvey to sit down on the steps until he was called to join him on the platform. Harvey hoped that Bellock would again be long-winded. The last thing he wanted to do at that moment was to be presented to thousands of Flurn as the solution to their perilous situation.

When Fromp sat down next to Bellock and was gazing up at him in adoration, Bellock began his address in a commanding and powerful voice that reverberated off of the gorge’s walls.

"My fine fellow Flurn, you well know the reason for which you have been called to gather this day. Our planet's existence and the security of all dimensions are now in grave jeopardy. You are all aware of the threat to our planet. The energy source for our orb clouds is degenerating rapidly as a growing number of humans bend their thoughts away from the life energy of the Unseen. While human thought was once infused with power, it has now begun to weaken, threatening our demise. But all hope is not lost. It has been retrieved and is with us this very day."

With these words, Bellock turned and extended a branch arm towards Harvey, motioning for him to join him on the platform. Harvey slowly rose and walked to Bellock.

Groans of disapproval and sighs of disbelief rumbled through the crowd. Harvey was certain that everyone could hear his unsettled gulp. It was exactly the type of reception he had expected because it echoed his own reaction when Bellock first told him why he had been brought to Ecclon. Bellock waited until the murmuring eased back into silence before resuming his address.

"Your reaction to the one retrieved from Earth is understandable. I will concede that his physical appearance is lacking, not what one typically equates with heroics and battles against dark powers, but please remember what our revered Gnarl the Deep once said, 'First impressions, though not impressive, may in the end impress us all.' This proverb, I am most confident, will ring true of young Harvey George, my selection for our present dilemma.

"I have been entrusted to lead the Flurn because your perception of me is one of unparalleled discernment and discretion. If you still believe this, I beg you to be confident in my choice. The boy needs your support to give him the courage and resolve required to combat the enemy. I realize that he is a green and tender shoot, but my search has been long and thorough in discovering the perfect human for this task."

Bellock paused and let the words he had spoken ripen in the minds of his fellow Flurn. After a temporized minute he began again.

"Yes, he is young, but his thinking is very deep and true, enough I believe to resist the deceptions of the Insips. My warp-hound, Fromp, had no difficulty in quickly scenting the thought energy of Harvey, a further confirmation that my choice is sound. I will conclude, therefore, with another adage from Gnarl the Deep, 'The eyes of a giant are blinded by the smallest grains of sand.'"

As he stared at the crowd, Harvey could tell that Bellock's words were changing minds. Heads were slowly nodding, conveying tacit agreement with Bellock.

Bellock concluded his remarks with a request and a blessing, "Would the Council of Elders please join me on the rock to speak privately with young Harvey. After our meeting, the leaders of your clans will share with you the particulars of our conversation. Thank you for the honor of permitting me to address you this day, and may the thoughts of the Unseen lift your leaves and run deeply in your roots."

With these words, Bellock turned to Harvey and informed him that the leaders of the twenty different Flurn clans would gather on the platform to discuss the particulars of his mission. Before Harvey had a chance to respond, the first Flurn was already atop the platform, and in short order, Harvey found himself feeling even more out of place, awkwardly standing in the center of forty appraising eyes.

12

A stouter and shorter Flurn, with a kind and tender-wooded disposition, named Merum was the first to speak. In a soft, almost caressing voice, he said, "I suppose we have little choice but to trust your decision, Bellock, but it still seems a brittle response to what we are facing."

"A bit of trust is all I need, and I thank you for it, Merum," Bellock respectfully replied with a nod.

Salix, a wispy Flurn who stood five feet taller than Bellock, spoke next. "I have known you long enough to realize that once you sow a seed you never uproot the plant, even when it is quite apparent that you are wrong. Since your decision has been made, it seems the only thing to do now is to sift through the grim details."

Salix's outer bark was rough and uneven, an accurate reflection of his ornery disposition. He was always quick with a criticism or pessimistic prognostication, but those who spent time in the same soil with him, knew that if you could ever get under his contrary exterior, you would find him to be as soft as balsa wood.

Bellock began, "Harvey must return very soon, and other than Fromp, he will be going alone."

"Alone!" shouted Salix. "How can you be so shortsighted and foolish? How in the name of Ecclon do you expect him to..."

Bellock abruptly interrupted Salix. The tall Flurn's tone would unravel Harvey's spirit even more if Bellock didn't check it. In a calm and controlled voice, Bellock completed Salix's thought. "How will he survive? One of the reasons I selected Harvey is because the enemy will initially take little notice of him. Who would? He is young and non-descript, and therefore, no cause for anyone to pay him much attention. This, I hope, will serve as his camouflage, allowing him to infiltrate the Vapid's stronghold and retrieve the book."

"And why do you suppose this attempt will be any more successful than the last?" snapped Salix.

"Lessons have been learned."

Merum had been staring at Harvey during the exchange between Bellock and Salix. He broke his gaze. Wearing an expression of genuine concern, he walked closer to Bellock and stated just above a whisper. "It is too much for one so young and inexperienced to handle. He needs more time to absorb everything. Yesterday, his worries orbited the concern of being accepted by his peers. Today, the future of all worlds rests on his shoulders. It is too much."

"I know it is a ponderous weight to bear," Bellock said, "but there is so little time. As you have, no doubt, observed, the light of the orb clouds has significantly decreased in previous days. The enemy is bending thinking even more rapidly than we feared. I had originally intended for young Harvey to stay with us for weeks, but now..."

Bellock stopped speaking and glanced at Harvey before looking back at the Flurn leaders and continued with a sigh. "He must return to Earth tomorrow. If we tarry any longer, it may be too late."

"But he is not ready, and how can you send him in alone? He will be walking into a warzone, blind and deaf!" Salix shouted yet again.

"Calm down, Salix. He will not be going totally alone. Fromp will be with him, and I believe he will be ready enough when the time comes for him to face the Vapid. I would not consider sending him against the enemy unequipped and ill-prepared."

The three Flurn had become so engrossed in their conversation that they failed to observe the whitening of Harvey's face. The weight of the words which he was hearing was just too much for him to support any longer. A few seconds later, the Flurn were interrupted by a thump on the ground. Harvey had fainted.

Bellock immediately went to his side and placed a rootlet hand on his forehead. He is alright. Only fainted. Too much too soon, I know."

"So, you are still confident in your choice, Bellock?" Salix condescended as they all looked down at an unconscious Harvey.

Seemingly unaffected by Harvey's passed-out and prone position, Salix continued without giving Bellock a chance to respond. "Who, may I ask, has the ability to equip and prepare him in such little time?"

"There is only one logical choice," replied Bellock, "the one who understands both of our worlds, and more importantly, the mind tactics of the enemy."

"You cannot mean Sheef," Salix gasped incredulously.

Bellock answered, "I can and I do. Sheef is our only choice. You must agree that there is no alternative."

"But can he be trusted after his turn to the enemy?" Merum asked.

Bellock remained silent for a moment before responding. "He turned back."

"Yes he did," Salix reluctantly agreed, "but metal once bent becomes all the easier to bend a second time."

"Perhaps so, but can you think of one better to train Harvey?"

With no quip or any type of response whatsoever from Salix, Bellock continued, "I do not feel that Sheef is in danger of falling under the influence of the enemy's propaganda a second time. I am not saying that it could not happen again. Heaven knows how susceptible humans are to the seduction of the Vapid, but Sheef's mind and thoughts are now protected by a formidable mental wall."

"A mental wall?" Salix asked.

"Yes, a mental wall, erected by Sheef himself. It is a wall of humility. He fell victim to the enemy's deceptions because he did not *think* that he could fall victim to the enemy's deceptions. Pride is a thick mist that obscures truth and invites delusion. This was the chink in Sheef's armor, but his foray into the camp of the enemy has mended it. His thoughts are now protected by his humility."

Salix was about to respond but was interrupted by Harvey's groggy recovery of his consciousness.

"It appears as though our young warrior has elected to rejoin us," Merum reported with a grin of relief.

Harvey slowly sat up, connecting the most recent events to the present. It took him a few minutes before he recalled the narrative of the last day and was able to determine what page of this strange unfolding tale he was currently on. He was still attempting to bring the world back into focus when he felt a puff of hot air on his right cheek.

An overly ripe odor followed on its heels. It was Fromp. There he sat with tongue splayed long, only inches from Harvey's face. Harvey lightly patted his head.

Merum had quickly taken to Harvey. Though he questioned Bellock, he knew in his heart after first meeting Harvey that the selection was correct. He knew all too well what Harvey was about to confront, and his fear for the boy's safety was even greater than that of Harvey's. Merum bent down and placed one of his rootlet hands on Harvey's shoulder and began speaking words of encouragement, not only for the boy, but for himself as well.

With a grandfatherly tone he said, "Harvey, I am grieved that so much has been placed in your pack to carry over rough and unpredictable terrain. How I wish it were not so, but in moments such as these, we must answer the call when it is given, no matter how unpleasant the call may be. Please remember, however, that a call such as yours is never given lest the strength to accomplish it is given as well."

Merum's words were absorbed by Harvey, releasing some of the tension in his neck and back.

"You must be wondering how it all can come down to someone so young. Consider how difficult it would be for one who has never seen a tree to comprehend its small beginnings. A seed, so small and insignificant. Ah, but what potential lies within! It waits for the appointed time, a time when conditions are perfect for it to sprout and break free. Roots burrow deep, pushing aside and splitting rock, while bough, branch, and leaf stretch and spread."

Merum stopped speaking and waited until Harvey looked up and met his eyes.

"Harvey, you are such a seed. If you were not, the wisest living Flurn would not have selected you. I believe that there is much potential and power lying dormant within you, waiting for the conditions to be just right for you to sprout and break forth into your purpose."

"But I don't know what I'm supposed to do. Fighting, darkness, and a, a, book?" Harvey stammered. "I have no idea what you all are talking about. How can I be the one for this?"

"One bite at a time," Merum said. "What you need to know at this point is that you are returning very soon to your world with Fromp. When you arrive, you will spend time with a man named Sheef. He has extensive knowledge of the enemy and how to combat him. He will train you well for the task which you have been given."

"Is Sheef human or like..."

"Like us?" Merum finished with a chuckle. "No, he is as human as you are, Harvey."

Here Merum turned to Bellock and asked, "Does he understand the extent of what would happen if the orb clouds ceased shining and Ecclon fell into darkness?"

"He does not. Presently he only knows how human thought affects our orb clouds, and that it is deviating from the thoughts of the Unseen."

Merum turned back to Harvey and said with increased gravity in his voice, "Harvey, Bellock has already shared with you how human thought from earth affects the amount of light generated by the orb clouds here on Ecclon, and how the light from these clouds sustains all life on our planet, including the Flurn. Strange as this all still must sound, you know this now to be true, but do you know the role of the Flurn and what would happen if they were no more?"

The question was rhetorical, so without giving Harvey any margin to answer, Merum continued. "Ecclon is known as the Gateway Planet, the door to all other dimensional worlds, and the Flurn are the ones who protect the gateway. As long as the Flurn exist, the worlds are safe, but if we were no more..."

"There would be no one to protect the other worlds," Salix solemnly interjected. "And now, Harvey, you begin to understand the depth of the threat and why I am not confident in this choice for leading the charge against the threat."

"Enough, Salix!" commanded Bellock. Your words are only making matters worse. Say something thoughtless like that again and I promise I will strip every leaf off of that twiggy head of yours!"

With a humph and scowl, Salix reluctantly submitted to Bellock's command.

Bellock looked to Merum and nodded for him to resume his explanation. "Dark forces known as the Vapid have for centuries thrived on your planet. They have grown in strength by feasting on the thoughts of humans when they turn away from the thought energy of the Unseen. Unfortunately, their appetites are never satiated. The more they consume, the more they desire, and the Vapid know that there is a veritable banquet to feast upon in the thoughts of creatures that dwell in other dimensional worlds, if only they could gain access to them. As of now, the Vapid are confined to Earth, but if something were to happen to the Flurn, there would be nothing to prevent them from taking over Ecclon and all of her doorways."

Harvey nodded as the mental haze that had disoriented him for much of the day began to dissipate.

Merum continued, "Since the vitality of the orb clouds is inextricably tied to the thinking of humans, the Vapid have been for countless years attacking human thought, using every lie at their disposal to turn people's minds away from the life-giving thought energy of the Unseen. And of late, the number of humans turning their thoughts away from the Unseen has increased significantly. This is why we suspect that the Vapid are using something to amplify the power of their deceptions."

"The book I heard you mention," Harvey guessed.

"Yes, it is a collection of lies infused with an incredible power to deceive. The Vapid are very skilled at deception, but a lie has no power over a human mind until it is accepted, believed, and declared. The more a lie is believed, and the more frequently it is spoken by a human tongue, the weightier it becomes, ever increasing in force to turn other humans away from the thoughts of the Unseen.

"We believe that so many humans have been collectively speaking aloud the same lies that they have now become powerful enough to materialize. The Vapid, apparently, have fashioned a type of parchment that can capture these deceptions. Binding the pages together, a book has been created."

"It almost sounds like the book created itself," remarked Harvey.

"It does, but the thinking of humans is the true author," said Merum. "Humans, by repetitively and collectively speaking these lies, created the book. Remember, Harvey, you humans are created in the image of the creative Unseen, who caused things to come into material being with mere words. Why would you not expect something similar to happen when millions of humans declare the same thing time and time again?"

"And you believe these Vapid things are using the book?" asked Harvey.

"Unfortunately, yes. When a Vapid reads from the book and speaks aloud the lies, its power to deceive is mixed with a human's power to deceive itself. The result is an incredible tangle of deception, turning many more away from the thought energy of the Unseen."

Bellock could see that the liquid in Harvey's cup was on the verge of dripping over its rim. "Merum, I think he has heard enough for now. Sheef will apprise him of the particulars during his training. For now, let us be about departing. Ecclon's time is waning. Harvey must leave soon, and so must we. We will depart shortly for the Shellows."

13

Bellock and the Flurn Elders led Harvey off the platform and into an open area to the right. All of the ground of Council Gorge was actually "open area" when it wasn't teeming with Flurn and hound. During the gatherings, however, the serene grassy meadow of the gorge was transformed into a Flurn forest, so congested with trunks and branches that if you were to wander into it, there is little chance you would be able to find your way out. You would be a bewildered captive of the Flurn forest until the gathering dispersed and the maze that had entrapped you got up and walked away.

Harvey didn't have to worry about this because the elders had instructed that a small clearing, encircled by some of the largest Flurn, be made. Here, Bellock and the Flurn Elders enjoyed a nutrient- rich repast. They gathered closely to one another, beyond Harvey's hearing, so that they might speak candidly about Harvey's mission and discuss what, if anything, could be done if the mission was unsuccessful. Sinking their roots deeply into the moist soil, they absorbed mineral-infused waters and conversed in hushed tones for hours.

Harvey, meanwhile, was sitting with an exhausted Fromp in the middle of the clearing. After the group had left the platform, Bellock released Fromp to romp with his fellow hounds. After tearing around the congested Flurn forest with a dozen other charged warp-hounds for an hour, Fromp returned to the clearing and collapsed next to Harvey. The warp-hound lay on his side, exposing his belly in hopes of inviting a scratch. Harvey soon took the hint and set his fingers to work on the indigo belly.

He scratched Fromp for a good fifteen minutes before stopping to take a bite of Kreen that Bellock had brought over to him. As before, a single taste satiated both hunger and thirst. Full and drowsy, he lay down and used Fromp's soft belly as a pillow. It wasn't long till he and the hound were soundly asleep.

Hours later, Harvey was awoken by the gentle shaking of Merum's rootlet hand.

"It is time for us to leave for the Shellows, Harvey. You will be on your way back to your planet before another day there has passed."

Those weren't comforting words. Though his knowledge of the Vapid was scant at best, the little he did know made him want to stay on Ecclon indefinitely.

Bellock, Salix, Merum, Harvey, and Fromp were soon up and on their way. Fromp took the lead, sniffing and zigzagging out in front. Bellock and Harvey were next, walking beside each other, shoulder to trunk, and rounding out the party were Salix and Merum.

Once they settled into their steps, Harvey turned to Bellock and asked him a question about a word that had been hovering in his mind since first hearing it.

"Bellock, what exactly are the Shellows?"

"The only way of returning to your world," answered Bellock.

"But why can't Fromp take me back?" Harvey wasn't sure why he said this because his first episode upon Fromp's back was not something that he wanted to become reacquainted with anytime soon.

"Fromp cannot take you back because... Well, truth and trunk be told, we do not know why, but warp-hounds can only open portals from other worlds. In order to exit Ecclon, one must use a Shellow."

As their conversation proceeded, the party walked through a narrow gap at the end of the gorge. It was so narrow that everyone had to walk in a single file line. The sheer vertical walls rose, leaning closer and closer to one another, as if the increasing height was creating an attraction between them that didn't exist at the base of the gorge where the air was thicker and more sensible. The attraction finally culminated in a kiss where the two walls touched each other.

Harvey had the feeling that at any moment the walls would crumble into one another, crushing and burying the entire party, and so he was quite relieved when the narrow gap suddenly widened, revealing a vista of rolling green hills, punctuated with what looked like enormous seashells.

Bellock stopped walking, halting Merum, Salix, Harvey and Fromp, and swept his rootlet hand before him. "The Shellow

Plains. Doorways to the worlds, and one of these, Harvey, will take you back home."

Harvey's eyes tracked with the motion of Bellock's hand, drinking in the grand panorama before him. The rolling hills were a vibrant and verdant green, like the countryside of Ireland, but rather than sheep dotting the landscape, there were thousands upon thousands of shells. Variegated in every nuance of the color spectrum, the shells were grouped together in myriad forms and shapes. Closest and to the left was a semicircle, filled with equally spaced maroon and cream colored shells. To the right, a trapezoid, its perimeter composed of a double row of amber shells.

It seemed to Harvey that every shape he had seen in a math book or doodled in the margins of his notebook paper was located somewhere on the vast plain: a square half filled, a solid octagon, a spiral with dozens of arms chasing one another in a clockwise direction. The shapes continued to the horizon, blurring as they outdistanced the range of Harvey's vision.

So overcome by the enormity and artistry of it all, Harvey let many minutes slip through his fingers before he realized the implications of what lay before him. When the realization did hit, it struck with such force that it momentarily dislocated the breath from his lungs.

"Each one of these leads to another world?"

Bellock's smiling eyes met Harvey's. He was obviously enjoying witnessing the walls of Harvey's understanding crumble, releasing a fresh curiosity to run wild. "You could spend a lifetime exploring what exists on the other side of the Shellows, and you would only be scratching the surface. The worlds of the Unseen are as the grains of the desert sands."

Salix stepped around the dumbfounded boy and handed Bellock a large cylinder.

"Thank you, Salix. It matters not how many times we send someone through to Earth, there are just too many to remember."

Harvey turned and looked at Bellock as he pulled out and unrolled a long piece of yellowed parchment.

"What is that?" asked Harvey.

"This," replied Bellock, "is the Shellway Chart, a map of what is before you. Without it, you might as well forget about ever making it back to your world."

Harvey glanced down at the unfurled map held by all three of the Flurn. The map was covered with hundreds of tiny shapes labeled with minuscule, indecipherable symbols, which Harvey concluded were the letters of an Ecclonian language.

"Ah, here it is, right in the middle of the twenty-sixth arm of the Meclo Spiral," Bellock said as he pointed out the location to the others. "Let us be off then. It will take at least a half day to reach it."

And so the party descended to the plain and began a trek to the Shellow that would take Harvey back to his world. A world which would only be the same in name, for everything he knew about it had changed forever.

Hours later the group arrived at a turquoise shell, very similar to a Conch shell resting on its side, and about the size of a delivery truck. Gaping wide at the bottom was an opening. Bellock halted the party about ten feet from the Shellow.

Looking into the Shellow, there was little to see, for just after the opening, the passageway turned sharply upward and wound itself into a tight spiral.

"Is it safe?" asked Harvey

"Safe? No, nothing is ever truly safe, but for the most part it can be trusted. It has been years since we have lost anyone."

Bellock's answer hardly reassured Harvey, but at this point he had little other choice but to grab hold of what was provided, and if trust was all that he was being offered, then trust was what he would have to take.

"So what do I do?"

"Walk and enter. That is really all there is to it, but let Fromp go first. He will lead you directly to Sheef.

"Does he know Sheef's scent?"

"No, even better, he knows his thinking. Every human has a distinct thinking signature. It is a type of fingerprint of thought. How do you suppose Fromp first found you? If all goes accordingly, you should appear at Sheef's front door."

"And if it doesn't go accordingly?"

"Some thoughts are better left unthought."

Apparently, Fromp had been through many a Shellow and thoroughly enjoyed the experience, for when Harvey looked to his right where Fromp was standing, he observed an animal in the throes of anticipatory anxiety. A restrained whine was pulling hard against its chain of obedience as a tremor developed in his hindquarters. It was clear that Fromp was waiting for a word of release from Bellock. Merum noticed Fromp's behavior also and said that if Bellock didn't release him soon, the quaking of Fromp's back end might rattle itself free from the rest of his body.

"Let us not delay for both Fromp and Harvey's sake," said Bellock. "Hesitation is the food of fear, binding one from action." Bellock announced this as much for Harvey as for himself, for he had quickly grown fond of the boy and feared much more for his safety than his tone indicated.

After he had said these words, the three Flurn gathered around Harvey, each placing a rootlet hand upon his head. Merum uttered a simple blessing, "To all directions which you go, may you be covered from above, lifted from below, and filled from within."

When Merum finished his blessing, Harvey turned to Bellock and asked, "Will we see each other again?"

"In our worlds I cannot say, for I do not know, but if not, we shall meet again in another world when we leave ours that one last time."

Harvey preferred not to think about leaving Earth "that one last time" and sincerely hoped that this final departure was not scheduled anytime soon.

Bellock looked down at Fromp and said only one word. Fromp turned and met Bellock's eyes with his, and Harvey thought he saw a slight grin momentarily appear along the gums of Fromp's snout.

"Hold onto his tail and keep holding on," commanded Bellock. "If you let go, who can say where you will end up." These were hardly the last words Harvey wanted to hear before entering a dimensional warp hole.

Fromp offered his tail to Harvey as a gentleman would do with his arm when escorting a lady, and as soon as Harvey gripped the furry lifeline, Fromp burst forth, shooting off with bullet velocity into the Shellow.

A second after entering the opening, both Fromp and Harvey were suctioned up and away into the spiraling interior. And with that, the mission to save Ecclon and all worlds had begun.

14

Harvey was stretched thin and taut, and then wound tightly into an infinitesimal tiny dot before completely disappearing. When he was vacuumed into the innards of the Shellow, it felt as if someone had grabbed his head and pulled it upward with superhuman strength, while his feet remained securely anchored to the ground, stretching his body toilet paper thin. And like toilet paper, he was wrapped round and round, growing ever smaller, as his elongated body followed the decreasing size of the spiraling interior.

During the entire episode, which only lasted a few seconds, he was unable to breathe, and just when he thought that either he would expire because of asphyxiation or was crushed to death, there was a tremendous pop, followed by the sensation of release. The pop turned out to be the sound of Harvey's body rapidly expanding back to its original size. Imagine how pleasurable and liberating it would feel to have been suddenly freed and allowed to "inflate" after being bent, twisted, and compressed into a speck the size of a microscopic, one-celled creature.

It wasn't until after he had passed through the Shellow that he realized that he was still firmly grasping Fromp's tail, and as ruffled and rumbled as Harvey felt from the experience, Fromp appeared to be entirely unfazed. Harvey surmised that this was yet another dimensional jump to add to the dozens that Fromp had previously made.

The enthusiastic warp-hound and Harvey were gliding with incredible speed through what can only be described as a grey void, and though it had color, it wasn't composed of any detectable substance. Harvey could feel no air pressure against his skin, and yet, he knew that he was traveling extremely fast. As for something to breathe, either there was some oxygen to draw upon or it simply wasn't needed.

If you were to ask him how much time had elapsed during his journey through the grey void, he wouldn't be able to honestly say. To Harvey, time seemed to have been forgotten in this place, as if it was of so little consequence and relevance that it had been dropped into the disposal of needless things and flushed away.

Perhaps this notion of time being a nonfactor was the result of Harvey having no desire regarding time as he moved through the void. We all become more aware of the passage of time when we desire something to last longer so that we might savor just one more "lick" of the enjoyable experience. Just think of the last days of any holiday break when the hours seem to pass like minutes, as the resumption of school, in all its bleakness, looms before us. And how acutely aware are we of time slowly dripping by, one monotonous drop at a time, when enduring something unpleasant, such as the droning math teacher who crawls through the muck and mud of a tortuous lesson on the difference between the associative and communicative properties.

The point is that Harvey, for the first time in his life, was without any desire for an experience to last longer or to be cut shorter. He, in a word, just "was". Now it would be wrong to assume that he was content, because that would mean that he was aware of a positive feeling - that of being satisfied - which would be something that he would desire to last longer, which as we already know, he did not. Harvey said later that he and Fromp might have flown through the void for minutes, days, or even years. In a place where the dimension of time is absent, how could one ever know?

After however long they traveled through the grey void, a thin green horizontal line appeared in the approaching distance. At first it was only thread thin, but quickly grew vertically from both sides into a massive wall, hundreds of feet, then thousands of feet, and kept expanding until it finally surpassed all "feets", obliterating every unit of measurement

It made absolutely no sense to Harvey, but the one thing that he did understand was that he and Fromp must have been traveling at a mindboggling speed, maybe even that of light, for the thin line to enlarge into such an enormous wall so rapidly.

How close was Harvey to the wall when he first realized that he was not slowing down and that at some point he would make impact with it? Distance in the void, like time and speed, was impossible to determine, and it really didn't matter anyway. What did matter was the inevitable and unavoidable fact that contact, hard contact, with the wall was quickly approaching.

"Emerald," he thought to himself. "It looks like a wall of emerald, and emerald is hard, very hard." Harvey's recognition of what it reminded him of only increased his already elevated anxiety about his impending union with the wall. And as he sailed on to what he believed would be a most painful experience, a peculiar thought sprouted in his mind. The human brain seems to wait for the most inopportune moments for its most bizarre notions.

He thought, "A bug, say a dragonfly, is buzzing about the business of searching for its next meal. Enjoying the rays of sunshine dancing upon its wings and the wind swaying its antennas, it's blissfully unaware of its approaching doom. A car is traveling at sixty-five miles per hour on a direct collision course with the dragonfly. The bug detects movement out of the corner of one of its bulbous, compound eyes; it's a smaller insect, lunch. The dragonfly adjusts its flight direction toward its prey, and then... SPLAT! Windshield smacks dragonfly. Dragonfly becomes abstract art. Is that my fate? Am I a bug on the way to my own demise? Will I hit the green wall with such a splat? I guess in situations like this it would be better to be a bug like the dragonfly. At least it didn't know what was coming. It enjoyed life right up till the end."

Just when this thought began to darken his future, a new thought surfaced and gave Harvey hope. "But Bellock must know what occurs when traveling between worlds, and he didn't seem at all worried about my safety. And Fromp, if I didn't know better, looks as if he actually can't wait to reach the wall."

Harvey thought this about Fromp because Fromp's legs were moving at a full sprint, even though they weren't making contact with anything at all, and his neck was stretched out to its maximum length, as if he was straining with all his might against Harvey's hold on his tail.

These thoughts about the nature of the impact with the wall were abruptly cut short when he suddenly hit and passed through it. Though colored like emerald, it lacked its solidity.

If you had been observing Harvey and Fromp enter the wall from the void, you would have probably described them as being absorbed by the wall rather than hitting it, and if you were one of those rare individuals who notices the tiniest of details, you might have observed that just before they entered it, the wall actually jumped out towards them and pulled them in.

Lime gelatin. It was as if he had fallen into the world's largest bowl of lime gelatin. Of course, it wasn't really gelatin, but at first the texture and consistency were exactly the same. I say "at first" because the longer Harvey was in it, the more its viscosity changed, becoming thinner and lighter.

Initially, it was a struggle to even move, but after being in the substance for about ten minutes, he found himself moving his arms and legs as you might do while swimming from one side of a pool to the other, and it wasn't long after this that he was able to easily walk around as if he was back on Earth. He had no idea whether the substance was changing states or he was. Either the material was becoming less solid or he was becoming more so.

And what was even stranger and more perplexing to Harvey was that he wasn't gasping for breath, when it was perfectly logical that he should be, considering that upon impact, his entire mouth, trachea, and lungs were filled with the green goo.

He wasn't straining for air. Actually, it was the complete opposite. He felt as if he had descended from a high mountain top where the air was thin and scarce, to sea-level where it was thick and bountiful, breathing the way he was really meant to for the first time in his life. With each passing second, his entire body brightened with more energy and spring.

As Harvey sensed the atmosphere becoming less solid, he did in no way sense it becoming less tangible. It's true that within a short amount of time he didn't have to struggle or swim in order to move, but he felt that there was still something around him, pressing in and covering him from head to toe. One thing was certain; he and Fromp were not alone.

Safe and secure is how Harvey felt. It reminded him of the days long ago before his mother became ill. When in instances of pain or fright - falling off his bike and scraping his knee, or being rattled awake in the middle of the night by the exploding boom of a clap of thunder - she comforted him by tightly cradling him in her arms. Those arms were a shield that protected him from any danger the world hurled his way, and as long as his mom held him, he believed he was safe. That was how he felt here, but to a much greater degree.

Earlier, when he was journeying through the grey void, he had no sense of time because he had no desire for the experience to continue or end, but in the green place, where he felt safe, secure, and at peace, he was very cognizant of the transpiring ticks of time.

Back on earth, Harvey had been through countless thunderstorms, but he, like most people, never grew comfortable in seeing lightning bolts or hearing thunder booms.

The problem is that there's just no way of predicting when they will strike, and if you're not prepared and are always caught off guard, how can you ever not be afraid? Another bolt is surely coming, and yet, it still causes a flinch or leap in shock when it does come.

That's the way it occurs on Earth. In the green place, however, Harvey wasn't surprised or caught off guard, because he could actually see the bolt of lightning approaching from a great distance.

It began as a tiny pinpoint of yellow light on the horizon, but rapidly ate up the distance in mere milliseconds to where Harvey was standing. It struck, but amazingly, it didn't knock him off his feet or burn his body. Instead, after entering his body, the lightning scattered into millions of miniature bolts, firing down every passageway and into every cell.

Death to life! Frankenstein's monster! The inanimate animated! And what had brought him into the world of the living? Lightning, electricity! It was as if Harvey, too, had been lifeless, and then a moment later, had been sparked alive. For many minutes his limbs shook in smaller tremors in the aftermath of the original quake.

Closely on its heels, a sensation of satisfied fullness and well-being bubbled from deep within. Like the effervescent carbonated response of a shaken and agitated soda when opened, Harvey feared that something might possibly froth out of his mouth, nose, and ears, or worse, he might burst if the bubbling continued for much longer.

He never had the chance to figure out what would have happened if he had stayed any longer, for at the height of this experience, an opening suddenly appeared in the floor, directly below him and Fromp.

They dropped down with a "whoosh" into a tube a tad wider than Harvey's arm span. They weren't in the tube very long before they were shot out like a spud from and potato gun, emerging into a world of blue skies, white clouds, and yellow sun. Earth!

SHEEF

15

"Down, Fromp! Come on, get down, boy! Yes, I'm glad to see you, too. Nothing like a dimensional leap to light a fire under a warp-hound. And what did that old piece of driftwood, Bellock, have you drag to my doorstep?"

Harvey heard all of this while face down in the dirt. Apparently, when you open a dimensional door, it's a very prudent idea to get your rear end out of the way quickly, because as soon as you step through the door, it slams shut with such force that a powerful energy burst is generated, capable of knocking down anything in front of it. One second Harvey was savoring the hills and trees of his familiar planet, and the next, what felt like a large foot kicked his backside, launching him airborne some ten feet skyward.

Arms and legs flailing, he had no time to get control of his body before his face touched down in the brown dirt furrows of a small garden. While still face down and wearing a tight fitting earthen mask, Harvey felt a hand shake his right shoulder.

"Are you alright? Can you move?"

Harvey couldn't immediately respond due to the air being knocked free and clear of his lungs. However, no bones seemed to be broken. The freshly tilled dirt had acted like a cushion, making his crash landing much less injurious than it could have been.

He responded to the shaking and questioning by rolling over on his backside and looking up into the face of a middle-aged man wearing a red baseball cap and a ragged, faded navy blue sweatshirt. It was a seasoned and genial face: the wrinkles in his forehead and the crow's feet around his eyes seemed to smile in concert with his mouth. A good and humorous nature was burrowed just under the skin. It was a face that you immediately liked, and though that of a stranger, it radiated a friendly familiarity.

"I guess that's the end of the peppers. No real loss, though. Never was much of a fan. Now if you had hit my tomatoes, then we might have something to talk about. I guess this proves that no matter how much you prepare, you just can't be ready for all eventualities. Built a fence to keep the rabbits out and a scarecrow for the birds, but it never crossed my mind to fashion something in order to safeguard the garden from a dimensional jumper." The man's words were thinly coated with a layer of faux irritation, weakly concealing his kind nature.

"Alright, why don't you try and stand up. I need to see if all of your parts are still intact and operational."

Here the man gently helped Harvey to his feet and whisked dirt off of his back and shoulders.

"Sorry about the garden. I didn't mean to," began Harvey. "It's just that when I came through the opening from..."

"You got bumped, didn't you?" the man asked with a chuckle. "Always dive to the right and roll. That's what I used to remind myself whenever I made a jump. That door packs quite a punch when it closes."

"Tell me about it," responded Harvey as he rubbed his rear end.

"John Sheefer," the man said as he extended his hand.

Harvey returned the gesture and said, "You're Sheef."

"That's what most people call me."

"Bellock told me."

"No doubt that he did. And you must be Harvey."

"You know my name?"

"Fromp brought me a message from Bellock over a week ago telling me that you would be delivered here soon. So... you're the one."

"I bet you were expecting someone bigger and older."

"No, not necessarily. I learned long ago to trust Bellock's discernment, and I know that what it takes to combat the enemy has very little to do with one's age or size. Now if my memory serves me correctly, I seem to recall that dimensional travel always made me famished. Would you like something to eat?"

Up until Sheef said the word "famished", Harvey hadn't even thought about food, but as soon as the word was uttered, the gates to his saliva glands were thrown wide, and his stomach awoke and yawned so loudly that Fromp's ears perked up in curiosity. Sheef heard the grumbling also and said, "Gastronomical response to a question. That's a new one for me. I'll take that as a yes. Why don't we go inside, and I'll see what I can rummage out of the pantry."

Harvey followed Sheef and Fromp into a small cabin which was built between two grassy hills in a shallow valley. A narrow stream gurgled below the leafy boughs of the cottonwood, oak, cypress, and willow trees that adorned its banks. The cabin had two bedrooms, a small living area, an equally sized kitchen, and one bathroom. It would be claustrophobic for a family, but more than adequate for one person.

Harvey took a seat in a roughly hewn chair which looked like it had been made out of pieces of discarded cedar. The top of the table only had half of its eventual boards on it, indicating to all who sat there that it was still in the process of being built.

"Sorry about the table. I keep meaning to finish it, but when there's only one person eating, what's the point in having another half?"

"No one visits you?'

"You're the honored first guest to grace my cabin and table since I moved here."

"And where exactly is here?"

"Somewhere out in the country. That's all you need to know. Few people, and even more importantly, few creatures, know where I am, and if you don't mind, I'd like to keep it that way."

"You mean the enemy, don't you? The Vapid things Merum told me about. There are places free of them?"

"Well, no place is completely empty of them, but they tend to concentrate more in certain areas than in others."

Harvey gave Sheef a quizzical look.

"After we eat, I'll explain it to you. I've always found that it's so much easier to wrap my brain around something if it isn't being distracted by a nagging stomach."

Sheef went into the rustic kitchen. There were no decorations on the walls, drapes on the windows, or knickknacks on top of the cabinets, evidence that the cabin was entirely bereft of a female's softening touch. He hunted through the refrigerator and pantry, emerging with the ingredients of a bachelor's entrée: a loaf of white bread, peanut butter, and grape jelly.

"Hope you like PB&J's. My diet is pretty basic. Not much variation here. What I buy is only what will last in between trips to town, which is two hours away."

"PB&J's are fine with me. I eat them all the time."

Harvey suddenly felt a connection with Sheef. Because of his mother's illness and his father's sales job, he had been left alone to fend for many of his own dinners. A peanut butter and jelly sandwich, served up on a paper plate, was his supper on numerous evenings.

Sheef sloppily slapped two sandwiches together. He poured two large glasses of whole milk and set them down on the half-completed table. As is the habit of many of the male gender, he ate most of his sandwich and downed his glass of milk without uttering a word.

After searching intently around his gums and teeth for any bit of peanut butter residue with his tongue, Sheef began his explanation of the preferred locations of the enemy.

"The Vapid and their minions, the Insips, gravitate toward those areas where..."

Here Harvey interrupted by asking, "The Insips?"

"Bellock didn't tell you about them?"

"I heard them mentioned, but he didn't tell me anything about them."

"Well then, let's back up a bit, shall we? The Insips, as I said, are the minions, those that actually do the grunt work for the Vapid. Their job is to echo or amplify negative thoughts generated by humans, as well as speaking their own."

"What do they say?"

"Sometimes they speak their own lies, but much of the time they don't have to. They simply agree with the lies humans have already told themselves. Humans are very prone to self-deception. We're all susceptible to our own lies, distorting our perceptions of other people and ourselves. Do you know what I mean?"

"Not exactly."

"Let me see if I can provide you with a simple illustration."

Sheef tilted his head sideways and searched for an example that Harvey could relate to. After a minute or two he began. "Imagine that a fourteen-year-old girl has been invited to the birthday party of one of her classmates. This girl has recently moved to town, and the classmate who invited her to the party is attractive and smart, very popular at school.

"The new girl arrives at the party where everyone seems to be having a good time, laughing and chatting away with one another. Everyone, that is, except her. She's standing by the drink table with no one to talk to, feeling lost and completely out of place. Luckily, the birthday girl, the one who invited her, walks into the room. 'Finally, somebody to chat with,' the new girl thinks. Instead of chatting with her, however, the birthday girl scowls and walks right on by.

"The new girl is distraught. Her thoughts about herself quickly sour. 'She hates me. Everybody does! Apparently I was invited to the party as some type of joke, since it's obvious to me that no one at the party likes me.' She is completely humiliated. But as is so often the case, there's more to the story. Here's what was really going on.

"Just that morning the birthday girl found out that her dad was being transferred to another city. Her family will have to move within the month, and she will leave the only home that she has ever known. Everything she's familiar with, including all of her friends, is going to be torn away from her. And to make matters worse, right before the party, she had the biggest fight she's ever had with her parents.

"Now let's return to the scene when she rushed past the new girl. She wasn't scowling at her at all; in fact, she was doing her best to hold back a flood of tears that threatened to break loose after seeing all of her friends. She hurried out of the room because she didn't want to make a scene and embarrass herself.

"The new girl's interpretation of the event is flawed to say the least, but it doesn't matter that her perception is a lie, for to her, what she believes about the incident has become her 'truth'."

"But it's not the truth," Harvey said.

"You're right," replied Sheef, "and the only way for her to see that what she believes is a lie is for someone, outside of herself, to reveal what's really going on. She has deceived herself, and by herself, she will most likely never arrive at the real truth. What makes the situation even worse, is that she doesn't just believe the lie, she feels it as well."

At this point in the conversation, Harvey wished that he was back in his grandfather's rocking chair with pickle in hand, that he might be able cognitively digest what he was hearing. After a few moments he asked, "Why does feeling it make it worse?"

"Harvey, a lie becomes more entrenched whenever it's mixed with strong emotion. This is why sometimes, even when people are shown the truth in a given situation, they can believe it intellectually and even begin to see the logic in it, but they still experience difficulty letting go of the lie. Lies entangled with emotions are very hard to unravel."

Harvey thought of his own life and wondered how many lies of his own making had him tied up.

"So, Sheef, where do these Insip things come in?"

"I was just getting to that. Insips can't read human thoughts, but what they can do is carefully observe and listen. If you watch the behavior of someone, it's not that difficult, especially if you have years of experience doing it, to deduce what they are thinking. Also, when people are alone and are frustrated, discouraged or depressed - emotions typically encrusted with self-deception - they frequently talk to themselves, allowing any Insip present to hear. And whenever an Insip surmises or hears a "meaty one", it gets excited because it knows it's about to eat."

"Eat?"

"They feed on negative thoughts. Any thought opposed to the Unseen and his true nature, or anything that degrades human dignity, is a dinner bell to the Insip. Negative thoughts and lies are to the Insip what bloody, raw meat is to wolves."

Struggling to understand, Harvey asked, "So that's it? They just feed on bad thoughts?"

"Hardly," Sheef replied with disgust. "They reinforce the lie and make it even stronger by agreeing and speaking it back to the human who first thought it. Enormous power is generated when two voices agree on something. When the Insip whispers the thought back, the person hears it and believes it even more, which in turn gives off even more negative thought energy, attracting other Insips to join the feast. This cycle, unfortunately, will continue, and the lie will become more entrenched and destructive unless something breaks it."

Beginning to grasp what Sheef was saying, Harvey was suddenly very alarmed. "Do you think I've been affected by Insips?"

"Without question. If you are part of the human race, then you're right in the middle of a war for your mind, which means that you, without even knowing it, have tangled with Insips on numerous occasions. "

Sheef paused for a moment to refill his glass of milk. It was then that Harvey realized that he had gotten so caught up in what Sheef was saying that he hadn't yet taken a bite of his own sandwich. The pause gave him opportunity to do so; however, when he looked down at his plate, there was no sandwich to be seen.

It didn't take long for him to figure out what had happened to his lunch. Strange noises implicated the guilty party. A series of overly moist licks, smacks, and slurps were coming from the kitchen floor where a certain warp-hound was mouth-wrestling the bottom portion of a peanut butter and jelly sandwich. When Fromp surreptitiously nabbed the sandwich from Harvey's plate, the top fell off and onto the floor. The bottom piece, which was thickly slathered with peanut butter, made it into the animal's gaping mouth.

The stickiness of the peanut butter behaved as glue, attaching the entire piece of bread to the roof of Fromp's mouth. Once it was set, it was a stalactite. With no opposable thumbs on his paws, Fromp was left with nothing but his tongue to try to dislodge the bread and peanut butter.

He shook his head up and down and side to side, while his tongue slipped in and out like a serpent's. This was followed by him rolling on his back and pawing vainly at his jaws.

"Serves you right, you thief," Harvey said while laughing. "You can jump from one dimension to another, but it looks like you've met your match with a sandwich. I should let you lie there and suffer."

The sight was pathetic. Fromp was frustrated and was now flailing around the room, but no matter how much he shook his head or body, it did nothing to free him from the sandwich's death grip.

"As funny as it is to watch him writhe around, I think it's about time we literally lend him a hand," Sheef offered while cracking up himself.

Sheef walked over to Fromp who was now panting heavily after a three minute bout with the sandwich. Sheef placed one hand on his head in order to calm him. He carefully inserted the other into Fromp's mouth where he wedged his fingers between the edge of the bread and top of the warp-hound's mouth. With a quick flick of the wrist, his fingers were a spatula that popped the bread free from the roof. Once Sheef's hand was removed, Fromp gulped down the mucus-saturated bread.

"Harvey," Sheef said between chuckles, "let me make you another sandwich while I finish telling you about the Insips."

"There's more?"

"The Insips aren't satisfied with only agreeing with a lie. They make the meal even juicier and delectable by mixing in their own.

Think of the human generated lie as the spaghetti and the Insip's as the marinara sauce on top. Make sense?

"Not exactly," Harvey replied. "You kind of lost me at spaghetti."

"Tell you what," said Sheef, "let's go back to the example of the girl at the party. She misinterpreted what happened at the party and latched onto the lies that no one likes her, she's awkward and unattractive, and she'll never have a close friend. She concludes all of this by declaring herself a 'loser'. The Insips agree with all of this and then layer on their own lies."

"So they take advantage of the situation," Harvey remarked. "They exploit the situation."

"'Exploit!' Impressive and excellent word choice," Sheef complimented. "She's already feeling down and out. Because her self-esteem is in shambles, it won't take much to nudge her further down the road of negative thinking, and believe me, the Insips are masters when it comes to negative nudging. Day and night they will reinforce the lie that no one likes her.

"Once this lie is solidified in her mind, it will provide the foundation for additional lies to be built upon. They will whisper to her that this present rejection will only get worse in the future. And after they speak this to her countless times, they will then tie the idea of not being accepted and loved by people to her not being accepted by the Unseen. With continual, skillful prodding, she will learn not only to harbor resentment against herself and others, but also against the Unseen."

Sheef stopped to let Harvey process. After a minute or so he asked, "Are you getting it?"

"I think so."

"Well, why don't you tell it back to me. Then we'll be certain that you really do understand it."

"Okay. The Insips do two things. They agree with and repeat the lies that humans come up with on their own, and then they mix in their own lies with these. Their desire is that human thought will be poisoned, hurting them and ultimately turning them away from the Unseen. Do I have it?"

"Don't forget about them feeding on negative thoughts and...?"

"And?" Harvey asked, eyebrows raised in confusion.

"The reason that you are here with me. Ecclon? Remember that business about the orb clouds, the Flurn, and the future of all worlds?"

"How could I forget," Harvey moaned.

He took a bite of his sandwich and slowly chewed the peanut butter, bread, jelly, and everything that Sheef had shared about the Insips before asking his next questions. With a lump in his throat and a hollow stomach, he wasn't sure that he wanted to know the answer, but he felt like he had to ask it anyway.

"What do Insips look like? Will I be able to see them?"

"Look like?" Sheef thought for a moment before continuing. "Think of a huge mosquito, anywhere from six to sixteen inches in length. Replace its membranous wings with something more like leather and cover its body with scales. As for color, black or brown, although I have, on occasion, seen a few colored the most revolting shade of pea soup green. Though trying to see Insips with human vision is impossible because our eyes can only detect the physical realities of our own dimension. Creatures existing on Earth, but operating in a different dimensional plane, such as the Vapid and the Insips, are invisible to human sight.

"Then how do you know what they look like?"

"It's true that human eyesight can't perceive them, but there are ways to enhance one's vision."

Sheef rose from his chair and walked into the living space where a small coffee table was located. Looking back over his shoulder, he asked Harvey if he would come help him move the table off of an area rug lying underneath the table. Harvey complied, but he couldn't remember if the lifting advice for heavy objects was "all legs and no back, or all back and no legs". In the end it didn't really matter because the table was much lighter than it appeared. Once the table was moved, Sheef slid the rug to the side, revealing a square door in the wooden floor.

"This is where I keep my other worldly items. If someone accidently happened upon any of these things, it could be harmful to their health and would definitely raise questions that I couldn't possibly answer. It's just better if I keep everything buried and out of sight."

Sheef descended down a five-foot wooden ladder into a tiny room with metal shelves affixed to the walls. Harvey wasn't invited to follow, so he wasn't able to get a good look at any of the shelf items.

Sheef knew exactly where the object he wanted was, and in less than a minute, he was up and out of the room, holding a small bottle in his hand.

"Here we are then. New eyes in a bottle, Harvey. A few drops and you'll be able to see what's lurking behind the curtain."

16

"What is it?" Harvey asked with a lopsided expression.

"Did you eat any of the Kreen fruit when you were on Ecclon?'

"I had some when I first arrived and right before I left."

"Do you remember how it affected your body?"

As Harvey recalled how the exhilaration had coursed through his body after taking only one bite, a contented grin momentarily graced his countenance.

"I can read from your expression that you remember the experience. The effects of Kreen on the human body aren't confined to Ecclon. This small bottle contains nothing else but Kreen nectar. A drop in each of your eyes and ears is all it takes to see and hear what other humans can't."

"Is it permanent?"

"Thankfully, no. How overwhelmingly burdensome it would be to always be seeing and hearing another world. One dimension is frequently more than my senses can handle. Think, for example, what it would be like if you had the ability to see and hear every radio and television signal being broadcast through the airways at any given time. And imagine if this capability was permanent. You could never turn off the sights and sounds."

Harvey's face colored with mild annoyance. "I can't think of a worse punishment. I love my times of peace and quiet when I can just sit and think."

"You and me both," Sheef agreed. "Let's be thankful then that the changes brought about by the drops only last for about three hours. I don't believe any person could survive very long if the effects were permanent. The Insips are motor mouths, lacking the ability to ever shut up."

"So you're telling me that if I were to put the drops in my eyes right now, I would be able to see these Insip creatures?"

"Yes and no. The Kreen nectar, as I said, will allow you to see them, but only if they're present."

"There's none around us right now?"

"There might be some here, but if so, not many. Do you remember where this conversation first began?"

Harvey tried to retrace his mental steps, but the conversation had taken so many unexpected twists and turns that he became lost when he tried to find his way back to the beginning.

"Not really."

"That's alright," Sheef chuckled. "I'm sure your brain is still reeling from everything that I've told you. Our conversation about the Insips began when I made the point that they tend to gather in some geographical locations more than others."

The mental fog in Harvey's mind began to clear, revealing the path back to the conversation's starting point.

"The reason I've decided to temporarily live in this area is that there tend to be fewer Insips here, and the power of the Vapid is weaker. I'm sure Bellock told you about my sojourn into the enemy's camp," Sheef sighed.

"For a time, I was under the complete influence and control of the Vapid, and even now, I'm still recovering from the ordeal. Bellock and I thought it best for me to recover in a place where the presence of the enemy is not so heavily felt."

Harvey was about to ask Sheef the details of what had happened, but then thought better of it. Harvey would let Sheef decide the time and place to share his story.

"Where, Harvey, do you suppose the Insips tend to congregate?"

"Well, since they feed on people's lies, I guess they would gather wherever there are lots of people." Harvey paused for a moment, and then offered, "Maybe the cities?"

"Very good reasoning. The Insips can't very well agree, lie, and feed on human thought if no humans are around. Since cities are places of concentrated, high populations, it makes perfect sense that Insips would be attracted there; however, this is not the only reason that they're drawn to the cities."

Sheef stopped speaking, rose from the table, and walked over to a cup on the counter which held an assortment of pens, pencils, and markers. He returned to his seat and handed a permanent marker to Harvey. He then reached into one of his pants' pockets and pulled out a quarter with his right hand, holding it out for Harvey's inspection.

"Harvey, I want you to take a good look at this quarter. Inspect it carefully. Be sure to take note of the date. Now, take the marker and place a dot or line somewhere on the coin, so that when you see it again, you'll know with certainty that it is the same coin."

Harvey had absolutely no idea what this had to do with the other reason for Insips gathering in cities, but after his time on Ecclon and the last two hours with Sheef, he had learned to go with the flow.

Once you've traveled to another world with a space retriever in order to learn from a tree that the fate of all worlds rests on your shoulders, someone asking you to put a mark on a quarter doesn't seem like a very strange request.

While Harvey was memorizing "1973" and placing a black dot on Washington's nose, Sheef got up and walked over to a small bookshelf in the living room. He returned a minute later with a book on gardening.

"Okay, now I want you to watch closely. I'm going to place the coin on the table and put this book on top of it. When I lightly tap my finger on the book, the coin will move through the solid wood of the table. If all goes well, you'll hear the coin hit the kitchen floor."

The trick worked precisely as Sheef had said it would. He placed the coin on the table, laid the gardening book on top of it, and tapped it with his index finger. A second later, Harvey heard the clink of a quarter as it landed on the floor. Sheef lifted up the book, revealing a table with no quarter.

"Alright, Harvey, pick the quarter up off the floor and tell me if it's the same coin."

Harvey bent down under the table to retrieve it, and sure enough, it was the same: a 1973, dotted-nosed quarter.

Sheef asked him once again, "Is it the same?"

"It is, but how did you do that? I saw you place the book on the coin. There's no way you could have grabbed the quarter from under the book. I would've seen you! I was watching the coin and the book the whole time."

"Exactly. You were carefully focused on those two things, but you weren't paying close attention to my hands or the sleeves of my sweatshirt. You were distracted away from what I was doing with my hands because you were so intent on watching what was occurring on the table. Let me do the trick again with another quarter. Like before, I want you to memorize the date and place a mark somewhere on the coin, but this time, keep an eye on my hands. Let me go over and get another book. The trick doesn't seem to work as well when you use the same book twice."

As Sheef performed the trick a second time, Harvey kept his eyes riveted on Sheef's hands and sleeves. At first, the trick proceeded exactly as it had before, and Harvey was beginning to feel a bit moronic at being fooled a second time, but then he saw it. It happened so quickly and deftly that he wasn't sure that what he thought he saw had actually taken place.

After Harvey had placed a dot, this time on Washington's ponytail, Sheef took the coin from Harvey in order to place it on the table, but in a split second, he dropped the coin down his right sleeve, while sliding out a different quarter from his left. He then quickly placed the different coin on the table and covered it with the book. When he tapped the top of the book, he let the original coin, the one with the ponytail dot, roll out of his right sleeve and onto the floor.

"Did you catch it this time?"

"I did! You had a second coin hidden in your sleeve, and that's the one you placed under the book. The one I marked, you dropped into your other sleeve and let it roll out onto the floor, making it appear that it had passed through the table. But I still don't get how you made the coin under the book disappear."

"Pick up the book and look underneath."

Harvey did as Sheef instructed and saw a quarter stuck to the bottom of the book.

"When I went to retrieve the book from the shelf, I quickly applied a smear of glue from a glue stick on the bottom of the book. Placing the book on top of the quarter and tapping it created enough force to stick the coin to the book, so that when I picked it up, it appeared as though the coin had vanished. "

Multiple light bulbs flickered on in Harvey's head. The mystery had been solved.

"So what is the lesson, Harvey?"

"The lesson?"

"Why did you miss it the first time?"

"I guess I wasn't paying attention to the right things."

"And that's because you were distracted by other things. So it is with humans who live in busy places such as cities. You see, people are so often ignorant of how their environment can both reveal and hide true reality. Take, for example, what happens when you get away from the hustle and bustle of daily life – all those distractions that can keep you from sensing what's really going on - and take time to enjoy the great outdoors.

"The natural world proclaims the artistry and creative genius of the one who made it. You can feel it nourish your soul when you stand on the shore of a placid mountain lake ringed by towering pines at the first light of day; when you look out into a massive canyon whose walls are painted by the sun's palette of oranges, pinks, and reds at sunset; or when you stand on the sands of a remote beach at night, beholding the glimmer of a million starry jewels.

"You feel something resonate deep inside, and though you may not be able to articulate what you feel, you know that it transcends your physical senses. A presence, much larger than yourself, has charged the atmosphere, and yet, you don't feel small and insignificant, but comforted by an intimate soothing that chases away all fear and anxiety. It is as though your soul has remembered a tune that it once knew, a tune that it was created to sing, but had been drowned out by the distractions and busyness of life and eventually forgotten.

"This is truth being unveiled through the natural world. Here, no concrete, steel, or glass obscures the Unseen's artistry, and so it is able to loudly proclaim His truth and existence. And when a human is in such a place, his or her mind can quiet down enough to hear the proclamation. Does this make sense? Do you know what I'm talking about?"

Harvey nodded. He knew exactly what Sheef was referring to. He had experienced it on the many walks through the woods and along Cypress Creek on his way to and from school. He had been late arriving to his first class on many a morning because he had stopped on his way to watch the sun peek its head over the tops of the trees to awaken the creek.

Sheef waited a minute or two before asking another question. He was letting Harvey enjoy the recollection.

"How do you think the Insips react to such places?"

"I would think that they wouldn't like them very much. Seems like they would want to stay away."

"They do for the most part. They are repelled by truth, so those areas which reflect the truth of the Unseen tend to send them packing. There are exceptions, of course. Some of the highly skilled Insips have been able to persuade humans that what they feel when they commune with nature is not a reflection of the Unseen, but some nondescript, abstract force, what some refer to as 'Mother Nature'. This erroneous notion can cause them, for lack of a better word, to begin 'worshipping' the mountains, trees, animals, and so on, instead of the One who actually made them."

Sheef pushed his chair away from the table and stood up and said, "Why don't we finish our conversation down by the creek. All this talk about the natural world makes me want to get out of this cabin and take some of it in. Do you like to fish?"

"I do but I only get the chance when we visit my uncle in Tennessee. He's the outdoorsman in the family, and he lives right on a lake."

"Well then, help yourself to the yellow fishing pole on the porch, and we'll see if we can catch something other than a PB&J for dinner."

Harvey followed Sheef onto the porch and picked up a small yellow fishing pole with a spinning reel that was leaning up against the porch rail. A silver spoon fishing lure was tied to the end of the line.

Sheef stuck his head back into the cabin and yelled for Fromp, who was so consumed with getting at the remaining peanut butter pockets in his gums and teeth, that he didn't even pay attention to the front door opening.

But at the sound of Sheef's voice, he scrambled to his feet and excitedly bolted through the partially opened door, swinging it wide open and knocking Sheef off his feet.

"Looks like I'm not the only one who got 'bumped' today," Harvey said with a smirk.

"Looks like it," Sheef agreed, laughing at himself. He got up, dusted himself off, and led the way down a trail to the stream. Harvey followed close behind, while Fromp crisscrossed the trail into the brush, leaping and snapping at dozens of dragonflies hovering in the afternoon air.

The trail soon ended, and they found themselves standing on the banks of a crystal clear stream. Their sudden appearance startled a number of fish, which darted from the open water to the protective overhangs of brush and tree on the other side of the stream.

"There are some nice brook trout in there, and the occasional rainbow if it's your day. Since it's just about dinner time for them, we should be able to catch a few. Cast your line towards the far bank, right next to the brown boulder. There's a deep hole there where the big ones like to lurk. When your lure hits the water, reel it in at a moderate speed."

Both Sheef and Harvey began casting and reeling under the softening rays of a tired sun. The water of the stream was so clear that Harvey could easily see the bottom, even in the deepest pockets. It was picturesque. Postcard worthy. The feeling one gets when being in a beautiful natural place - what Sheef had just described when they were in the cabin - is what Harvey experienced then. He sensed something encircling and supporting him, and he quickly recognized it. It was the same presence which he felt when he was in the green place.

"No," thought Harvey, "I don't believe that those Insips would like it here one bit."

Sheef was just about to begin explaining why the Insips are so drawn to the city, when something broke the water on the other side of the stream. A record breaker of a rainbow trout launched out of the water like a missile exploding out of a silo. Gleaming from the light of the late afternoon sun, the silver lure hung from the trout's lower lip. But the line didn't lead to Sheef's pole. The jerk was so sudden and hard, and the moss-covered rocks which Harvey was standing on so slippery, that it didn't take much to pull him over and in. Dropping unexpectedly into different environments was becoming an all too familiar experience for Harvey.

17

As soon as the fish broke through the water, Sheef knew not only what had happened, but also had a pretty good idea as to what was about to happen. It was the largest trout that he had ever seen in the stream, large enough to destabilize even the most seasoned angler, much less a one hundred twenty pound thirteen year old caught totally off guard. Harvey wasn't in any way positioned for a major bout with a monster trout. His pole didn't even have the opportunity to bend into the familiar semicircular shape characteristic of a quality fish fight.

The first tug on the pole turned out to be the last. Harvey should have immediately let go when he was pulled off balance, but for some unknown reason, instead of letting go, he gripped the pole even tighter.

He would have enjoyed the ride if he had been atop the water on a pair of skis, instead of being submerged and struggling for air. He was dragged at least fifty feet upstream before the line finally broke, freeing him to float to the surface like a detached fishing bobber.

The chain of events unfolded so quickly that Sheef had no time to help Harvey, not that he himself was in any condition to render any aid, for as soon as Harvey was thrown off balance and jerked into the water, Sheef was overcome by an uncontrollable fit of laughter, which had to fully run its course before he could to do much of anything again.

The manner in which Harvey surfaced only added fuel to Sheef's spasmodic hysterics. The tip of the fishing pole surfaced first, slowly rising out of the water like a submarine's periscope, followed by Harvey's raised right hand, still firmly gripping the pole's handle. Finally, his wet and matted head, accentuated with sprigs of riverweed, emerged from the deep like a newly formed island already sprouting vegetation.

Up until this point, Sheef was still a bit unsure about Bellock's decision to choose a thirteen- year-old boy, but when Harvey opened his mouth and said with a grin, "At least I saved the pole!" Sheef knew, then and there, that the right decision had been made.

"Here's a young man with a sense of humor, who's both courageous and tenacious. That's something that I can definitely work with," Sheef thought to himself.

Seconds after Harvey went in, Fromp followed. It wasn't concern for Harvey's safety that induced him to leap into the water, it was just the water. Warp-hounds love to swim and will splash in for the flimsiest of reasons. After Harvey surfaced, Fromp swam circles around him, barking and biting at the water.

Harvey couldn't believe it. It was the second time in less than a week that he had been dragged, drenched, and laughed at. Although this time, the culprit was a trout and not a rascal of a warp-hound.

Harvey did his best to swim, fully clothed, with only his left arm and legs. His right hand was occupied with holding the pole out of the water. Sheef waded into the stream, trying to lend him a hand, but was still laughing so hard that he had to concentrate on keeping himself from falling in the water as well.

When he finally did recover enough composure to utter an intelligible sentence, he said, "Here you are, all worried about the Insips, when the real threat to your life turns out to be a trout!"

It wasn't the wittiest thing to say given the humorous nature of the incident, but it didn't take much humor at all to cause Sheef to double over again in a second fit of hysterics.

It was only when Harvey had finally beached himself like a walrus on the bank that Sheef asked if he was alright. When Harvey attempted to respond that he was fine, he too was overwhelmed by the humorous chain of events. They laughed together until the hilarity of the situation sputtered and died.

Fromp emerged from the stream drenched and dripping. He shook violently and then sat down. For the next ten minutes no one spoke a word. Harvey and Sheef remained still as turtles, sunning themselves in the warmth of the last light of day.

Sheef finally broke the stillness by standing up and searching for some quality skipping stones along the water's edge.

After finding a few that looked as though they had been designed for optimum skipping, he said, "The water is moving a little too quickly to get many skips. The game I like to play is to try to get one really good skip in the middle of the stream that causes the stone to fly clear out of the other side, hitting my chosen target. Keep your eye on that medium-sized tree to the left of the brown boulder."

Sheef bent his knees, wound back his right arm, and let the stone sail. It touched down in the middle of the stream and then sprung back to life as it leapt up and over the boulder, flying just to the right of its intended target. Sheef's entire body leaned to the left, as if altering his posture would someone change the flight path of the stone.

"Missed it by a hair. Here, you give it a try, but mind you don't fall in again," Sheef said with a good natured pat on Harvey's back.

Harvey took the offered stone from Sheef but was unsuccessful in his first skip attempt. He did much better with subsequent skips and actually hit the tree twice in the course of about a dozen throws. Sheef was skipping stones right along with Harvey, and in short order, a little competition developed between the two of them as they selected various targets for each other to try to hit. About halfway through their competition, Sheef resumed the conversation about the Insips.

"Harvey, remind me why the Insips are attracted to the cities."

"They like the amount of people there and all of the distractions."

"Distractions are the key. Remember the coin trick, and how you were fooled because you were so focused on the book and the coin and not on my hands? All those people compressed into a small area can become a powerful distraction.

"Recall what I said about how our environments can reveal or hide truth. In the city, you primarily have an environment which reflects the creativity and ingenuity of man. There is absolutely nothing wrong with men constructing buildings and roads. These are things that we need in order to keep our society properly functioning. The problem is that cities - little worlds of concrete, steel, and glass – can blind and numb people to the presence of the Unseen that is sensed when they commune with nature. They are so consumed with the frenetic, high-paced life inside a man-made, concrete terrarium, that they can easily become oblivious to anything larger or more meaningful than their own fight for survival.

"Like an ant operating only by instinct in its daily toil, or an ostrich with its head buried in the ground, unaware of the threat of attack, distracted men and women of the cities become easy victims for the deceptive and destructive aims of the enemy.

"This is not to say that there aren't many people in the cities who are aware of the Unseen. There definitely are, but the point I'm trying to make is that it is generally easier for the Insips to deceive and keep people ignorant of the Unseen's presence and existence because of the distracting nature of the city environment.

"But enough about Insips for now. Let's get you into something dry and slap together some more PB&J's. Tomorrow we'll pick up some groceries and see if we can't add some variety and color to our meals."

"We're going into town tomorrow?" Harvey asked with a startled look.

"Not going to town. We're headed to the city. Classroom lecturing is over. It's time you received some real-world experience."

18

Considering what was in store for Harvey the following day, he thought that getting much sleep was out of the question. However, almost immediately after hitting the pillow, he was fast asleep. Flying through voids and gelatinous green walls, in addition to falling into a frigid stream, had significantly run down his batteries. His slumber was so deep that he snoozed away the hours far below the layer of dreams, awaking rested and reenergized.

They had a breakfast of stale cornflakes with no sugar and questionable milk. Harvey actually felt some curdles from the souring milk on his tongue, but he not only refrained from saying anything about it, but finished his bowl and helped himself to a second. He was famished and knew that he would need plenty of sustenance to carry him through the day.

When they finished breakfast, Sheef grabbed two large backpacks to hold the groceries he planned to buy in the city and the bottle of Kreen nectar.

"Don't want to forget this. You'd miss all the fun," Sheef remarked as he picked up the bottle and tossed it into one of the unzipped backpacks.

He then called to Fromp who was curled up at the end of Sheef's bed. "Come on, Fromp. We can't very well travel without you."

Fromp sprang as a spring from the bed and flew ten feet through the air into the living room, where he slid across the wooden floor and slammed into Sheef's legs.

"And he's safe!" Sheef shouted.

"You're going to bring Fromp with us to the city?"

"There's no way in the world that I'm leaving this hound alone in my cabin. He's ten years old, still relatively young for a warp-hound. Their life spans are very similar to those of humans. Like a ten-year-old child, he is brimming with energy, and believe me, the last thing you want to do is leave an animal his size cooped up inside with no constructive way of releasing it.

"I used to work with another warp-hound about Fromp's age, and made the mistake one day of leaving him all alone in my apartment. It was only for an hour. Needless to say, when I returned home, the place was destroyed: seven holes in the sheetrock and all the carpets had large chunks bitten out of them. That little incident cost me over two thousand dollars and got me evicted from the apartment building. And you may not have encountered it yet, but Fromp has a mischievous side to him that reveals itself when you least expect it. It's always a good idea to keep an eye on him."

As Sheef spoke, Fromp calmly sat on his haunches. His tongue was languidly hanging from his mouth, while his large brown eyes spoke innocence and disbelief to the actions of the destructive warp-hound Sheef had just described.

"Don't believe that look for a second, Harvey."

Fromp tilted his head to the side in an attempt to feign even more innocence.

"But more importantly," Sheef continued, "there's no easier nor faster way to travel. Warp-hounds aren't limited to only opening up doorways between dimensions. They can also create short warp holes between any two geographical points."

"You mean Fromp could create a doorway from wherever we are to a tropical island?"

"Sure he could. You could be surfing, sunning, and napping under palm trees within minutes."

At that moment, Harvey had never wanted anything more in his life-to be able to escape to a tropical paradise in order to splash around in the surf. It sounded so wonderful, not just because going there would mean he could act like a kid and not have to worry about Insips, Vapid, and saving the world, but because he knew it wasn't a possibility. Things become all the sweeter when we know that they are unattainable.

"Unfortunately, we're not going to a tropical island today, but to the major hub of hustle and bustle and distracted people – the big city."

He followed Sheef and Fromp outside. This time, though, they didn't take the path to the right which led down to the stream, but instead, walked straight ahead to a line of pine trees one hundred yards away.

The tall grass around the cabin was still wet from early morning dew, so that by the time he reached the pine trees, Harvey's pants and shoes were quite damp.

On the other side of the trees was a large meadow filled with yellow and orange wild flowers. Harvey followed Sheef to the middle of the meadow where he stopped and instructed Harvey to stand still. He commanded Fromp to sit, and then kneeled down on the ground so that he could look directly into the animal's eyes. Sheef stared intensely at Fromp for a least a minute before breaking his gaze and standing up.

"I was thinking him a thought of where I want him to take us. The sights, sounds, and smells of a particular city I have in mind. You see, warp-hounds don't hunt or track by using their noses to scent what they're after. They use their minds to hone in on thoughts."

"And he knows now which city you want to go to?"

"He does, and he'll get us there, no doubt about that, but exactly where in the city, I can't say with certainty. Don't worry, though, he's not going to have us appear inside of a brick wall or anything like that. He typically warps to an open area. As I was linking my thoughts to Fromp's, I thought of a park in the middle of the city, so it's likely that's exactly where we'll end up. Let's just hope that it's too early in the morning for Fromp's mischievous side to be awake."

Sheef made three clicking sounds with his mouth and then shouted four words. "Take us there, Fromp!"

Harvey braced himself in anticipation of being picked up by Fromp's tail and spun silly as had occurred when he was first transported to Ecclon, but this time, no furry tail reached out in his direction. Fromp did, however, begin rotating rapidly in pursuit of his tail as he had done when he warped Harvey to another dimension.

Within seconds, an eight foot whirlwind of wildflowers and dirt was spinning only feet away. Harvey watched the mini-tornado increase in speed until he was distracted by what sounded like barking above his head. He looked confusedly at Sheef who pointed to the very top of the whirlwind. There was Fromp wildly barking. His front paws and head were hanging over the edge of the cycling vortex. The whirlwind was spinning rapidly, but somehow Fromp was no longer moving, he was just hanging there as if it was nothing out of the ordinary.

Suddenly, the whirlwind leaned towards the ground. Apparently, Fromp's weight on only one side of the whirlwind caused it to capsize. Though still spinning quickly, the entire moving column of wind fell and thudded sideways on the ground.

Fromp excitedly hopped out and stood before a large rotating circle. The image of the meadow of wildflowers on the other side of the circle began to blur and fade. A different image came into focus. It was a city skyline behind a landscape of trees and grass.

"Your shortcut to the city. Looks like Fromp is taking us directly to the middle of the park. We'd better hurry up and go through. This door will only remain open for another twenty seconds or so, and Fromp won't have enough energy to open another one for at least an hour."

Stepping through the portal was no different than walking out the front door of a house. One second Harvey was in the meadow, the next he was in the middle of an enormous metropolis.

Everything appeared to be fine until Harvey recognized an animal looking at him from a grassy area about fifty yards away. It was a very large dog with an extremely long tail, violently swishing the air. The dog appeared to be grinning. Apparently, the side of Fromp that Sheef had warned Harvey about was awake and well.

Up until this point, he had not looked down, but when he finally did, he realized the particular fix that he and Sheef were in. The ground wasn't green and smooth, but blue and wavy, gently moving beneath their feet. They were standing above the water in the middle of a large pond. Somehow, Fromp had managed to warp himself safely to the bank, while sending Harvey and Sheef to the center of the pond.

There's a brief moment in a cartoon when a character realizes that he has just run off a cliff into nothing but empty air and momentarily stands suspended in the air before falling. Harvey and Sheef experienced such a cartoon moment. When they both realized where they were, they had just enough time to glance at each other and exchange looks of shock before dropping.

They came up gasping for breath and shouting oaths of a certain hound's demise. When they reached the bank, Fromp greeted them both by licking their dripping faces.

Sheef addressed Fromp with a raspy voice while placing a leash on the animal. "You measly warp devil. If we didn't need you for getting around, I'd make you into a rug for my cabin."

Obviously Sheef didn't mean what he said, but it sure felt good to say it.

"Well, let's get walking. Hopefully the exercise will dry us out a bit."

Walking single file, with Fromp sheepishly leashed behind Sheef, they were soon surrounded by a cacophony of car horns and the crumbs of a thousand conversations.

"City life," said Sheef, "there's nothing like it. So much culture to savor. I love all the different people tossed together in one giant concrete bowl."

"But isn't much of it distractions for the Insips."

"Yes, but it doesn't mean that the distractions themselves are bad or that this city isn't incredible. Large cities, such as this one, remain wonderful places to live. In fact, if not for my incident with the enemy, I would probably live here. You need to know that distractions don't necessarily make a place bad, they just make the Insip's job easier."

They walked five blocks to an open plaza enclosed by skyscrapers. People were walking in every direction, many of them acting as if no one else in the plaza even existed.

"So busy and distracted," Sheef observed. "Most are lost in their own little worlds. Even the sight of a large purple dog barely turns heads."

Sheef directed Harvey to a bench with an excellent vantage point from which to people watch.

Sheef unzipped one of the backpacks and pulled out the bottle of Kreen nectar. He unscrewed the eyedropper top and placed a drop in each of his eyes and ears. He then handed the eyedropper to Harvey.

"Remember, you only need one drop in your eyes and ears. Any more and the effects will last for the entire day, and trust me, three hours with open eyes is more than enough. Initially it will sting a little, and your vision will blur for a minute or two, but both of these effects will quickly pass. Whatever you do, don't stand up right away. Seeing two dimensions simultaneously wreaks havoc on depth perception and balance. It will take your mind ten minutes or so to adjust."

Harvey took the eyedropper from Sheef with a shaking hand. He was shaking so badly, in fact, that Sheef worried that Harvey might poke his eye out or puncture an eardrum. Slowly, he lifted the quaking dropper to his right eye. He could see a tear emerge from the bottom of the dropper. Time seemed to drag as the drop slowly grew to the size and weight that would allow it to detach and fall. The anxiety- laced anticipation was too much to bear, so Harvey decided to hurry along the process of growth and detachment by shaking the dropper. It did the trick.

The impact of the first drop was accompanied by a stinging sensation. Harvey quickly applied the other three drops and tightly closed his eyes.

He heard multiple high-pitched voices speaking all at once. Some were soothing and kind, while others were harsh and accusatory. When he opened his eyes, everything before him was distorted and blurred: a watercolor painting with too much water applied. It looked as if the lines surrounding objects and people had been erased, allowing the colors to escape and mix with one another. But as Sheef had said, this was momentary. Within minutes, things began to sharpen and redefine themselves.

What Harvey saw jolted him backwards, nearly flipping him over the bench. He immediately shut his eyes.

"It's alright," Sheef said while gently placing a hand on Harvey's back. "I reacted exactly the same the first time. Take a moment or two to relax and get adjusted. Nothing's going to hurt you."

It took Harvey a few minutes to catch his breath and calm down enough to reopen his panicked eyes. When he finally did, he slowly panned his head from the left to the right, capturing the panorama before him.

“Tell me what you are hearing and seeing,” Sheef calmly said.

“Voices, thousands of whispering voices. And the people... Some have what look like light coming out of them. They’re glowing brightly.”

“And the others?’

“There are more of them, but light’s not coming out but going in. They’re not glowing like the others. They’re shadowy,” Harvey whispered.

“What you’re seeing are life givers and life takers. The people that you see giving off light are the ones who are attuned to the thought energy of the Unseen, and this light and life energy – the same that powers the orb clouds of Ecclon – is flowing out of them, affecting anyone close by. The more life energy that flows out of them, the brighter they glow.”

“Do those close by know that they’re being affected?”

“They may not know exactly what’s going on when one of these glowing people is nearby, but they definitely sense that something is different. Usually, it’s very positive, and they feel more alive, but if a person is deeply controlled by the Vapid, he or she might grow hostile and angry in the presence of one of the glowing people.

“The others, the ones you said are shadowy, they are the life takers. They’re not attuned with the thought energy of the Unseen. No light flows out of them. Instead, they suck up any life energy around them. Being around people like this is draining.

Everything is about them. They're self-absorbed. They dominate conversations, always redirecting the attention and energy back on themselves. Think of the first group as suns and the second as black holes."

Harvey had wondered more than once, why he sometimes felt energetic around some people and drained around others. Now he knew.

"Do you see the Insips?"

Harvey saw them alright. Hundreds were buzzing about the heads of people in the plaza. Some were hovering only inches away, while others had landed and appeared as though they were feeding.

"I see them everywhere."

"Look around you, do see any close by?"

Harvey looked 180 degrees to the left and saw nothing, but when he turned the other direction, he saw two large Insips, each close to a foot long, hovering next to his head. They were leathery with beady yellow eyes. Small but menacing teeth filled their mouths. Harvey's heartbeat quickened as his breath went shallow.

"What do I do? Are they reading my thoughts? Do they know who I am and what I'm doing here?" Harvey said with rising panic in his voice.

"Calm down. I saw those two Insips arrive a few seconds ago. Remember, they can't read thoughts. Now listen carefully and do exactly what I tell you. Look directly into their eyes. Like dogs and cats, they can't stand when a human stares directly at them. It makes them feel exposed and vulnerable."

Harvey lifted his eyes and stared squarely at one of the Insips. The creature let out a squeaky moan and flew a few inches to the right, trying to break away from Harvey's stare. Harvey kept his eyes riveted on the Insip. It tried a second time to break away by shifting to the left. When this failed to stop Harvey's stare, the Insip looked at its partner and then back at Harvey. It then let out a wicked hiss and flew off in a huff. The other Insip quickly followed.

"You confused and frightened them for the time being. However, they'll be back with reinforcements. We should be long gone before that happens. Now tell me what you hear."

"I can hear voices, but I can't understand anything. There are just too many. Everything is all jumbled up."

"It's very important, Harvey, that you hear what they're saying. What you need to do is isolate a person with only one or two Insips."

Harvey looked around the plaza. The non-glowing people definitely had more Insips around them. He spotted a woman across the plaza who was sitting on a bench by herself. A large Insip was hanging upside down, its talons clinging to her hair. Its mouth was mere centimeters from her ear.

"What about the woman alone on the bench?" Harvey asked as he pointed across the plaza.

"That's perfect. Casually walk over there and take a seat next to her, but don't look at the Insip this time. You want it to stay so that you can hear what it's saying. Concentrate your thoughts and hearing on it. Try to block everything else out. I'm going to stay here. There's not enough room for all three of us on the bench. If I need to communicate with you, I will transmit a thought directly to your mind. Take a sip of the nectar. It will allow us to communicate with each other telepathically."

Harvey took a small sip of the nectar and then walked to the other side of the plaza. He tried to walk casually as Sheef had told him to do, but passing through a swarm of whispering and hissing Insips was an experience he wanted to shorten rather than prolong.

When he finally made it through the horde and reached the other side, he politely said to the women on the bench, "Excuse me, but do you mind if I sit here?"

The woman made an attempt at a weak smile and replied, "Oh no, go right ahead."

Harvey thanked her and sat down about two feet away. He resisted the temptation to look at the Insip which was still hanging upside down on the right side of her head. Staring straight ahead, he tried to appear as if he were studying a group of pigeons hopping around in the middle of the plaza. He concentrated on listening to nothing but what was next to him. Within seconds, he could clearly hear the whispers of the Insip.

19

"You're right. Sanders is out for your job. And you've been such a good a boss to her. You were so understanding when she came in late last month, and that performance review you gave her this year, such laudable praise for an average employee. And how does she thank you? She goes ahead and steals the biggest account of the year.

"What talent does she have for marketing cereal anyway? That new Toasted Grains and Fruit account-she was only chosen because she flatters Anderson. A first class suck-up, that's what she is. She'll say anything to anyone if it will advance her career. The idea for the cereal account was yours in the first place. You should be the one who's getting all the credit and praise, and she knows it, too.

"Did you see how smugly she looked at you during today's meeting, sitting right next to Anderson? But isn't that the way it's always been? People never giving you what you deserve. You should be the one running the department and not that idiot Anderson. Think of how much money would come rolling in if you were in charge.

"But do your coworkers recognize your brilliance and the good you do for them and the company? No, they just conspire against you, gossiping behind your back. It's best you don't trust any of them. Look out for no one but yourself. Sanders is conniving. Better to take her down before she does it to you.

"You know how to make her life difficult. The next time she comes in a minute late with another excuse about her colicky baby crying all night, dock her pay. Show her that you're not one to be tangled with. And, don't forget, you know ways to get someone fired."

Harvey clearly heard all of this from the Insip as if it was speaking directly to him and not to the woman. He couldn't hear what she was thinking, but he could tell by her tightening and souring countenance that the words were being received and taking root.

When he first saw her across the plaza, he noticed that she was one of the life takers. Shadows were swirling about her as light and life energy were absorbed. And now it was only getting worse. The more she listened and accepted the lies of the Insip, the darker the shadows colored.

"Oh, what is that?" Harvey thought to himself. A putrid odor, like that of rotting meat, drifted into his nostrils. He looked under the bench, expecting to see a dead animal or someone's unfinished lunch from a week ago, but there was nothing but concrete.

He hoped that it was a transitory smell that had stopped in front of the bench to catch its breath before heading to other areas where it could offend. Unfortunately, it didn't seem to have any inclination for moving on.

It wasn't until Harvey observed the behavior of a dozen or so Insips hovering nearby that he realized the source of the putrid odor. He saw them simultaneously tilt their heads up to scent the air. Once hooked by the scent, they spun around with appetites aroused. It was the woman's thoughts. The lies of the Insip were already beginning to fester and rot, releasing a foul, sewer stench. For the nearby hovering Insips, the dinner bell had been rung.

Their eyes locked onto the woman's head. Multiple screeches of delight accompanied their mad flight towards her. Within a matter of seconds, the Insips landed, completely covering her head.

Harvey resisted the temptation to turn and look, but with his peripheral vision, he could see the Insips jostling against each other. They made loud slurping noises as they fed off the woman's negative thought energy. It wasn't long before they were spewing their own lies and deceptions.

Suddenly, the woman turned on Harvey with a hatred that he had never seen before and said with seething vitriol, "Who are you and what do you want? Just leave us alone. Go away!"

The shock of what she said and how she said it was so disturbing that Harvey found himself unable to move. He wanted nothing more than to bolt away from the woman and her nest of Insips, but his legs had turned to jelly and refused to respond.

Whatever it was about Harvey, the woman didn't like it at all. Since he wasn't moving, she decided to get up and leave. She angrily grabbed her purse and jumped to her feet, but before bolting off into the crowd, she bent down, tilted her head, peered into Harvey's eyes, and snarled. It was the most frightening look he had ever seen, and he knew that it was something other than the woman that had looked at him.

Sheef watched the entire episode unfold from his bench across the plaza, and though he couldn't hear what the lady had said to Harvey, he was able to surmise the tone and flavor of her words by the manner in which she departed. When Harvey's face blanched snow white from shock, Sheef shot a thought at him straight across the plaza.

While still immobilized with fear, Harvey heard a familiar voice. He turned to the right expecting to see Sheef, who he assumed had walked over and taken a seat next to him while he was preoccupied with the woman, but when he turned, he only saw an empty bench. Glancing back across the plaza, he saw Sheef still seated.

"It's the Kreen nectar. He's linking to my thoughts," Harvey said to himself as he made eye contact with Sheef.

There were a few seconds of silence before Sheef's thought message broke in again.

"Harvey, just stay seated until your body and mind settle down. Once you catch your breath and your thoughts, send back a message explaining what happened."

It took about five minutes for Harvey's agitation to subside. He did his best to focus all his mental energy in the direction of Sheef as he projected his first thought across the plaza.

"Sheef, it was terrible. The Insip that was hanging on her head before the others came, spun its deception so well that I was beginning to believe what it was saying. At first I was disgusted by its voice and the lies that it was spewing, but by the time it finished twisting everything around, I was enjoying the sound of its voice and actually buying its lies."

Sheef volleyed back a thought to Harvey. "They're very good at what they do, and even if you know the techniques to defend against their deceptions, you can still be taken in. But I don't want you to worry. There's no one on this planet who knows how to combat this foe better than me. During my time with the Vapid, I received quite an education on the Insips, including how to exploit their weak spots. I promise to train you well and arm you with the weapons you will need to repel them, but let this be a lesson and a warning to you. Never think that you are beyond their ability to deceive, and never, ever let your guard down around them, even for a second."

Harvey sent another thought to Sheef, but the rate at which he thought the thought had significantly increased. If Harvey had actually spoken the words, he would have been gasping for breath.

"Sheef, the way that woman spoke to me... I've never heard anything like it"

"Harvey, slow down. What you witnessed wasn't her. I mean it was her voice, but it wasn't her speaking. All of those Insips injecting their venom into her mind totally overpowered her thoughts. They were speaking through her. Now, it's important that you tell me exactly what she said."

The thinking rate of his thoughts momentarily returned to normal, but as he recalled the words that were spoken to him, it again increased.

"She, or they, asked me who I was and what I wanted."

"Did they say anything else?"

"They told me to leave them alone and go away. Do you think they know what we're up to?"

"No, but somehow they knew you were aware of their presence, and their questions to you indicate that their suspicions were aroused. There's no doubt that they'll report back to whatever Vapid they serve and inform him of what happened."

Panic overwhelming the tenor of his thoughts, Harvey asked, "What do we do?"

Sheef's thought was loud and stern. "We need to get out of here immediately. If their Vapid Lord is nearby, he will send out a search party to comb the city. If he catches you here and now, it's all over."

"A Vapid Lord?"

"I don't have time to explain. Back to the park as fast as possible without running. The last thing we want to do is draw attention to ourselves."

Harvey got up and walked quickly over to Sheef and Fromp who were already heading back to the park.

Walking at a hurried pace, it was difficult to navigate around the pedestrians clogging the sidewalks. Harvey collided with several shoulders and bellies. He felt like a pinball being bounced between the machine's bumpers.

He had a difficult time keeping up with Sheef and Fromp, and on two occasions, he briefly lost sight of them. No words were spoken until they were two blocks from the park.

Panting and out of breath, Sheef directed Harvey's attention to a clump of bushes to the left of the pond where they had first arrived.

"Fromp can open up the portal in the middle of the bushes. They should hide him and what he's doing well enough so that no one will take notice."

Walking at their current pace, they would reach their target in less than two minutes, but it would take Fromp another minute to open up the warp hole back to the meadow. The good thing was that Sheef wouldn't have to waste time thinking to Fromp where he wanted to go. At the command of "back", Fromp would immediately know the destination.

They were delayed by heavy afternoon traffic on the last two streets they had to cross before reaching the park. Harvey observed Sheef's facial muscles tense as the seconds ticked by. Sheef knew that it was likely that the Insips had already given their report to their Vapid Lord and that a search party had been deployed to look for Harvey.

Sheef pressed the crosswalk button on the traffic light post for the fifth time. He knew that additional presses did nothing to shorten the time before the sign changed, but poking at the button released some of his skyrocketing anxiety. Finally, the electronic, ghostly image of a pedestrian appeared on the crossing sign. Sheef and Fromp resumed their brisk walk while Harvey remained motionless.

Felt, heard, and saw. In that order, Harvey sensed its approach. Up until this point, Harvey had never really experienced what could be labeled as utter hopelessness or despondency. It is true that he experienced bouts of sadness due to his mom's illness and the emptiness of much of their family life. He had not experienced, though, the kind of despair that makes one feel trapped in an emotional quicksand that, regardless of how much he fights against it, it continues to sap life and pull him deeper down into darkness. This horrendous bleak and empty feeling is what washed over Harvey's body and left him standing dumbfounded and frozen on the curb.

For most of the day, a pleasant breeze had been blowing across the city, moderating the temperature, but at the same moment the dark feeling enveloped Harvey, the air grew still. The atmosphere became heavy with heat and humidity.

And the sound, which came closely on the heels of the atmospheric change, was that of a massive inhalation of air. The noise caused Harvey to turn around and look back towards the plaza. A forty foot billowing black cloud filled the street that he had just come from and was quickly advancing in his direction.

It wasn't until Sheef and Fromp had made it to the curb on the other side of the street that Sheef realized Harvey wasn't with them. He looked back and saw Harvey standing in the same spot that he had been seconds ago. He cupped his hands around his mouth and shouted.

"Run! Harvey, run now!"

Fromp contributed his own shout by barking shrilly, and it was the bark and not Sheef's voice, that snapped Harvey out of his stupor. He shook his head and began running as fast as he could across the street. The cross walk sign had already changed to "Don't Walk" so Harvey was forced to pivot around two moving cars. As soon as he made it to the curb and joined Sheef and Fromp, they all sprinted off across the final street, running as fast as their feet and paws would carry them.

There's an unspoken rule that most people are aware of regarding what shouldn't be done if you ever find yourself in a situation in which you are being chased on foot: whatever you do, don't turn around to look at the thing pursuing you. Violating this rule will slow you down and increase your chances of being caught. This is all perfectly logical, but logic doesn't always prevail in such situations.

Whatever was behind Harvey was terrifying, and he knew that if he were caught, some form of pain would probably be inevitable, so doing anything foolish at this moment, such as turning around, would only increase the likelihood of the unknown pain becoming a reality. However, just like the proverbial cat, Harvey's curiosity got the better of him. In the middle of the last street before the park, he turned back and looked. What he saw stopped him dead in his tracks.

The billowing dark cloud was three blocks away, but given the speed at which it was traveling, it would engulf Harvey within the minute. When he turned his gaze upon the cloud, it appeared the same as it had when he first saw it, but as he continued to look, it began to change.

The dark clouds dissipated, revealing a beautiful tropical beach, and sitting on the beach, building a lovely sandcastle, were his mother and father. They were laughing and smiling, and when they saw Harvey, they invited him to come and join the fun. An enormous grin lifted the corners of his lips.

Immobile in the middle of the street, he began to feel that his entire body was becoming lighter, so light that at any moment he might lift off the ground and float effortlessly over to the beach.

This feeling of lightness moved through his entire body, beginning in his feet and then rising all the way to the tips of his hair. Five seconds later, though, he couldn't even think straight.

The letters making up the words of his thoughts became so jumbled that he couldn't even remember his name.

Sheef had already reached the bushes, and Fromp was in the process of opening the warp hole. For the second time, Sheef realized that Harvey had been left behind. He turned around and saw Harvey in a dream-like state, slowly swaying back and forth in the middle of the street.

He shouted at the top of his lungs, "HARVEY, KEEP RUNNING! DON'T LOOK AT IT! KEEP YOUR EYES ON ME!"

Harvey could barley hear Sheef call his name. His words sounded remote and thin, like they were spoken from the bottom of a deep pit.

Sheef continued to shout, but Harvey could no longer hear him. The sucking sound of the thing behind him had replaced every other noise in the city.

Sheef knew all too well what was happening to Harvey. The Vapid Lord was luring him in, and if he didn't do something quickly, everything might end before it began.

Running back into the street at full speed, Sheef crashed into Harvey, knocking him off his feet and jolting him out of his stupor.

Harvey landed on the asphalt right in front of a moving taxi, which slammed on its brakes, stopping inches from Harvey's head. Curled in a fetal position while grabbing his right knee, he began to moan and shout.

"My knee! Sheef, what are you doing? Why'd you hit me?"

There was no time to respond. The black cloud was now only a football field away. With a surge of fear-induced strength rifling through his body, Sheef bent down and scooped up Harvey. He threw him over his shoulder with fireman alacrity and sprinted for the now opened warp hole.

Sheef ran as fast as he could, but age and the extra poundage on his shoulder were taking their toll. The cloud was moving faster now, and Sheef knew that making it to the bushes and through the hole would be close. He reached down deep and found one remaining burst of energy.

When they were less than five feet from the warp hole, the leading edge of the cloud morphed into the shape of an arm. The hand at its end elongated, and skeletal fingers lunged for Sheef's legs. They grabbed him around his right ankle as he jumped into the warp hole. Once the hand made contact with his body, it ceased being gaseous and turned hard and solid.

Sheef and Harvey could see the meadow with wild flowers only inches away, but when Sheef leaped through, he felt something violently latch onto his leg, causing him to trip and fall into the meadow. They made it through, but so had the arm and hand.

When Sheef fell and hit the ground, Harvey was flipped off his shoulders and into the dirt. Sheef was lying face down and clawing at the ground. He did his best to get a firm finger hold on the soil, but the grip of the hand on his ankle was too strong, and Sheef soon found himself losing the battle as he was dragged backwards.

20

Harvey had no idea that something had grabbed Sheef as they were warping back to the meadow. Given the speed at which he was running and the instability due to the extra weight on his shoulders, Harvey assumed that Sheef had simply tripped, and it wasn't until he heard him cry out in pain that he realized something was wrong.

For a brief moment, bewilderment was Harvey's only response to what has happening to Sheef. This reaction was understandable considering what was occurring from Harvey's perspective. He too was lying on the ground, and when he turned around in reaction to Sheef's screams, he couldn't see the arm and hand which had reached through the portal and were still attached to Sheef's ankle. The only thing that he could see was that Sheef, for some reason, was sliding backwards.

Bewilderment became comprehension when Harvey rose to his feet and saw the reason for Sheef's backward movement. He ran toward the hand without having any idea of what he was going to do to it when he reached it. Luckily, he didn't have to figure it out.

Snarling with fangs bared, Fromp darted around Harvey's legs and attacked the arm. When Fromp clamped his teeth on the arm's wrist, Harvey heard what sounded like bone being crushed.

Fromp's bite separated the hand from the arm. Sheef, who was no longer moving, looked back and saw the stump retract through the hole. A second after it disappeared, the warp hole closed. The hand, which was still clinging to Sheef's ankle, turned gaseous and vanished.

Sheef sat up and began rubbing his ankle. "Well, it doesn't get much closer than that," he said as he grimaced in pain.

There was blood seeping through the bottom of his pant leg where the nails of the skeletal hand had dug deeply. Sheef lifted his pant leg to inspect the injury. Five puncture wounds had left their mark.

Fromp had already begun treating the wound in the only way he knew how. As soon as Sheef had lifted his pant leg, Fromp's tongue was out of his mouth and onto Sheef's ankle, lapping up the oozing blood and applying a salve of saliva.

"That will definitely leave an interesting scar. At least the enemy didn't get away unscathed, and it looks like I owe you one, Fromp," Sheef said as he patted the warp-hound's head.

"You think you can help me get back to the cabin?" Sheef asked Harvey as he shakily stood up.

Harvey nodded and positioned himself so that Sheef could use his body to take the weight off of his right ankle. Once stabilized with his human crutch, Sheef limped back to the cabin. Harvey helped Sheef get settled on the couch in the cabin's living room.

"I need you to go into the kitchen and open the cabinet next to the sink. Bring me the bottle of rubbing alcohol, the roll of gauze, and the largest bandages you can find."

Harvey followed Sheef's instructions and was soon back at the couch where he spent the next few minutes helping Sheef clean and dress the wound. When they were done, Harvey sat down next to Sheef and asked the question that had been weighing on his mind since they had returned.

"Sheef, what was that thing?"

"That was one of the Vapid Lords, and a very powerful one I might add. You see, every Insip serves a Vapid, a creature that, as you just witnessed, has the ability to alter its substance and shape. Basically, these are the brains of the operation, and each Vapid oversees a certain territory and commands a horde of Insips. The most powerful Vapids, known as 'Lords', tend to be found wherever there are highly concentrated human populations.

"Like the city."

"Like the city. They're consumed with nothing but hatred for the Unseen, and anyone who has his or her thoughts inclined towards Him. Their goal is to wage war using every weapon of deception at their disposal, and as I'm sure Bellock told you back on Ecclon, they're not content to restrict their warfare to Earth. Their hope is to expand the battle beyond Earth and into every other dimension."

Ever since arriving back at the cabin, Harvey's head ached. As Sheef talked about the Vapid, the pressure behind his forehead increased to the point that beads of sweat began to appear on his face. Immediately, Sheef knew what was happening and felt guilty for not addressing it sooner.

"Your head's hurting isn't it?"

"How did you know?"

"I'm sorry, Harvey, I should've have warned you about this. I guess the attack by the Vapid kind of distracted me. The reason for the headache is that the effects of the Kreen nectar are wearing off. Your mind is readjusting. The headaches will lessen each time you use the nectar.

"I've got some lemons on the kitchen counter. Slice one in half and squeeze the juice from the entire lemon into a glass. Drink it all. It will make you pucker like crazy, but the acidity of the juice will quicken the readjustment of your mind and alleviate the headache."

Harvey did as he was told and found that Sheef was correct on both counts: his face squinted from the puckering and the headache was soon gone.

After Sheef had dressed his injury, and they had both rested from their ordeal with the Vapid, they headed down to the stream in the hopes of catching dinner. The original plan had been to fill up the backpacks with groceries while in the city, but obviously that plan had been scrapped. Now, with even the peanut butter and jelly provisions running low, they were much more serious about landing some trout.

Because of Sheef's wound, it took them twice as long to reach the stream, but unlike the day before, this time Harvey walked back to the cabin dry and carrying a stringer of six nice-sized brook trout.

While he was fishing, he tried to enjoy the beauty of the stream, but it was mostly in vain. The images, sounds, and feelings from his encounter with the Vapid Lord kept bullying themselves to the forefront of his mind, pushing aside and silencing most of his other thoughts.

Sheef filleted the fish and seasoned them with salt, pepper, and a squeeze of lemon. Not long afterward, they dined on trout that had been swimming less than two hours before.

After he finished his first two fillets, Sheef said, "Beats peanut butter and jelly any day. These half dozen practically jumped straight from the stream and into the pan, and that, my young friend, is what makes them so delicious. The fresher the catch, the better the taste."

Sheef couldn't imagine how traumatic the events of the morning had been for Harvey. It had been traumatic for him, and he was an adult with experience with the enemy. Such an event would mentally and emotionally paralyze most grown men, much less a thirteen year old.

He could tell by Harvey's silence and the serious expression on his face during their time fishing, and now at dinner, that he was trying to process and make sense of what had occurred. Sheef's remarks about the fish were a failed attempt to try to lighten the mood, but he soon realized that the best course of action was to face it head on.

"What's on your mind, Harvey?"

To be truthful, Harvey would've preferred not talking about it at all and forgetting the incident entirely, but since this wasn't an option, he thought it would be best to get his thoughts and growing fears out of his head and out in the open.

It took a while before Harvey began talking, and when he finally did, his words came out slowly and were interspersed with pauses and sighs.

"Before I even saw the Vapid cloud approaching, I had this horrible feeling. If you hadn't shouted at me and got me running across the street, that feeling might have killed me."

"Death is unlikely, but describing the feeling you experienced with that term is actually quite accurate. Think about it logically. If the Unseen is the source of life-giving thought energy, then it makes perfect sense that a power that stands in stark opposition to Him would project the other side: death-giving thought energy. You see, when you remove life, all you're left with is death.

"How would you describe a person, for example, who is fully alive, vibrant, and healthy? Would they not be hopeful and optimistic, moving forward and rising up? If so, then what about a person who is not dead physically, but is so emotionally and mentally? Wouldn't they exhibit the opposite characteristics of the fully alive person, despairing and pessimistic, moving backward and sinking down?"

Sheef paused before continuing, which confused Harvey. He couldn't tell if Sheef's last question was merely rhetorical, or if he wanted a response.

Since he couldn't figure it out, he reacted in the manner in which most people do in similar circumstances. He remained silent and nodded. Whether or not Sheef interpreted this as an agreement to his point or an indication that Harvey was ready to move on, Sheef soon began speaking again.

"If it is true of people, why would it be any different for other intelligent beings? Shouldn't we expect that a power opposed to the Unseen would project the same feelings as the person who projects mental and emotional death? This is what you experienced today. And believe it or not, there is something good in it."

"I can't imagine what that would be."

"From this point forward, you will know when a Vapid Lord is nearby, and it's always a good idea in battle to know where the enemy is."

Harvey looked down at his plate and began lightly poking his remaining trout with his fork.

"Sheef, when I looked at it for the second time, I think I saw my parents."

Sheef sighed deeply before gently responding.

"I'm sorry, Harvey, but I can assure you that you didn't see them. It was a trick. Unlike the Insips, the Vapid have the ability to deceive with images as well as words. They are masters at twisting mental pictures to their advantage, using them to draw humans into their clutches. And what is the saying about pictures and their worth?"

"That a picture is worth a thousand words."

"Exactly. Do you know why?"

"Not really."

"Images often bypass the mind and go straight to the heart, where emotions can be easily manipulated. Let me ask you this, did you want to join your parents?"

"I did. They were together, building sandcastles on the beach. My mom looked great, just like she use to look before she got sick. I wanted more than anything to run over and join them."

"And you would have, too, if I hadn't knocked you back to reality. If you had lingered a moment longer, you would have walked over to join your parents on the beach, only you wouldn't be making sandcastles with them right now. By the time you realized that it was all an illusion, you would be securely in the hands of the enemy."

"So I should thank you for slamming me to the pavement?" Harvey asked with raised eyebrows.

"I'm sorry I hit you so hard, but the Vapid was reeling you in, and I knew that I had to apply significant force in order to break the line."

"Well, thanks for saving me, but I hope you won't have to do that again."

"Me, too."

Harvey was becoming somewhat unnerved as he formulated his next question. He wasn't even aware that he had tightly waded up the napkin in his lap.

"Sheef, I know you said that the Insips can't read thoughts, but what about the Vapid?"

"They can't peer into your mind any more than the Insips can."

"Then I don't get it. That Vapid Lord created images of my parents. He must have gotten into my head somehow."

Sheef shook his head as he responded. "They are skilled at what they do. That's for sure. Comes from years of practice. The Vapid Lord didn't read your mind. He threw out a lure, like the spoon you used to catch the trout. The lure was just a generic mom and dad. It was your own mind that supplied the faces and the other details."

"But how would he know that I've always wanted to go to the beach, especially with my parents?"

“He didn’t. Like I said it was a lure. Come on, what kid wouldn’t want to go the beach? And who does every scared child want comfort from? Mom and Dad, right?”

Harvey nodded.

“So there you go. You’re frightened, so you want Mom and Dad, and low and behold, there they are in a place you’ve always wanted to visit. It was the perfect lure.”

“You’re right.”

“About what?”

“The Vapid being very skilled. How will I ever...?”

“One thing at time, Harvey,” Sheef interrupted. “Your training hasn’t even begun yet. When the time comes, you’ll know how to fight. For right now, let’s get these dishes cleaned and put away.”

Sheef collected the dishes and scraped the scraps into a bowl he had set out for Fromp. After clearing the table, he suggested to Harvey that they should sit out on the porch and finish their conversation. A fatigued warp-hound sluggishly followed them onto the porch and was soon curled into a sleepy indigo ball of fur at Sheef’s feet.

The sky that evening was ablaze with a million pulsating stars. From where they were sitting, Harvey could easily hear the snorts and grumbles of the stream behind the cabin as it bedded down for sleep, and for the second time in recent days, that sense of the Unseen’s comforting proximity soothed his frayed nerves.

Sheef took time to point out some of his favorite constellations before revisiting the events of the day. When that conversation finally did resume, it was Harvey, and not Sheef, who began it.

Glaring unblinkingly at the clump of trees which they had passed through on their way to the meadow that morning, Harvey said, "I'm scared, Sheef, really scared. I mean, I've been scared since Fromp fetched me to Ecclon to meet Bellock, but after today, I really don't think I can do this."

Sheef noticed that tears were pooling in Harvey's eyes and were about to overflow their banks.

"Harvey, you were chosen for this task, not because of your age or size, but because there is something special about your mind and the way you think. With training, you will not only be able to resist and combat the enemy, but you will be able to free many of those who have been deceived and imprisoned by his schemes. But more importantly, I can tell that your head and heart are inclined towards the Unseen. You can rest assured that He is close to you, and that you will not be doing this alone. By the way, did Bellock, by chance, share any of Gnarl the Deep's proverbs with you?"

"I remember something about impressions and sand?"

Sheef smiled playfully and said, "I think there's probably more to it than that, but considering everything that has recently been dumped on you, I'm impressed that you remember even two words.

"Impressions and sand... I believe you are referring to two of Gnarl the Deep's more quoted sayings."

While searching his memory for the two proverbs, Sheef squinted his left eye and bit his lower lip.

"I think I have them. *'First impressions, though not impressive, may in the end impress us all.'* And the other one.... *'The eyes of a giant are blinded by the smallest grains of sand.'* I think that's right. Even if I didn't get the wording exactly correct, the meaning is abundantly clear. Bellock couldn't have chosen better proverbs for you, and I feel confident in saying that there may never have been a more fitting recipient for such words. Who knows, when this ordeal is all over, even some of the Vapid Lords may find themselves quoting them."

"But what do I do about my fear? I mean, it doesn't just go away. I feel like when I face the enemy again, I'll be so scared, I'll become paralyzed and won't be able to do anything."

Sheef paused before replying and placed a calming hand on Harvey's shoulder. "Let me remind you again that you won't be facing the enemy alone. The Unseen will be with you. But there's something else you need to understand, something that I need to remind myself of. The Vapid and the Insips can't hurt you mentally or physically unless you give them something to work with."

"What? How can you say that when the Vapid Lord almost tore your ankle off," Harvey challenged. "You didn't give it anything to make it attack you like that?"

"Actually I did," Sheef replied with a sigh. "I gave it my fear. The Vapid, as I mentioned before, can't read thoughts, but they're very adept at sensing emotion, especially fear. And this particular Vapid sensed my fear of being caught. Just before I leapt for the warp hole, I had this intense fear that I was going to be caught and dragged back into his clutches. And what happened?"

"Just what you feared would happen."

"Exactly." Sheef elaborated, "There are very few people who really understand fear. Fear has substance to it. It's material that can be used, typically in a harmful way, to create things and shape one's future. Think of a potter who begins with a lump of clay. At first the clay is nothing but a mound of water and earth, but it has the potential to become something more in the hands of the potter. Fear is like this, and the Vapid are very talented when it comes to using it to shape things which they can use against us."

"You mean it was your fear that created the arm and the hand?" Harvey asked in disbelief.

"Yes it did. As incredible as it sounds, it used my fear of being caught to create something that could harm my physical body. If I hadn't handed it my fear to work with, it wouldn't have had anything to use to stop me. But the opposite is also true."

"The opposite?"

"The opposite of fear, which is hope. Hope is material that can be used to create and alter our futures in a positive way."

"So the secret is to hope and not to fear."

"You got it. But obviously that's something easier said than done."

"Then how do you do it?"

"By replacing lies with the truth."

"But that doesn't make sense. If you know what's true, then why are you still afraid?"

"I'm in the process of learning the truth and untangling the lies, and old habits die slowly. Unfortunately, learning to do this doesn't happen overnight. It's one of those incremental, little by little, bit by bit things."

"But I don't have time for 'bit by bit'."

"Well, I guess that means we'd better get started first thing in the morning, which also means that we'd better call it a night."

21

Harvey woke the next morning to the sounds of Fromp's incessant barking and the smell of sizzling bacon. The sound woke him, but it was the smell that drew him to the kitchen where he found Sheef serving up a hearty breakfast of eggs, bacon, hash browns, and toast. Smiling while manipulating a spatula like a conductor's baton, Sheef invited Harvey to sit down and eat.

"When did you go shopping?"

"Fromp and I warped over to a twenty-four-hour grocery store on the West Coast early this morning. I hope you like eggs and bacon."

His mouth was watering so much that Harvey was afraid that if he opened his mouth to respond, he would drool all over the kitchen floor. A large smile would have to do.

Fromp was outside in the yard, and all during breakfast, he never once stopped barking. Halfway through his meal, Harvey asked Sheef what was wrong with Fromp.

"Finish up your breakfast first, and then we'll go outside and you can see for yourself what all the fuss is about."

Harvey was happy to comply, and after they'd finished breakfast and placed their dishes in the sink, they walked out onto the porch.

Fromp was bouncing and leaping as he ran in circles around the yard in front of the cabin. Every few seconds, he would nip at something in the air.

Laughing at Fromp's antics, Harvey said, "What in the world has gotten into him? He's acting like a nut. Look at him. He's biting at nothing."

"Are you sure there's nothing there to bite?" Sheef said as he pulled out the bottle of Kreen nectar. "Unlike humans, warp-hounds don't need any help to see things in other dimensions."

Harvey reluctantly took the bottle after Sheef had placed drops in his own eyes and ears.

After the incident yesterday with the Vapid Lord, Harvey wasn't all that enthusiastic about opening his eyes so soon. "Is this really necessary?"

"Only if you want to learn how to fight."

"Well, when you put it that way, I don't really have a choice. Do I?"

"Not really."

Harvey placed the drops in each of his eyes and ears as he had done the day before; however, this time the stinging sensation was not nearly as bad.

When his eyes were dimensionally opened for the second time, he saw a familiar creature ping ponging around the yard, doingits best to escape the frothing mouth of Fromp. It was an Insip. Initially, Harvey was frightened, but his fright quickly uncoiled itself into relief when he realized that it was only one Insip.

Harvey turned to Sheef and asked, "What's it doing here? Did it follow us through the warp hole?"

"No, Fromp and I picked it up when we went to the grocery store this morning." Sheef laughed to himself at the possible misinterpretation of his sentence. "I mean, we captured one when we were in town. We didn't pick it up from one of the aisles in the store."

The image made Harvey laugh. He pictured himself shopping in just such a store. "Let's see, on this aisle we have cereal, oatmeal, chips, bread, and a malevolent, fanged monster."

"Sheef, this may be a dumb question, but why in the world did you bring an Insip here to the cabin? I thought you were trying to stay clear of them."

"I am, but you can't really learn how to fight one if you don't have one to practice with. Besides, as long as we can see it, one Insip can't do much harm. Once the enemy is exposed, much of their power to deceive is lost."

Believe it or not, watching the Insip fly for its life was actually funny and entertaining. Harvey could never have dreamed that he would, only one day after being scared silly by the Insips on the lady's head, now be laughing at these very same creatures.

"But I don't get it. Why doesn't it just fly off and get away from Fromp?"

"It would if it could, but it's trapped."

"I don't see a fence or a leash."

"There's no leash, but there is something like a fence all around the little bugger."

Harvey squinted and looked carefully for anything that resembled a fence. Squint and concentrate as he might, he failed to recognize anything like what he was looking for, and he was just about to ask Sheef if he was sure about what he had said, when he noticed something peculiar occurring in the air.

For the briefest moment, the image of the oak tree on the right side of the yard and the rising sun above it seemed to blur and vibrate. Then it was normal again. A second later, the same thing happened to the image of the clouds directly above the yard. And as he continued to watch, this same phenomenon of what he was looking at becoming fuzzy and shaking for only a millisecond, happened again and again.

"You see the warping don't you?" Sheef asked.

"Different things in the yard keep getting blurry."

"It's a warp field. Fromp created it to hold the Insip. He did the spinning thing that he always does to open up a warp hole. Once the doorway was created, he bit into the space-time fabric which surrounds the opening and dragged it all around the yard. It's what we call a warp wall, a containment field that can temporarily hold what other walls cannot."

"So how long will it last."

"I would say that we have a little over an hour remaining, so let's not waste any more time."

As Harvey followed Sheef into the yard, he asked Sheef one more question.

"When the wall is gone, won't the Insip flee back to its Vapid Lord and tell him where we are?"

"Not if it's dead."

Sheef led Harvey to the middle of the containment field where he began instructing him on how to combat the Insip. He also commanded Fromp to stop chasing the Insip and sit down next to him. Sheef had to repeat himself four times before Fromp finally obeyed.

"I almost forgot, before we begin we both need to drink some Kreen nectar. We have to be able to communicate with each other by only using our thoughts. Can't have the Insip listening in on our conversation.

They both took a small swig of the nectar, after which Sheef began speaking again.

"The first thing you need to do is call the Insip to yourself. Remember, the Insips can't read your mind. They base their agreements and lies on what they hear you say out loud and by observing your behavior. What really attracts them is when you say something very negative about yourself, your situation, other people, or the Unseen."

"But look at it. It's still buzzing around like a maniac. It's not even paying attention to us," Harvey said.

"Trust me. It will. Its food is negativity, and these things are always hungry. I'm going to sit down on the porch and coach you from there. I don't want to distract the Insip from attacking you."

"Thanks a lot."

"Don't mention it. Why don't you loudly say something disparaging about yourself."

"Like what?"

"I don't know. Like you're stupid or ugly, or that everybody hates you. They love that kind of stuff."

Harvey thought for a moment about what do say as Sheef and Fromp walked back to the porch. From the porch, Fromp's ears stood at rigid attention, never taking his eyes off of the Insip. His body was quaking. More than anything, he wanted to go and finish off the Insip. Obeying Sheef by remaining on the porch was almost unbearable for him.

"Alright, anytime now, Harvey. The wall won't last forever."

"Hold on. I'm thinking... Okay, I've got one."

Harvey opened his mouth and shouted out the negative words. "I hate myself! I'm always getting things wrong. I'm such an idiot!"

The Insip stopped its erratic flight and hovered in the air. Its head snapped in Harvey's direction. A moment later, it landed on his right shoulder and began speaking.

With a soothing yet accusatory tone, it said, "You're right. You do muck things up most of the time. But it's not your fault, must be your teachers and parents. Aren't they the ones who are supposed to be training you to be successful? If you're always failing at things and making mistakes, then they must not really care about your welfare."

Sheef had placed three extra drops in each of his ears so that he could hear what the Insip was saying. This would mean that he would be listening to the sounds of another dimension for the next twelve hours, but in order to coach Harvey from the porch, he really didn't have a choice in the matter.

Sheef thought to Harvey, "Okay, Harvey, this Insip doesn't know anything about you, your family, your friends, or your teachers. It's just speaking in generalities, hitting on points that usually work with kids your age. It's using one of its favorite tactics of trying to get you to see yourself as a victim."

"What do I do?"

"Start declaring the opposite. You know that what it's saying is a lie, right? Your parents and teachers want the best for you, and making mistakes is just part of growing up. Mistakes are really some of the best teachers for gaining wisdom. Go positive with the truth."

Harvey began speaking loudly what Sheef had said.

"No, that's a lie. My mom and dad care deeply about me. I know that they want me to succeed. And my teachers are always willing to give me extra help whenever I need it. Anyway, there's nothing wrong with making mistakes. Besides, how can I learn to do the right thing without sometimes doing the wrong thing? And I'm not stupid. I was the only one who made a 100 on the last math test."

Harvey's words hit the Insip like a heavyweight boxer's punch. The force of the truth declaration hit it so hard that it was sent flipping backwards off his shoulder. It hit the ground not far from the porch. Fromp whined and licked his chops.

"Alright, try it again," thought Sheef. "Say something really hateful about your sister."

"But I don't have a sister."

"Who cares? The Insip doesn't know that."

Harvey conjured up the image of someone who might look like his older sister if he had one and began loudly speaking again.

"She makes me so mad! I can't believe my sister said that I stole money out of Mom's purse. She's always making up stuff about me. Sometimes, I just wish that she was dead."

"That's good, Harvey. You just called it to dinner."

The Insip, which was still on the ground, shook its head and then bared its fangs. This time it didn't land, but hovered right in front of Harvey's face.

With seething words it said, "You know why she can't stand you, don't you? She's jealous because she knows that you're your parents' favorite, and she'll stop at nothing to make your life miserable."

Sheef broke in with a thought. "It's using the sibling rivalry thing. They love to divide and weaken families, turning them against each other. Go ahead and knock that thing out of the air."

Success and victory in battle, though still just training, were beginning to alter Harvey's perception of himself. For the first time since Bellock had referred to him as a warrior, the word didn't seem quite so foreign and distant to him. Obeying Sheef's instructions, Harvey reared up and swung with words that hit the Insip right between its eyes.

"No, it's not true that she hates me. She's my sister and we've done so much for each other. And my parents don't have favorites. They spoil and love on both of us all the time. I don't want her dead. She's my sister and I love her!"

The first five sentences had sent the Insip reeling backwards for a second time, but when he uttered the last sentence, it was as if a major league batter had just made contact with the Insips head. It was a line drive, straight into the warp wall, where the Insip hit, whimpered, and crumbled to the ground.

"Oooo...nicely done, Harvey. I like your technique," Sheef thought to him from the porch where he was silently cheering like a sports fan.

Harvey continued for another ten rounds with the Insip. Each time Harvey said something negative to attract the Insip, the creature just couldn't help itself. It had to fly back every time and start in with its lies, and every time, Harvey walloped it with the truth of the matter.

After the last exchange, the Insip staggered slowly back into the air. It had finally figured out that it was being played with, and it didn't like it. It snarled and screeched, staring down Harvey with its yellow beady eyes. But just as it was about to streak toward Harvey's head, Sheef gave a simple command to Fromp.

"Go get it, boy!"

The animal leapt off the porch and only hit the ground once before bouncing up in the air to snatch the Insip. He bit down hard, forcing a shrill cry out of it. When he came back down, the Insip hung limply out of either side of his mouth. For good measure, he violently shook the thing in a death rattle.

"I think it's dead, Fromp. You can drop it now," Sheef said from the porch.

Fromp let the Insip roll out of his mouth and onto the grass. Even though it was dead and no longer a threat, Fromp continued to growl.

22

The daily schedule for the next week was almost exactly the same. Harvey would rise to the sounds of Sheef cooking breakfast, rattling, and jingling all the way with pan, plate, and fork.

Once the dishes were washed and put away, they would go out and sit on the porch where Harvey would open his eyes to another dimension that was becoming increasingly familiar to him by placing Kreen drops in his eyes and ears. After a few tips from Sheef, he would enter what they were now referring to as the "warp court", where he would battle a fresh Insip that Fromp had fetched earlier in the morning.

With Sheef coaching him from the porch, Harvey continued to hone his combat skills by repelling and neutralizing the enemy. And as happened on the first day, when the Insip was worn thin from fighting, Sheef would release Fromp to finish off the job.

On the fifth day, after witnessing Fromp crush and shake the life out of yet another Insip, Harvey had a thought that awakened his conscience. Using Kreen nectar telepathy, he asked Sheef if it was necessary to end each of the training sessions with such a violent death.

"Sheef, does Fromp really have to kill them like that? I mean, they're practically dead anyway. Can't he just injure them enough so that they can't make it back to their Vapid Lord? Maybe maim them by clipping their wings?"

Sheef took a few seconds to gather his thoughts before responding to Harvey's question.

"Harvey, do you have any idea how today's training session is unlike previous ones?"

Harvey gave Sheef a quizzical look and thought for a moment about the morning session. Nothing seemed any different about what he was doing in the warp court, but he decided to scan the yard carefully. Perhaps there was something he missed. He walked over and examined the lifeless Insip that Fromp was pawing at to ensure that it was actually dead.

"I don't see anything different. I fought the Insip just like I did yesterday, and Fromp killed it just the same, too."

"I want you think back to the coin trick. Do you remember why you were fooled the first time I performed the trick?"

"I was distracted by what you were doing with the book and the coin, and not paying attention to what you were doing with your hands and sleeves."

"The distraction blinded you to what was really going on?"

Harvey nodded his head in agreement, but still had no idea what Sheef was getting at.

"Harvey, did you know that lions use a strategy of distraction in order to stage a surprise attack? A lion will reveal itself in front of a herd of gazelles, for example. The herd will so focus its attention on the threat before it that it becomes blind and deaf to what is occurring to the sides and behind. If only a few of the gazelles would look to the sides and back, they would observe the tall grasses being slightly agitated, an indication that something is closing in on their position by stealth and camouflage. But none of the gazelles break their attention away from the obvious threat that they can clearly see before them, and so, they never see the rear and side attacks coming until it's too late."

The hair on Harvey's neck stood on end as he had a most unsettling thought. There was only one reason that Sheef would have referred to the lion trap: there was more than one Insip in the warp court today.

Harvey slow turned 360 degrees. He scrutinized every inch of the yard, looking for any sign of another Insip, but the only one he could see was the dead one that Fromp was now playing with.

"Sheef," Harvey said with actually words rather than thoughts, "are you telling me that there is more than one?"

"Just like the lions," Sheef said slowly with eyebrows raised.

"But I've looked around the yard twice now and haven't noticed anything. Maybe the Kreen nectar is wearing off."

"No, your eyes are good for at least another hour."

"Then where?" Harvey yelled.

"All too often we're blind to things because they're too close to us."

Harvey turned another circle, but once again, nothing. His frustration and fear were growing, and he was in no mood for Sheef to be speaking in riddles.

With growing exasperation, Harvey said, "I don't know what you're talking about. I've looked around the yard twice. There are no more Insips! "

"If you're right about that, then where did the notion of not letting Fromp finish off the Insips come from? You don't suppose you came up with that on your own, do you?"

"You're telling me that an Insip made me think that?"

"Think about it. Why would you want to allow a creature, which you know will stop at nothing to destroy you and every other human it encounters, a chance to escape and make it back to its Vapid Lord?"

"I guess it doesn't make sense."

"No it doesn't, so are you ready to find out what's hanging on the back of your shirt and whispering sweet nothings to you?"

"Are you telling me that I've had Insips on my back the whole time you were going on about how lions attack? You could have told me!"

"Calm down. There are only two."

"ONLY TWO! And that's supposed to calm me down? Well, what do I do?"

"What do you mean?"

"How do I get rid of them?" Harvey shouted.

"The same."

"The same? What kind of answer is that, Sheef?"

"Do what you did to the others to repel them. Begin speaking the truth."

"I don't know how to speak truth about what they said!"

"What they said to you is deceptive. Reveal their true intentions."

It was a few minutes before Harvey's adrenaline subsided enough for rational thinking to return. It took him another few minutes to gather his thoughts. No longer shouting, but very assertive, he began, "I know you're there and you can hear me. You will be shown no mercy. You're evil and bent on my destruction. You attempted to trick me into believing that you shouldn't be killed by the warp-hound, so that you might escape and flee back to your Vapid Lord where you would wallow at its feet and tell him where we are. You're strategy has failed and now you must die."

Harvey heard two thumps on the ground behind him, followed by the sounds of Fromp's jaws closing. He looked down at one of the mangled Insips. Its eyes were wide with shock.

Harvey rejoined Sheef on the porch and took a seat in a rocking chair next to him. For more than five minutes, he didn't say anything. He stared at the court, replaying everything that had occurred with the three Insips. He was processing every aspect of the training session, trying to determine how and why he had let his guard down. Finally, he turned to Sheef, and with a pronounced exhalation, said, "I can't believe that they got to me. I never saw it coming."

"You rarely do. That's why you always have to keep your guard up."

"But how? They were hanging on my back where I couldn't even see them."

"You don't have to see them to know that they're present. There are ways other than sight to detect their presence. Anytime an unusual thought seems to appear out of nowhere, suspect that an Insip might be the cause. Examine the thought. If it's negative, especially if it tears you or someone else down, and it seems to contradict something that you know to be right and true, then it's very likely that an Insip is behind it.

And never forget that you are always most vulnerable to being deceived by the enemy when you think that you're no longer vulnerable to being deceived."

"Is that what happened to you?"

"It is. Like you, I was selected by Bellock and brought to Ecclon by a warp-hound."

"Fromp?"

"No, her name was Penpix. She gave her life trying to save me from the Vapid."

Harvey reached down to stroke Fromp's head, thankful for how much loyalty and courage he had shown to Sheef and himself. He felt confident that if it came to it, Fromp would probably do for him what Penpix had done for Sheef.

"So how did it happen?"

"Like I said, I thought I was above being deceived. Bellock first tasked me with going after the book. I trained extensively with Bellock himself, and when I returned to Earth, I was cocky and looking for a fight. I was so confident that I would be able to find and destroy the book without the enemy ever laying a thought on me. I basked in my own glory of saving the world."

"But I don't get it. How could you be deceived after so much training with Bellock? You must've known all of the enemy's tactics."

"I did know most of their tactics, but the problem is that with all of the training, I never learned how to combat my own arrogance. You see, I was getting very close to the stronghold of a particularly powerful Vapid Lord by the name of Nezraut. Bellock and I came to believe that it was this Vapid Lord who possessed the book. I knew the enemy couldn't stop me if I refused to give him anything to work with. He must've known this as well. Apparently, he detected my pride, for pride is what he used against me. I could've just gone after the book and that would have been the end of it."

"Then why didn't you?"

"Because my arrogance opened the door wide for the Insips to come in and make themselves at home. I don't know how they latched on without me seeing them. It was probably very similar to how those two hung on your back, but it doesn't really matter where they were when they deceived me, only that they were able to do it. Rather than just retrieving the book and leaving, I decided to fight and try to destroy Nezraut, but I didn't count on there being so many Insips. It wasn't until after I escaped from Nezraut that I learned that he wasn't merely a powerful Vapid Lord, he was the most powerful Vapid Lord. That's why there were so many Insips."

"How many?"

"Hard to say with any certainty, but I know that thousands attacked me, and these were only a tiny fraction of Nezraut's minions."

"So the lie that they fed you was that you shouldn't leave quickly but stay and fight."

"And because of my arrogance, I thought I had a really good chance of success. But once you accept one lie, those that follow are much easier to swallow."

"What was the next lie?"

"Well, when I saw these enormous clouds of Insips swirling around what must have been Nezruat, my thoughts began to turn against Bellock. I thought to myself, 'Why isn't he here to help? Why did he send me in alone to fight against such large numbers? He must have known the odds and realized that the chance of survival was extremely low, and that's why he sent me in instead of going himself.' Before I knew it, in my mind, Bellock had betrayed me. Do you see how the two lies are related?"

"Not really."

"Bellock never told me to fight Nezraut. I accepted that suggestion from the Insips because it appealed to my pride, and once I accepted it, the Insips were able to make me believe that Bellock had sent me to my death by getting me into a fight I couldn't possibly win. And you can probably guess what happened next."

"I can?"

"I began to give off negativity, ringing the dinner bell, and when I did, dozens of Insips descended upon me. This was just the beginning of the downward cycle of accepting more lies, giving off more negativity, and inviting even more Insips to feast and deceive. It wasn't long before I was their prisoner. Mind you, I wasn't being held by any physical walls, but mental walls that I created myself. There was nothing holding me prisoner but myself. I could've walked away at any moment, but I didn't want to. I had come to hate Bellock and no longer saw the Vapid Lord as evil. In my deluded thinking, I saw Nezraut as the virtuous one, seeking to liberate us from the exploitive and oppressive Flurn. My mind was so twisted that I actually believed it was Bellock, and not Nezraut, who was consumed with gaining access to the other worlds in order to fulfill his own ambition and greed.

"Penpix opened a warp hole and tried to drag me into it just to get me away from all the Insips, but I didn't want to go, and so I fought her. The thing is, she was so loyal to me, that she wouldn't fight. And so..."

Sheef's voice broke and quivered so much that he had to stop talking in order to regain enough composure to continue. Glassy and red eyed, he haltingly resumed his narrative.

"Penpix died by my own hand. My thinking had become so twisted and warped that I perceived those who cared about me the most to be my enemies, and dealt with them as such. All the while, Nezraut was grinning and sinisterly laughing in the background."

"How did you escape?"

"Bellock and Fromp came for me. They risked their very lives in order to kidnap me and take me back to Ecclon. I spent months there recovering. Bellock patiently helped me untangle all the lies. When I finally returned to Earth, he suggested that it would be wise for me to live somewhere far from the Vapid's presence."

"Like in this cabin in the middle of nowhere," Harvey interrupted with a grin.

"Precisely. It's been the perfect place for my recovery and recuperation, and it was proceeding quite well, I might add, until you came along."

When he said the last sentence, Sheef smiled and playfully tousled Harvey's hair.

A distant rumble of thunder interrupted their conversation. They were both so engrossed in the conversation that they failed to see that the weather was rapidly turning for the worst. From the east, ominous, towering black thunderheads were moving toward them. A chilled wind from the storm blew through the porch.

Sheef stood up and began moving the lighter and unsecured items on the porch inside.

"Help me get this stuff in the cabin before the storm hits. From the looks of it, this one could be really bad."

NEZRAUT

23

The storm struck with a fury. Hailstones mercilessly pounded the cabin's tin roof. Gale to hurricane force winds halted the fall of raindrops and redirected them horizontally into the cabin's windows, rattling their panes.

It rained and thundered for the next two hours, and when the storm had finally exhausted itself, it left in its path downed trees along the stream and around the meadow. Although the storm had moved on to other areas to uproot and rattle, slate-colored, low hanging clouds remained.

As they surveyed the storm's damage from the porch, Harvey could tell that something had unnerved Sheef, who remained silent, staring off into the distance.

Harvey alternated his glances from his feet to Sheef and back again, hoping that Sheef would pick up on this nonverbal cue from his peripheral vision and share what was on his mind. When Harvey's strategy failed, he resorted to a more direct approach.

"Sheef, what is it?"

After a slow and pronounced sigh, Sheef said, "That storm. There was something more to it than we could perceive with our eyes. I don't know how, but the enemy was mixed up with it. I get the sense that our location, and worse, our intentions have been discovered, and that this was a type of warning for us to stay away."

"If you're right, and the Vapid know about our location and intentions, then they know about me. But how could they know? None of the Insips have escaped and nothing followed us here, at least I don't think anything did."

"Nothing would need to escape or follow us here, if it was here the entire time."

"What do you mean? You think there's been something spying on us since I arrived?"

"Or before," Sheef said as he sighed deeply and ran his fingers through his hair. "The truth is, Harvey, I don't know what I'm saying. Maybe I'm just being paranoid since our encounter with the Vapid Lord in the city."

Harvey could tell by the sound of his voice that Sheef didn't believe a word of what he just said.

And Sheef, realizing it was useless to remain standing on the porch and worrying about something he could do nothing about, said, "Harvey, it's about lunch time. Why don't you grab a pole and head down to the stream. I've always had good luck after a rain. Maybe all the racket on the water makes them hungry. But you go on without me. I've got a few things to take care of inside."

Harvey grabbed the pole and did as Sheef suggested because he didn't really believe that it was a suggestion. Apparently,

Sheef needed some time alone to sort out whatever else he was worrying about.

When Harvey arrived at the stream, he couldn't believe the scene before him. Many trees that had beautified and softened the banks had been toppled by the high winds. At least half of the trees had fallen into the water. Harvey couldn't imagine hooking anything but a trunk or branch. There was, however, an open area in front of one of the few remaining upright trees. He walked over to the spot and unhooked the lure from the pole.

He was about to make his first cast into the middle of the stream when he heard a rustle from the opposite bank. About half way up the hillside was a line of bushes, brambles, and stickers. It was the type of overgrowth that would catch you like a spider's web if you were ever brave or foolish enough to venture into it.

He could tell by the occasional shaking of the bushes that something was moving inside the growth. He concluded that it must've been something small, a squirrel or a rabbit, which could navigate around the prickly maze.

He didn't hear anymore sounds for the next half hour, and he soon forgot about the noise in the bushes, being numbed by the steady, rhythmic cadence of his casting and reeling. After two dozen casts, he hooked and reeled in a small brook trout which would have to be thrown back.

The fish had partially swallowed the hook, so it would require a little more time and effort to get it out without permanently hurting the fish. He placed the fish on the bank and knelt down, his back now to the stream, to work on getting out the hook.

While two of his fingers were wiggling around in the fish's mouth, he heard the rustling sound again. He spun around quickly, and for a split second, he thought he saw two green luminescent eyes staring back at him from within the sticker growth.

The sight jolted his body, pulling his fingers slightly backward. The hook's barb pierced his index finger and sent a sharp pain through his hand. He did his best to momentarily ignore it. Holding the fish with his left hand so that the hook wouldn't sink any deeper, Harvey carefully lifted his finger off of the barb.

While staring at the bushes on the opposite bank, Harvey worked to remove the hook from the trout's throat. When it was dislodged, Harvey tossed it back into the stream. For many minutes he strained his eyes, scrutinizing the bushes for the two green lights, and just as he was about to dismiss what he had seen as a figment of a fatigued imagination, they appeared again.

It was not his imagination. They were definitely eyes, and based on how high they were off the ground, they belonged to an animal at least four feet in height, clearly not a squirrel or a rabbit.

When the animal moved again, its movements violently shook the bushes. Whatever it was, it didn't seem to care that its cover had been blown. Harvey felt that the animal wanted him to see it.

He expected the eyes to disappear again as they had the first time, but they didn't. In fact, not only did they remain, but they seemed to be getting larger, which could mean only one thing. The animal was moving in his direction.

Harvey slowly backed away from the stream, never taking his sight off the green eyes. His retreat, however, was halted when he bumped into a tree. He jumped out of his skin for the second time that day, but was relieved when he realized what it was.

A growl from the bushes directed his attention back across the stream. The eyes were no longer alone, but had been joined by two rows of snarling, pointed teeth. The animal would soon emerge from the bushes.

Harvey looked back towards the cabin. He thought that if he ran at full speed and didn't look back, he would be able to make it there with time to spare. The animal, even if it was fast, would still have to swim across the stream.

The snout of the animal cleared the edge of the bushes, and Harvey could see strands of saliva hanging down from its jaws.

"It's now or never," he thought to himself as he prepared to bolt up the path to the cabin. But just as he was about to take his first step, a massive arm tightly wrapped itself around his chest. Harvey let out a bloodcurdling scream that could be heard for miles. Thrashing and kicking with all his might did little, for whatever had grabbed him from behind was far stronger.

By now, the entire head of the animal had emerged, and it appeared as though it was preparing for an attack. The free hand and arm of the thing which held Harvey from behind, picked up a small boulder and hurled it across the stream. The snarling animal in the bushes had no time to react. The boulder made direct contact with its head.

The sound of cracking bone was followed by a piercing yelp of pain and the noise of a hasty flight from the bushes. The yelps quickly faded as the animal scurried away into the distance.

With the threat of attack now gone, Harvey looked down at the arm and hand that was wrapped around his chest. He recognized them immediately, for there was only one creature that he knew of who had wooden arms and hands.

This recognition occurred at the same time that the arm released him. Harvey turned around. Standing before him was a very familiar Flurn.

"Bellock!" Harvey exclaimed, "Is it really you?"

"Greetings from Ecclon, my young friend. It appears that the time to act is shorter than we had first thought. Where is Sheef? I must speak with him at once."

24

Harvey's emotions were mixed at seeing Bellock. On the one hand, it was Bellock, the illustrious sage and leader of the Flurn with whom he had quickly developed a friendship, and who introduced him to a fantastical world of danger and adventure. But on the other hand, his appearance on Earth could only mean that things were going very badly and that the time to act would be sooner rather than later. The two walked up the path to the cabin as if they were back on Ecclon traveling to Council Gorge.

"I can't believe you're actually here."

"I wish that it was under better circumstances, Harvey."

"How long have you been on Earth?"

"Not long. I arrived near the stream just before you walked down to fish. I apologize for not revealing my presence sooner, but I had to confirm my suspicions."

"What suspicions?"

"That the enemy had found out about you and was watching."

"You mean that animal in the bushes was sent by the Vapid?"

"I can assure you that it was no creature from this planet. It was not on the hunt for just any prey, but was specifically sent to find and attack you."

Harvey's gulp was audible. He hadn't thought about it when it occurred, but as he reflected upon the nature of those green eyes, he had to agree, they were not of this world.

"And I suspect," said Bellock, "that there might be other types of eyes watching you even now."

When they reached the cabin, Harvey ran inside to tell Sheef about their unexpected visitor. Sheef walked out on the porch with a look of dumbfounded shock.

"Bellock, what in the world are you doing here?"

"It is progressing far more quickly than I predicted. But we dare not talk here. Obviously, I cannot fit into your home. Is there a place free of trees?"

"There's a large meadow not far away, but why?"

"It may be nothing, but there is the possibility that not all the trees are what they appear to be, and we must not take any chances."

Fromp, who was worn out from his morning tussle with the three Insips, had stayed in the cabin with Sheef while Harvey went fishing. Curled up tightly in a furry ball at the end of Sheef's bed, his ears went rigid at the sound of his favorite voice.

Bolting through the open cabin door, Fromp leapt from the porch directly into the trunk of Bellock, who had been the recipient of numerous such greetings, and thus, was expecting at any moment the exuberant greeting of his warp-hound. Fromp jumped with his paws splayed wide, so that he landed on Bellock in a type of embrace. Bellock returned the gesture in similar fashion by wrapping his large branch arms around Fromp's quivering body.

Bellock found it difficult to get any words out because Fromp's slathering licks and gentle gnawing of his bark were tickling the noble Flurn and making him laugh.

It was many minutes before Fromp's tornado of affection subsided enough for Bellock to be able to set him down on the ground. Though no longer embraced by his master, the warp-hound still maintained contact with Bellock by leaning heavily against his trunk.

Bellock lovingly petted Fromp as he said, "No better way to brighten a grim situation than with a greeting from a warp-hound."

It wasn't long, however, before Bellock's smile was erased by the dark and weighty reality.

"Sheef, this meadow you mentioned, might we go there now."

"It's just over there," he said as he pointed in the direction of the line of trees, many of which had been blown over by the storm, marking the edge of the meadow.

Nothing else was said until they reached the middle of the meadow. Bellock took a few moments to observe the surrounding trees.

Sheef asked, "So what's this all about Bellock? It must be pretty serious to bring you here to Earth."

"The orb clouds are failing more rapidly than the Council had originally predicted. We thought that Ecclon had a least one of your earth years left before the planet went dark."

"And now?"

"A fraction of that. Two earth months, maybe less. You know there is only one thing that could accelerate the process like this."

"The book."

"We believe now that there may be more than one copy, with multiple voices declaring their words over the human race. There is simply no other explanation. Too much thought is turning away from the Unseen in too short of time. But there is more. The Council believes that the enemy has something else afoot."

Typically it was Harvey who was the one prone to quizzical looks, but this time, it was Sheef's turn.

"Sheef, the evidence is mounting that the Vapid have been devising an additional strategy to take control of Ecclon. It looks like they are formulating plans to stage an actual attack against the planet. As the light of Ecclon fades, the Flurn will correspondingly grow weaker, making them vulnerable to attack and unable to mount much of a defense."

"But how? The primary power of the Vapid and the Insips is to twist thoughts into deception, not to wage traditional warfare in another dimension."

"Unless they are given enough fear to work with."

"True, but even if every human on Earth was deathly afraid of the Vapid and spoke aloud their fears so that the Vapid could materialize and unleash a physical attack, how could they ever reach Ecclon?"

"Our first and foremost concern has always been the continued survival of our planet by keeping the orb clouds burning brightly, but we all knew that it was only a matter of time before the Vapid figured out a way to reach Ecclon. We simply did not anticipate that it would be so soon."

"But only a warp-hound can open a doorway to Ecclon."

Bellock didn't reply, but instead stared at Sheef, letting Sheef's last statement be the answer to his own question.

"Are you telling me that the enemy has warp-hounds?"

"Not exactly like Fromp, but something similar. Perhaps it is a hybrid that the Vapid has bred with dogs of your planet. A number of warp-hounds have disappeared from Ecclon in the past few years."

"How many went missing?"

"At least five litters."

"But it doesn't make sense. If you can't get to Ecclon without a warp-hound, how could the enemy have even reached the planet?"

"They could not," said Bellock in a grave tone. "Someone from Ecclon must have brought them to Earth, and I am quite certain as to who that might have been."

"Who would do such a thing?"

"Someone who has rebelled against my authority for years. A Flurn who desires to rule, rather than serve, Ecclon. His name is Crawn. He has been conspicuously absent from the last three Flurn gatherings."

"I can't believe he would betray his fellow Flurn."

"Pride and the pursuit of power have a way of contorting things into the inconceivable, and we are all susceptible."

"You don't need to remind me of that," said Sheef with a sigh.

Bellock responded to Sheef with words heavy with compassion. "Lessons learned, wisdom gained, and character formed, my friend."

Sheef received the comfort with a nod.

"But enough about this," Bellock said resuming his serious tone. "How these warp-hounds came to be is not the present issue. They exist and increase the threat."

"How many of these things do you think the Vapid have?"

"I do not know, Sheef. I was not even entirely positive that they existed until today."

"Today?"

"I observed one down by the stream. It watched and then attempted to attack Harvey.

Sheef looked over at Harvey, both stunned and angry.

"Harvey, why didn't you mention this?"

"I didn't have the chance. It just happened, and since then, you and Bellock have been talking."

Sheef realized that the tone of his voice was unwarranted. Harvey had done nothing wrong. The reality was that the edge in his voice wasn't because he was upset at Harvey, but concerned about his safety.

Sheef turned back to Bellock and asked, "The Vapid can conceivably open a portal to Ecclon?"

"There have already been reports of activity on the outskirts of the Flurn settlements."

"Sounds like reconnaissance."

"My thought exactly. It appears that something is probing for weak spots in preparation for an attack. However, the warp-hounds may not be the Vapid's only weapon. Sheef, have you ever wondered why Flurn rarely warp to other planets?"

"I've never really thought about it."

"In the time before I sprouted, a young Flurn by the name of Thraysek warped to your planet. He had heard the stories from the Flurn elders about Earth and Ecclon's connection with it. Unfortunately, he was not content with merely hearing about Earth. Curiosity got the better of him and held more sway over his will than maturity, and he decided to violate Ecclonian law and warp to Earth without the approval of the Flurn. He never returned, and his acorns were never recovered."

Piecing together what Bellock had said about wanting to speak away from trees and his story about the missing acorns, it suddenly became clear to Harvey. He burst out, "Are you saying that there might be evil Flurn?"

"It is very probable, Harvey. Like the warp-hounds, these dark Flurn are most likely a twisted distortion. They would have to be significantly less intelligent, though, so that they could be easily controlled and commanded."

Sheef walked about five feet away before turning around and walking back to where Bellock and Harvey were standing.

"Let me get all of this straight," Sheef said to Bellock. "The Vapid have been accelerating the decline of the orb clouds on Ecclon by turning vast numbers of people's thinking away from the thought energy of the Unseen by reading from multiple copies of the book."

Bellock nodded.

"But apparently the enemy is not taking any chances. As more humans turn away from the thoughts of the Unseen and Ecclon begins to see its very existence wane, the Vapid will open up a secret offensive. When the light is almost extinguished on Ecclon, the enemy will use hybrid warp- hounds to open up warp holes and attack the planet with hordes of dumbed down Flurn. Is this basically it?"

"That about summarizes it."

"But there's something I don't get. Why doesn't the Vapid just wait until the orb clouds go dark and the Flurn die? Then there would be no resistance."

"Nezraut knows that the Flurn are aware of what the Vapid are doing to the orb clouds of Ecclon, and after your encounter in the city, the Vapid certainly know that someone is coming again for the book. Even if we can destroy the book and reverse what is happening to the orb clouds, the enemy still has a plan to take Ecclon. Besides, the Vapid would much rather see the Flurn die by their own hands, than have them simply wither away due to lack of light."

Their conversation was briefly interrupted by the creaking of tree branches on the far side of the meadow. An hour before, Harvey wouldn't have given such a noise a second thought, but in light of what Bellock had shared about the possibility of there being dark Flurn, every creak of branch and limb from that point forward would put him on edge.

"I'm sure it's only the wind," Sheef said without much conviction in his voice.

"What I still do not understand," mused Bellock, "is how the Vapid discovered Harvey so soon after his arrival back on Earth."

"Our trip to the city certainly didn't help keep him hidden."

"The city?"

"I took Harvey there as way of introducing him to how the Insips do their dirty work. While we were there, we had an unscheduled encounter with a Vapid Lord and were very close to being caught."

"But how would it have known about you and Harvey being in the city?"

"When the Insips Harvey were observing left, they must have reported what they saw directly to their Vapid Lord."

At this point Harvey narrated to Bellock everything that had taken place when he was observing the lady on the park bench, including how they suddenly looked at him and asked who he was and what he wanted.

After Harvey finished his narrative, Bellock scratched the area on his trunk that would have been a chin if it were a human face.

"It is still hidden within the mist, as Gnarl the Deep used to say. It makes so little sense. Those Insips should not have known that Harvey was aware of their presence and watching them."

Bellock studied Harvey for a moment as if he was sizing him up for a new suit.

"Harvey, did anything unusual happen to you when you passed through the Shellow on Ecclon and warped back to Earth?"

Harvey looked at Bellock with a puzzled expression.

Bellock must have accurately read his face, because he clarified the question.

"I apologize, Harvey," Bellock said with a ripple of laughter, "I suppose my question is rather ridiculous. What has not been unusual for you since all of this began? I should have been more precise. Allow me to rephrase the question. When you stepped into the Shellow, you should have immediately been transported back to Earth. Is that what occurred?"

"No, not at all. Fromp and I were somewhere in between for... Actually, I don't know how long we were in between."

"The duration of time is not important. Tell me exactly what happened, and please do not leave out any details, no matter how insignificant they may seem to you."

Harvey shared everything he could remember about traveling through the grey void and entering the green wall.

"And you say that while inside this green wall, a bolt of lightning struck you, releasing electricity to every part of your body. Sheef, did you know anything about this?"

With a cut of irritation in his voice, he said, "No I didn't. Like you, I'm hearing all of this for the first time."

"I'm sorry, Sheef. I didn't think there was anything to tell you. I just assumed that my experience was what everyone experienced when traveling back to Earth."

Sheef's countenance and voice softened as he replied. "Believe me, Harvey, it's not. It's alright. I don't think if you had told me it would have made a difference anyway, because I haven't a clue as to what it all means?"

"It means," said Bellock, "that Harvey was consumed by the Unseen and had a very intimate experience with His power and presence."

"That was the Unseen?" asked an astounded Harvey.

"Few have had the privilege of traveling to His realm, and even fewer have been absorbed into His very being and had His power course through their physical bodies. Harvey, you have been touched and marked by the Unseen in an incredible way. This can only mean that your role, if this is even possible, is more important than ever, and that the situation we are facing is dire."

"But what does all this have to do with the Insips being aware of him?" asked Sheef.

"Like an illuminated light bulb, young Harvey seems to be radiating the light and life of the Unseen so intensely that he has become detectable to the Insips and the Vapid."

Both Bellock and Sheef looked intently at Harvey, which made him extremely uncomfortable.

"What? Why are you two looking at me like that?"

Sheef stopped staring at Harvey and turned to Bellock.

"But if Harvey is detectable to the enemy, won't it be difficult for him to infiltrate Nezraut's stronghold and remove the book?"

"More than difficult, said Bellock. I would say it is impossible. The only chance of success is to cheat the enemy of its reaction time. Fromp will have to warp you and Harvey far enough away from Nezraut's stronghold so that Harvey will not be detected by him or his minions too early, but you will need to be close enough to observe his activities. Sheef, I will need your eyes to tell me what moves and preparations are being made for a possible assault against Ecclon. After you are in position and have done your reconnaissance, Harvey and Fromp will warp to the heart of Nezraut's fortress."

"What about me?" asked Sheef.

"You must stay behind and wait. If Harvey and Fromp are not successful and are caught, you will still be able to provide me with the intelligence I require. Also, I am not sure that you are sufficiently recovered enough to come face to face with Nezraut once again."

After Bellock said this, dead air hovered above the meadow where they were all standing. No one knew what to say next, especially Sheef. Harvey decided to break the tension by changing the subject, saying the first thing that came into his mind.

Slapping his hands together and with a smile on his face, he said, “So, when do we start?”

Harvey’s strategy worked. Both Bellock and Sheef were knocked out of their worried cogitations and redirected to Harvey.

“Well, Harvey, since you asked, I suggest as soon as possible. The enemy now knows that you are here, and, undoubtedly, what you are about. The quicker you leave the better. I myself must return to Ecclon and prepare the Flurn for a possible attack. “

“Alright then,” said Sheef. “Harvey, you and I will return to the cabin, grab a quick meal, and gather some provisions. I agree with Bellock about getting out of here as soon as possible. I would much rather go on the offense against the Vapid than wait here until we’re surrounded and trapped like rabbits.”

25

In the middle of the meadow, Fromp opened a warp hole to Ecclon for Bellock. When his master walked through, Fromp didn't even attempt to follow. As much as he loved being by Bellock's side, he knew now that his task was to stick close to Harvey.

By the time they made it back to the cabin, the sun had already set. Sheef hastily assembled a half dozen bologna and cheese sandwiches. He and Harvey each ate one while scurrying around the cabin, gathering only the essentials that they thought would be needed for reconnaissance and infiltration. Sheef tossed the rest of the sandwiches in his backpack with a few apples and a box of crackers.

"I've got two canteens hanging on a peg in my bedroom. Why don't you fill those up with water. Where we're going you'll definitely be glad we brought them."

"And where exactly is that?"

"To a place where Nezraut is somewhat free from reminders of the Unseen. Do you recall our conversation about how the natural world reflects the creativity and artistry of the Unseen? All things that He created on Earth bear His fingerprint, but this is especially true in regards to living things. Areas that are lush with green plants and teem with animals on land and in water, shout His name most loudly. To mute these shouts as much as possible, Nezraut, unlike the majority of other Vapid who dwell in the large population areas, has chosen a place that is barren and arid. Hating life, he has fled to an area where death quite often has the upper hand."

"Like the desert?"

"Yes, like the desert, so make sure you fill those canteens to the top."

Harvey filled the canteens and placed them with the backpack and other supplies on the half-finished kitchen table. Sheef moved the coffee table and folded back the carpet which covered the hatch to his hidden floor room. He descended the ladder as he had done before and returned holding two full bottles of Kreen nectar.

"We used up most of the other one. Here you go. Now you have your own," Sheef said as he tossed Harvey his own bottle. "Go ahead and put that deep in your pocket. Without Kreen, you'll be as blind as a bat against the enemy."

As Harvey shoved the bottle to the bottom of his right pocket, he heard the sound of creaking outside the kitchen window, followed by something rattling against the roof on the back of the house.

His hand frozen in his pocket, he shot a glance at Sheef, who slowly picked up the backpack and canteens and placed their straps on his shoulder.

"Maybe it's just the wind again, blowing tree limbs against the house," offered Harvey.

"I would agree if I had any trees close to the house. Nearest one's about twenty feet away."

"Do you think it's the dark Flurn Bellock was telling us about?" Harvey whispered.

"Could be. I need to get a look outside. The windows in my bedroom have curtains I can peer around without being seen."

Sheef tiptoed through his room and stood with his back to the wall on the left side of the three bedroom windows. Harvey tentatively followed.

"Harvey, turn off the lights."

Harvey flipped off the only switch in the room. The light of a full moon seeped through the fabric of the sandy brown curtains. Sheef slid his hand between the window and the curtain, creating a gap large enough for him to see a portion of the backyard.

"I don't see anything," he whispered.

He then opened the curtain wide enough to fit in his entire head, allowing him to scan the entire backyard.

"No, there's nothing out there. Probably just an owl. They sometimes perch on the eaves of my roof.

But as Sheef said this, Harvey saw the unmistakable shadows of limbs and branches appear on the tops of the curtains and slowly move downward. Harvey frantically searched for his voice, which had fled at the sight of the shadows. After what seemed to him like an eternity, he finally found it and whispered across the room to Sheef.

"Sheef, there's something on the roof, and it's not an owl."

Sheef tilted up his head as all three of the windows shattered simultaneously, exploding under the force of swinging branches.

With only a second to react, Sheef dropped to the floor, covering his head from the flying fragments of glass.

Harvey backed into the wall opposite the windows and squatted down in an attempt to stay out of reach of the four black branch hands that where whipping about the room like uncontrolled fire hoses.

Unlike the Flurn of Ecclon, these cultivated by the Vapid appeared as though they had been charred by fire. They were covered with jagged bark, capable of effortlessly slicing through muscle and bone. Grey thorns, like miniature shark fins, protruded through the bark.

Looking out through the broken windows, Harvey could clearly see the upside down faces of the dark Flurn. The scratching noises on the roof were caused by their rootlet toes digging into the shingles, anchoring them so that their trunks and arms could hang over the edge.

Where Harvey had observed wisdom and grace in the faces of Bellock, Merum, and Salix, these Flurn projected nothing but vicious hatred, empty and purposeless.

If you were to ask these Flurn, assuming that they had the ability to understand language, the reason for their hatred, they would be unable to give you any cause before venting their rage on you for merely existing. Like rabid dogs that have lost touch with any semblance of reasoned animal thought, these dark Flurn didn't think, but acted out of a contemptuous instinct: a venomous animosity for all things.

Still crouched under the broken windows, Sheef shouted, "Harvey, get out of here! Go to the living room!"

Harvey immediately complied and was soon followed by Sheef who scurried across the floor on hands and knees, dodging grasping hands along the way.

Fromp was in the living room, growling and snapping at the front door. Thrashing noises on the windows and walls could be heard in every direction.

Sheef ran to one of the front windows and briefly looked out.

"These things have us completely surrounded. There's no way we're getting out of this cabin without being caught. Fromp will have to open a warp hole right here in the living room."

Sheef called for Fromp so that he could think to him their warp destination. Fromp, however, was reluctant to obey. He was behaving solely on instinct, which told him to protect Sheef and Harvey by attacking the threat pressing in on them. Sheef ran to the door and grabbed Fromp's head with both of his hands so that he could hold it still long enough to make eye contact with him and send a thought.

Fromp's anxiety was somewhat quelled when he realized what Sheef wanted him to do. Immediately after Sheef successfully transmitted his thought, the entire east side of the cabin was lifted off of its foundation and raised about fifteen feet in the air. The sofa, tables, chairs, bookcases, and two humans and a warp-hound, slid across the wooden floor and into the kitchen. Everything slammed into the wall, creating a pile of furniture, arms, legs, and paws.

While they tried to free themselves from the pile, the east end of the house suddenly fell to the ground, followed quickly by the west side being raised into the air. This caused everything to slide back across the floor to the opposite wall. And as happened before, the raised side violently dropped back to the ground. This was followed by the north end being lifted and dropped.

The dark Flurn were attempting to shake their prey out of the cabin. This seesawing of the house continued, and the sensation for everyone inside was like that of being on a ship at sea during a raging storm.

Harvey and Sheef tried to stand up a number of times, but it was nearly impossible because the angle of the floor was continually shifting, and the chaotic movement of the pile of household debris threatened to sweep them off their feet at any moment.

Fromp was trying with all his might to grip the wooden floor by digging in his nails, but rather than slowing him down, the nails acted like ice skate blades, causing him to slide across the floor faster than Sheef and Harvey. The strained look of panic on Fromp's face as he glided uncontrollably by would have set Sheef and Harvey into fits of hysterics if imminent peril wasn't literally knocking on the door.

After Sheef collided with the east wall for the fifth time and was hit in the jaw by the corner of the coffee table, he knew that he had better think of a solution to their predicament quickly. If not, they would all be victims of murder by furniture or shaken out and into the hands of killer trees.

During their next slide through the living room, Sheef lunged out and tried to grab Fromp's tail. Unfortunately, the moving couch hit the warp- hound's head, sending his entire body spinning away from Sheef's outstretched hand. On the next pass, Sheef latched onto his tail and slowed him down enough to give him the command.

Yelping loudly at the hard tug on his tail, Fromp turned around to see what had halted his motion. Looking directly into his eyes was Sheef, who yelled, "Now, Fromp, Now!"

Fromp did his best to run in the required circular pattern to open up a dimensional warp hole, but once again, his nails failed to gain any grip on the slick floor. He tried to compensate for the lack of traction by moving his legs even faster, which did nothing but make him look even more comical.

"Harvey, we need to get Fromp on something so that he can gain traction. Help me grab the living room rug on the next slide."

The rug was wrapped around two of the kitchen table's legs, and on the next pass, Harvey, who was lying flat on his stomach, reached out and snagged one of the rug's folded up corners. Sheef grabbed hold of Harvey's leg, and using his body like a ladder, climbed up until his head was even with Harvey's. He reached out and got his own hold on the rug.

Unfolding a large area rug is difficult enough when a floor is flat and stationary, but when it's convulsing in the manner of a carnival funhouse, the process is nearly impossible.

It took them four trips from one side of the cabin to the other to completely unfurl the rug, and another two to get Fromp up and on it.

Sheef again shouted for Fromp to open the warp hole. Fromp was initially confused by the command. Why would Sheef be asking him so soon to do the same exact thing that had just failed? But when he felt his nails dig into the carpet fibers, he knew immediately what to do.

Faster and faster he chased his tail, and it wasn't long before Harvey saw the familiar sight of a warp whirlwind beginning to form. Yet this time, it was books, plates, silverware, and other odds and ends, rather than dirt and leaves, that were sucked into the swirling vortex. And since Fromp was creating it atop the still sliding carpet, it resembled a tornado moving unpredictably across the flat and level plains of Middle America.

When the warp hole was finished and ready to transport everyone, Sheef shouted to Harvey over the clamor of household debris clashing against walls and the racket created by the dark Flurn outside, still violently rocking the cabin.

"I don't think Fromp can tip it over like he did before. We're going to have to jump through it."

"Sheef, are you serious?" Harvey screamed. "We'll be killed if we try to make it through. Look at all that debris!"

"It's that or these Flurn creatures!"

The room, which had been darkened by the now shattered lights, was suddenly lit by moon beams from above. When Harvey and Sheef looked up, they saw that the entire front half of the roof had been ripped off by five or six of the twenty foot Flurn. Razor sharp, thorny arms and hands filled the cabin.

Slamming down their massive rootlet hands to crush and flatten, the dark Flurn were making craters in the wooden floor, and before long the holes outnumbered the non-holes.

Harvey fell into at least five of the hand craters, and though he tore his pants and badly scraped his legs on the splintery perimeter of the holes, miraculously, he didn't once twist his ankle.

Sheef, however, did not fare so well. The force of the floor being smashed was so intense that large spear-shaped fragments of wood were jettisoned into the air like metal shrapnel from exploding hand grenades.

Harvey followed Sheef as he dashed around holes and hands to catch up with the warp hole that was still spinning erratically around the living room, but it seemed that each time they were a second away from making the jump, it would spin off into another area of the cabin.

When the warp whirlwind spun itself into one of the corners of the room and stalled there, temporarily trapped between the two adjoining walls, Sheef knew this was their best, and perhaps last, opportunity to get away before everything in the cabin, including the two of them, was crushed.

They were only five feet from the corner of the room with the warp hole when a root-hand smashed down in front of Sheef, shattering the floor. Since Harvey was following, he had a second more of reaction time and was able to swerve around the hole, but without that extra second, Sheef was unable to make the evasive move. His right leg went down, braking the motion of his body and causing him to fall headfirst. He was able to quickly free his foot from the hole, but when he attempted to get back on his feet, he felt a searing pain in his left thigh.

A one-foot wooden shard, which had been launched when the Flurn smashed the floor, was sticking out of his upper leg. Harvey had no idea why Sheef didn't get back up and make the jump until he saw the chunk of wood lodged in his bloodied thigh.

Courage and focus took command of Harvey's will and mind; there was not the slightest hesitation. With unwavering action, he reached down, wrapped his arm around Sheef's waist, and yanked him to his feet. Whether it was caused by an adrenaline surge, the unforeseen effects of absorbing so much Kreen nectar in the past few days, or a combination of both, Harvey had never felt so much strength ripple through his muscles.

Yelling over the din of the swirling warp hole and the smashing of wood, Harvey screamed, “Hold on to me tightly! We’ll have to make the jump together!” And with that, they flung themselves in, blurring and then blending in with the rotating chaos.

26

If you have ever been outside when a severe thunderstorm is venting its fury with bolts and booms, then you have probably also experienced what it's like to be on the receiving end of its gale force wind. When the speed of wind exceeds forty miles per hour, hearing anything but the sound of the wind becomes increasingly difficulty. The storm intercepts the sound of a dog barking or a parent yelling for you to come inside, for instance, before it can reach your ears. Disregarding all civility, it hurls the sound far behind you, where it can never again be recovered. It's not that you have become briefly deaf. You simply can't hear any other noise but one - that of the storm's roaring wind. And if the winds continue to intensify, this roar is soon followed by a more substantial body of force that can easily knock you off your feet.

When Sheef and Harvey entered the whirlwind, their hearing was overwhelmed and their feet were knocked out from under them. The sensation was similar to that of falling into a raging river, frothing from rapids atop, while twisting from currents below. The hydraulics of moving water are so powerful that anything entering the river is immediately rotated from vertical to horizontal, and then shot uncontrollably downstream, but in this instance, it was the element of rushing air, rather than water, that did the rotating.

It would be bad enough if it was only Harvey and Sheef caught in the swirling vortex, but to make matters worse, there were other objects recklessly flying as well. Unlike Dorothy who had to contend with flying houses, farm animals, and fragments of windmills during her tornado ride in the *Wizard of Oz*, Harvey and Sheef had to avoid being hit by high velocity silverware, plates, the entire contents of the food pantry, and wooden floor splinters.

Traveling so quickly in such a tight circular trajectory, it was very difficult for them to defend themselves from hurtling household goods and cabin flotsam. Harvey successfully tilted his head to the left in order to avoid a can of green beans, but this only served to put him in the line of fire of a trio of tuna fish cans, which popped his chest with machine gun rapidity. A hard blow to the gut from a canned ham and he was gasping for breath in a doubled over fetal position. However, the ham is probably what saved his life, for just as he bent over in pain from being hit in the stomach, one of the dark Flurn's thorn-covered branches sliced through the whirlwind, only inches from his head.

Soon, more and more branches were violently slicing down. Watching the close shave to Harvey's head, Sheef knew that if they didn't get out of the rotating vortex in the next few seconds, they would both be cut and seriously injured, or the warp hole would collapse and there would be no escape.

Remembering how skydivers can slightly increase or decrease their speed and alter their direction of flight by manipulating their arms and legs, Sheef reached out and grabbed Harvey's pant leg to get his attention.

Because he knew that any words he shouted would immediately be muted by the roaring air, he didn't even attempt to yell to Harvey what he wanted him to do. Rather, when Harvey looked back, Sheef thrust out both of his arms towards the middle of the whirlwind. His arms created drag and slowed the upper part of his body, causing his legs to whip out and into the warp hole. Once his legs entered the hole, they were pulled through, dragging the rest of his body free from the swirling mess.

After watching, Harvey understood exactly what to do and followed Sheef's lead. Soon he was whipped, dragged, and sucked out of the frying pan and into the fire.

27

Because they were flung out into the warp hole while their bodies were still horizontal, and lacked the ability of a cat to right itself, they slammed down onto the hard desert floor while still on their sides.

Fortunately, Sheef landed on his right, not on his left, thigh, which might have driven the wooden floor fragment even deeper into his leg. The hard hit, though, still sent a surge of pain through his body, beginning in his thigh wound and traveling all the way to his face, where it culminated in a contorted grimace.

He sat up and tightly wrapped his hands around the chunk of wood. At least four inches of the large splinter were buried in his flesh, but surprisingly, there wasn't much blood surrounding the puncture wound.

"Can you pull it out?" asked Harvey as he briefly glanced at the wound before turning away in disgust.

Sighing and gasping between words, Sheef said, "If I pulled hard enough, I could probably get it out, but it would be like pulling a plug out of a dam, and most likely kill me. As painful as it is to have a giant toothpick lodged in my thigh, it's better than yanking it out and possibly bleeding to death. I know one thing for certain; I'm not going to make it any distance under my own power."

"Fromp can carry you."

"Fromp?"

"I rode on his tail to Council Gorge when I was on Ecclon. He coiled his tail up into a seat."

Laughing only increased the throbbing pain in his thigh, but upon hearing how Harvey had ridden upon Fromp's tail, his reaction to the comical image that he conjured up in his mind was more than he could control. Half laughing and half anguishing in pain, Sheef asked, "And you actually rode on it?"

"It took a while to get my balance, and it was pretty bouncy, but I finally got the hang of it."

"I'm sure that our old faithful warp-hound would be willing, but I don't know if he could support my weight. I must have at least eighty pounds on you. But we can worry about that later. For right now, I need to see to this wound and figure out where Fromp dropped us."

Sheef pulled a large pocketknife out of his pants and handed it to Harvey. He then instructed him to make his long-sleeved shirt sleeveless. Harvey was reluctant to do so for fear of nicking Sheef's skin with the tip of the blade.

"Harvey, what's the hold up?"

"I don't want to accidently cut you."

"I've got a chunk of wood the size of a cucumber in my leg. I'm not really concerned about you scratching my shoulder."

Harvey saw the logic in his reasoning and hastily cut off the sleeves, which Sheef took and wrapped around his leg, stabilizing the wooden fragment in place.

"That should keep it from moving around and doing any further damage."

The full moon was casting an eerie blue glow on the desert landscape, a nightlight over barren terrain. They stood in the middle of a horseshoe shape, a semicircle of mountains to their backs and sides. Before them, the ground sloped slightly downward. The terrain, but for one feature - a towering sandstone spire rising hundreds of feet into the air - was empty and indistinguishable. Pointing to the rock tower, Sheef said, "Like a finger pointing us to the enemy."

"That's where Nezraut is?"

"Not in the sandstone formation, but in the walls of the canyon below it, though I suspect that the tower wasn't formed naturally by wind and erosion."

"You think Nezraut made it?"

"Too much of a coincidence is often much more. A tall but narrow rock formation, which looks strikingly similar to a tower, and just so happens to be located directly above the Vapid Lord's stronghold? I don't think so."

"But what would he use it for?"

"Probably some sort of antenna that Nezraut is using to broadcast his deceptions."

"You mean like a radio station."

"Very similar, but probably in the dimension that the Vapid and the Insips operate. It's the only thing that makes sense to me.

Anyways, I wish Fromp had warped us a bit closer. The canyon has to be a good eight miles away."

"Couldn't he just warp us again?"

"He could, but opening a warp hole is exhausting. If we asked him to open another one so soon, it would completely drain him, and who knows how long it would be until he was able to warp you into Nezraut's stronghold. Besides, when he gets fatigued, he loses accuracy. He wouldn't have to be very far off to warp you midair, hundreds of feet above the canyon floor."

A sharp yelp pierced the silent desert air, followed by a sustained howl. Soon, what sounded like hundreds of coyotes, were unnerving the placid atmosphere.

Fromp, who had been lying next to Sheef since they arrived from the cabin, stood up at the sound. Every hair on his back went rigid. A low growl and muffled "woof" could be heard.

Harvey looked at Sheef who was drenched in moonlight and still sitting on the hard-baked desert floor. "Are there coyotes out here?"

"Not sure, but I've heard enough coyotes and wolves in my life to know that whatever's making those sounds is neither."

"You think they could be Nezraut's warp-hounds?"

"That would make sense. What better way to protect your hideout. But look on the bright side. Fromp will warp you directly inside the stronghold. Most likely, you'll never have the opportunity to tangle with any of them."

"You're assuming that they're only guarding the outside."

"Believe me, once you're inside, demented warp-hounds will be the least of your worries."

"That's encouraging to know."

"Just telling you like it is, Harvey. The better you know what you're up against, the better off you'll be. But let's quit with the chatter and get a move on. I don't want to be caught out here in the open when the sun comes up."

Harvey helped Sheef to his feet and supported him while he wobbled stationary on one foot.

"Squinting from the pain in his thigh, Sheef said, "Don't think bouncing on a tail seat is an option. Maybe it won't be so bad if I ride on Fromp's back.

Sheef called Fromp over and transmitted a thought to him, but this time it wasn't concerning a destination to travel to, but rather, a position to travel upon. When he finished thinking this thought, Fromp's ears perked up as he coiled his tail into circular seat.

"Sorry, Fromp, can't ride up there. Too much weight on my part, and too much bounce on yours. Maybe another time, but for now, why don't you carry me on your back."

Fromp responded by dejectedly uncoiling his tail and lowering his head.

Harvey helped Sheef get situated on Fromp's back. It was easy to tell by the expression on Fromp's face that the load on his back was more than his suspension was designed for, but as always when faced with a difficulty, Fromp bowed up with strength and met the challenge.

Once Sheef was secure on Fromp's back, he said, "Harvey, lead on toward the tower. We need to reach the edge of the canyon before the east goes pink."

Although the jarring wasn't as bad as it would have been if Sheef had ridden on Fromp's tail seat, the constant shifting of the animal's walking body sent rhythmic pulses of pain from his wound to his head. Sheef determined that it would help matters if he distracted his mind by occupying it with something other than the unpleasant sensations related to his injury.

"How are you feeling, Harvey. Are you afraid?"

Initially, Harvey thought that a more ridiculous question couldn't have been asked. How could he not be afraid? Despite the teaching and training he had received, he was still a very inexperienced and naïve teenager walking into the lair of a supernatural foe who was a master manipulator of fears, lies, and truth. He should've been paralyzed in mind and body, but for some inexplicable reason, and defying all logic, he wasn't.

"It's weird. I know I should be scared out of my mind, but for some reason, I'm not. I know there's a strong possibility that I won't survive what I'm about to attempt, and I may never see my family again, but I'm not that scared. Maybe all the Kreen I've been using during my training has begun affecting my emotions."

"It's not the Kreen, Harvey. It's the Unseen."

"What do you mean?"

"I mean that He's very close to you. Look, there are only three reasons why you wouldn't have much fear when you are about to confront an adversary as powerful as Nezraut. The first is that you've lost control of your mental faculties, and you're entering into such a dangerous situation with little trepidation because you're not in your right mind."

"Meaning that I'm crazy?"

"Yes, but obviously that's not what I believe. I'm only exploring possibilities. If you were going crazy, you would've exhibited other signs of it before now, but I haven't observed you making random farm animal sounds, attempting to eat rocks, or any other such irrational behavior, so I think it's safe to mark temporary insanity off the list. Another possibility is that you want to die."

"Like a death wish?"

"Exactly, but the problem with this idea is that people with a desire to die typically are hopeless, having nothing to live for, but this hardly describes you. One of the things that has been so surprising to me is that you haven't become despondent or discouraged for any real length of time. You have your entire life before you, a purpose, and your family to see again. Scenario number two works out no better than the first, which leaves us with the only remaining reason."

"The Unseen."

"Something outside of yourself is comforting you in such a way as to make you courageous. It's beyond, above, and greater than what you could conjure up on your own."

"Well, if what you say is true, then I can't really lose, can I?"

"What do you mean?"

"If I'm successful, I help save Ecclon and the future of all the other worlds, but if the worst were to occur and I died, it would actually turn out to be the best."

"How so?"

"I would probably get to go back to that green place."

"The Unseen's realm?"

Harvey nodded.

Sheef smiled, amazed by such mature wisdom uttered by one so young.

"You're absolutely right, Harvey. There's really not a losing side. Death would almost be a gain."

The realization that it was a win- win situation, settled as dew on his heart, softening the contours of his face and lightening his limbs.

It took them most of the night to make it to the southern edge of the canyon. If Sheef wasn't injured, they could've easily cut the time in half, but Fromp had to walk slowly to reduce the jostling of Sheef's body, and they had to stop a number of times to let the warp-hound rest.

When they finally arrived, it was just before dawn. Half a mile west of the tower formation, on their side of the canyon, they came to a ten foot wide ledge, thirty feet below the top of the canyon. Sheef had discovered the ledge during his first visit.

Two scrawny, twisted trees and a cluster of scrubby bushes scrapped out an existence in the sandy, nutrient-depleted soil of the ledge, which could only be reached by carefully climbing down a steep fifty degree slope. Sheef hobbled off of Fromp and limped to the edge of the canyon.

"That ledge is my reconnaissance perch and your disembarking point.

"Why can't we just stay right here?"

"There's no cover. We'd be spotted soon after sunrise up here. The bushes down on the ledge will conceal us well enough.

"But you can't climb down there with your leg wound."

"Who said anything about climbing? My plan is to slide on my rear."

Harvey examined the rough and rocky terrain of the slope. "You really think your leg can handle sliding down that?"

"Maybe not, but what's the alternative? We can't stay here much longer, and I can't very well climb down with only one good leg."

"But look how steep it is. If you lose control, you could easily roll right off the ledge."

"Then it might be a good idea for you and Fromp to go ahead of me and act as a safety net if the slope gets the better of me."

Harvey was the first to go. He squatted down on his hands and feet as if preparing to play crab soccer. In this posture, he shimmed down the slope. By the time he reached the ledge, both of his hands were striped with cuts and scratches from acting as brakes on the coarse ground. Fromp came next, trotting casually down the slope with tail curled high as though he was walking on level ground.

Sheef tentatively lowered his body into a modified crab soccer position, with his injured left leg sticking straight out in front of him and resting on the ground. With both hands behind, ready at any moment to check his speed, he began his descent. For the first ten feet things went relatively smoothly. Harvey breathed a sigh of relief. To him, peril had been avoided, and the twenty feet left to go would proceed exactly in the same manner as did the first ten.

It was the scorpion's fault. Not that it ever had any malicious intent to harm Sheef, and it's likely that it never even noticed him cautiously working his way down the slope. The same could not be said about Sheef. He noticed the scorpion and responded in the manner that most men in his situation would have. He jumped out of his skin and screamed like a frightened little girl.

If the jump had occurred while walking on horizontal ground, he would have quickly recovered from his scare and squashed the scorpion, laughing at his overreaction, but he wasn't on horizontal ground, and a scream, rather than a chuckle, followed his movements.

His jerky jolt of a response to the scorpion is what caused his hands, if only for a second, to leave the ground. This brief interruption of his hands acting as brakes on the steep slope, was all it took. Within seconds, his body was sliding down the sand and rock slope as if he were racing on a sled down a snowy hillside.

Harvey had momentarily turned away from watching Sheef in order to study the other side of the canyon where Nezraut's stronghold lay hidden. Ever since arriving at the canyon, he had felt the same dark presence which he had encountered in the city. It hovered heavily over the canyon floor, saturating the air to the point that it was almost tangible. He sensed that a grave emptiness was reaching out its talons, hungrily grasping for his heart and mind.

The sounds of tumbling rocks jolted him back to the world of wounded friends precariously descending canyon walls. When he looked up, he saw Sheef, no longer cautiously navigating his way one purposeful and secure limb placement at a time, but racing rapidly down to the slope.

Later, when Harvey thought back on the incident, he didn't remember thinking about what to do. His split-second reaction to the possibility of Sheef going airborne off the ledge was instinctual, his thoughts and movements reacting with lightning fast alacrity to the situation.

He called to Fromp, and when the hound turned in response, Harvey met his eyes with the same focus and intensity that he had seen Sheef use whenever he transmitted thoughts to Fromp. The warp-hound immediately understood and knew what to do. He anchored himself to one of the two trees by wrapping the end of his long tail around its trunk.

A small avalanche of rocks, caused by Sheef's downward slide, tumbled onto the ledge. Harvey knew that they would have only one attempt. If Fromp missed his target, Sheef would make his final "warp" to another dimension.

So much dust had been kicked up by Sheef's uncontrolled descent that Harvey was having a difficult time actually discerning his falling body. If it were not for the frantic screams for help, you would never guess that a suffering human was concealed in the dust ball.

When Sheef's body finally hit the level ground of the ledge, it did little to reduce his speed. It did, however, alter the orientation of his body. As he slid feet- first onto the ledge, his right foot made contact with one of the small bushes, causing him to turn 180 degrees. He was still on his back, but now he was racing head-first across the ledge and toward open air.

Realizing it was now or never, Harvey screamed to Fromp. "Now, Fromp! Grab it!"

With mouth agape, Fromp lunged for Sheef as he flew by. He bit hard into the protruding piece of wood in Sheef's thigh and a good chunk of his pants, but the speed and inertia of Sheef was so fast and powerful, that Fromp, who dug in his nails as aggressively as possible, was unable to slow him down. Sheef flew off the ledge, five hundred feet above the canyon floor with nowhere to go but down.

And this would have been his final destination if not for the tenacious jaws of a faithful warp-hound. Fromp was still gripping the large wooden splinter and a section of Sheef's pants between his teeth, and his long tail, the end of which was still tightly wrapped around the tree trunk, was now stretched to over twice its original length, The agile tails of warp-hounds are primarily composed of muscle and are endowed with an unbelievable elasticity. This is a crucial characteristic considering the myriad positions and contortions it must be shaped into during its many dimensional missions.

Sheef and Fromp were about ten feet away from the side of the ledge when the tail reached its maximum stretch and went taut. They were jerked to a stop, and the fragment in Fromp's mouth was abruptly yanked backwards. The subsequent pain experienced by Sheef was so intense that the word "excruciating" was found wanting.

For a split second, they were suspended in midair. When they did begin to fall, their connection to the tree trunk by way of Fromp's tail, caused them to swing as a pendulum back towards the ledge's side. Their violent collision with the wall dislodged rocky fragments, which fell away and disappeared from sight, echoing into silence in the depths below. The silence was broken by Sheef's cries of pain which were mixed with Fromp's guttural growls as he tried his best to maintain his bite on the wood and pants.

Harvey stood on the edge and looked down. Ten feet below dangled Fromp and Sheef, in that order and upside down. Harvey got down on his stomach and grabbed hold of Fromp's tail, and though he pulled with every muscle fiber in his back and arms, the combined weight of hound and human was just too much.

Sheef heard the sound of shuffling rocks above and lifted his head to the side, looking up the canyon wall. He could see Harvey's arms hanging over the ledge, straining to lift a weight far beyond his ability.

"It's no use, Harvey," Sheef shouted hoarsely in pain. "You'll never be able to lift both of us. I'm going to think a thought to Fromp. Then try again. You should be able to do it."

"Think a thought to Fromp and then I will be able to do it," Harvey thought to himself. "How will that make it any...." Harvey froze in mid question, suddenly realizing what Sheef was planning to do.

"Sheef, don't do it. There's got to be another way!"

"There is no other way!" Sheef insisted. "Together we weigh too much. Fromp's tail and teeth are bound to give out soon."

"You can't tell him to let go," Harvey screamed in panic.

"If I don't, then both Fromp and I die, and without a warp-hound, you'll stand no chance of getting into Nezraut's stronghold."

Harvey's countenance hardened as his next words were squared with an obstinate resolve. "Sheef, I'm not going to let you fall! Just give me a second."

"Sorry, kid, it's not your call to make, and we're about out of seconds."

Sheef let his head fall back down in order to rest for a moment before looking up again to meet Fromp's eyes. As soon as he made eye contact with Fromp, he began thinking the thought.

Fromp received a powerful mental image of him opening his mouth and releasing the wood and pants. The warp-hound whined. Obeying the thought would violate his strongest instinct to protect, even with his own life, those he loyally served and loved. He tried to resist, but the thought was heavy and persistent, pounding incessantly upon his mind. He knew that it would quickly wear down his instinct, and in the end, he would reluctantly obey Sheef. He felt his jaw muscles loosen. The stick slipped an inch. “Good boy, Fromp. Let it all go now,” Sheef whispered, still looking intently into Fromp’s eyes.

He then turned away, letting his head hang loosely. He expected the release and fall at any second, but when five seconds passed and he was still dangling from the ledge, he turned back to face Fromp. A fiery determination was burning in his eyes. His jaws were violently clenched. Obviously, Fromp had changed his mind, and he now had no intention of letting go.

“Fromp, I said let go,” Sheef yelled. His words and volume had no effect on the animal’s resolve. He tried thinking the same image that he had sent just a minute ago, but Fromp’s mind rejected it, bouncing it back to its sender. When the thought he had just transmitted to Fromp reappeared in his own mind, Sheef knew that it could mean only one thing. A much more powerful thought had entered Fromp’s mind, blocking and deflecting all others.

A minute prior, when Harvey saw Sheef stare at Fromp, he knew that he was thinking the thought for Fromp to release his bite, and he also knew that the only way to save Sheef from falling, was with a stronger counter thought.

He had no idea if it would work, but it was the only thing he could think of doing. He jabbed his hand into his pocket and pulled out the full, unopened bottle of Kreen nectar, which Sheef had given him back at the cabin. Hastily pulling out the cork, he lifted the bottle to his lips.

During the days of training, he and Sheef had barley used a quarter bottle of the nectar. Just one small drop into the eyes and ears is all it took for a human to see and hear another dimension. Sending a thought to another human could be done after only swallowing two, and Kreen wasn't even necessary in order to think a thought to a warp-hound.

Harvey had no idea what would happen if he ingested more than a couple of drops, but he reasoned that more Kreen would result in stronger thoughts, and stronger thoughts were exactly what was needed in order to save his friend.

Once he set the bottle to his mouth, he didn't pull it away and let it fall to the ground until it was completely empty. All five ounces were immediately absorbed by his blood stream.

A rush of explosive energy, a wave of concussive euphoria, and a surge of superhuman strength flooded his body. Trillions of neurons glowed white hot in his brain. All of his thoughts were suddenly so well shaped, dense, and deeply rooted, that he felt confident he could solve the most perplexing mathematical equations and untangle the knottiest of riddles.

However, the preeminent thought in his mind at that moment had little to do with math or puzzles. He created an image of Fromp tenaciously biting into the wood and pants, and then projected it to Fromp. The supercharged thought streaked downward like a meteorite before impacting the warp- hound's brain.

Harvey's thought was so strong, the images and colors so compelling and vivid, that Fromp could do nothing but immediately obey. Sheef's image of Fromp releasing his bite and letting him fall was expelled from his brain.

The effects of the over indulgence of Kreen nectar weren't confined to his brain. All the muscles in his legs, arms, and back were awash with unbridled power. His skin was rapidly rising and sinking as if his blood had begun to boil.

He reached out and once again took a firm hold of Fromp's bushy tail, pulling with the same amount of effort which he had pulled the first time he tried to lift Fromp and Sheef, but this time it felt as if there was no weight hanging from the tail.

Fromp's rear end shot upward, rising so quickly that Harvey had no time to move out of the way. The furry backend made full and flat contact with his face, knocking him backward, and sending Fromp and Sheef somersaulting over his head and crashing down on the ledge behind him.

Sheef's body was crumpled up in a heap of shredded clothing and blood. Harvey's forceful yank had saved Sheef from falling to his death, but had also dislodged the wooden fragment from his thigh. The plug had been removed, allowing the blood to flow freely.

Grimacing in pain, he pressed the palms of his hands into the wound in an attempt to stem the oozing blood, but the wound was too large and the damage to the artery too extensive. Even with zero medical training, Harvey knew that Sheef would soon bleed out and die. He figured that since it had already saved his life once today, maybe it would work a second time.

"Sheef, your bottle of Kreen. Where is it?"

"In my left pocket," Sheef said while wincing in pain. "But why?"

"Never mind, just lie back and try not to move."

Sheef was in no position to argue. He lay flat on his back, too weak now to press his hands on the wound, and fell into a delirious, half- consciousness. Harvey fished in Sheef's pocket for the bottle. He threw aside the cork and poured about half of the contents directly into the thigh wound, which immediately began to fizz effervescently like the chemical reaction of baking soda and vinegar. Sheef's only reaction was a slight twitch. Before long, a white gelatinous goo filled the wound. The bleeding had stopped.

Three hours later, Sheef was still unconscious. With no one's imminent death facing him, Harvey decided to lie down and rest. The energy expended during the escape from the black Flurn, the hike through the desert, and the action on the ledge, finally caught up with him, and soon after shifting his body into neutral, he was fast asleep.

28

Sun and shadow danced upon Harvey's closed eyelids. Dream or reality? Did he even want to know? He was coming out of a deep sleep, rudely aroused by the unrelenting pinpricks of a harsh sunlight.

His back ached. Something large and hard was pressing in on his left shoulder. With eyes still closed, he reached back with his left hand to remove whatever was causing the discomfort. His hand raked through sand and rock until it reached the object. Upon touching it, he immediately knew what it was, and also knew the answer to the question. It wasn't a dream. The hazy incongruence of the last day and night cleared as the pieces fell into place. The annoyingly bright light, sand, and empty bottle were the incontrovertible pieces of evidence, informing him of where he was and what he was doing.

Harvey opened his eyes, temporarily blinded by the white desert light. He turned his head to the right, following the sound of a familiar voice and saw Sheef sitting with his back against one of the trees. Fromp was standing in front of him with the wooden shard, which Sheef was unsuccessfully trying to wrestle away from him, still firmly clenched in his mouth.

"It's about time you woke up. I was beginning to wonder if you were still breathing."

"What time is it?"

"Close to noon I'd say. I lost my watch when we were warp-whipped out of the cabin."

"How's your leg?" Harvey asked as he got up and walked over to join Sheef under the tree.

"It's stiff, but thanks to whatever you did, there's no pain, and even more importantly, it's no longer bleeding."

Harvey observed the wound which was now completely filled with a hard white substance.

"What is it?" Harvey asked.

"Don't know. Might be some type of scab or new tissue growing. Whatever it is, it reminds me of cauliflower."

Sheef straightened out his leg and readjusted his back against the tree before looking directly into Harvey's eyes.

"So, would you mind filling me in on what exactly happened and tell me why I'm not dead?"

Harvey recounted everything that had occurred from the moment Sheef and Fromp flew off the cliff to when he passed out in exhaustion.

"You drank the entire bottle?" asked a dumbfounded Sheef.

"I didn't know what else to do. It was the only thing I could think of."

"But the entire bottle!" Sheef said, smiling and laughing.

Relieved to see that he wasn't upset, Harvey began to laugh as well.

"When I saw you thinking the thought for Fromp to let go of the wood in your leg, I knew the only way to possibly save you was to send Fromp a stronger thought."

"Your thought obviously did the trick. I've been trying to get Fromp to release the chunk of wood for the last half hour, but he won't so much as let me budge it."

Sheef again grabbed firmly onto the end of the wood and yanked it, but as he did so, the pressure of Fromp's bite increased, and a very low growl rumbled deep in his throat.

"See what I mean? You'd better think him a 'release' thought before he tears a jaw muscle."

Harvey's brain, still flush with the effects of Kreen, launched another power-punch thought. Within seconds, Fromp let the salvia-drenched wood drop to the ground. Sheef picked up the piece, wiped the drool on his pants, and while still staring at it, said, "That was great thinking, kid. I wouldn't have thought of it. And thanks for not listening to me. Resourcefulness and bravery... Bellock certainly did choose well."

Even more powerful than a Kreen-infused thought were Sheef's words. Harvey's father, so consumed by the demands of his sales job and the health of his wife, had found it difficult to spend time with his only child, a prerequisite for recognizing achievement and speaking the corresponding words of encouragement and pride. Harvey wasn't even aware of the empty place in his heart until Sheef's praise filled it.

Embarrassed at tears forming and preparing to roll down his cheeks, Harvey looked away from Sheef to a clump of bushes at the edge of the ledge.

"Sheef, shouldn't we move behind the bushes?" Harvey said without turning around to look at him. "Weren't you worried about being spotted in the daylight?"

"You're right. Here, give me a hand up."

Harvey took Sheef's outstretched hand and easily pulled him to his feet.

"Easy there. Don't want to injure my newly healed leg. Remember, until that Kreen wears off, you'll have superhuman strength in those muscles of yours."

Both crouching down like cavemen, they scurried over to the scrub bushes on the edge of the cliff. The bushes were naked of most of their leaves, allowing Sheef and Harvey to easily see through to what was on the other side. By looking down through the bushes at an angle, the canyon floor was clearly observable. What they saw almost caused Harvey to take his first tumble off the ledge and Sheef his second.

The canyon floor was thickly coated with the erratically swaying branches of a million black Flurn. From their perspective on the ledge, it looked as though angry swells in a black ocean were being further agitated by the bluster of a raging tempest. And throughout this sea of darkness twinkled thousands upon thousands of glowing green eyes.

"Sheef, are you seeing what I'm seeing?"

"I'm seeing it, but finding it hard to believe. Looks like Nezraut has cultivated a forest of those pleasant, thorny Flurn who paid us a visit back at the cabin. That canyon is easily two miles wide and five long, and every square foot is covered with one of those creatures."

"And the green lights?"

"You know as well as I do what they are."

"I was really hoping you wouldn't say that."

"I'm sorry, but hope won't change the fact that every pair of your so-called 'lights' is set atop a snarling, fanged snout."

Though they couldn't hear the sounds of what was occurring below, they could tell by the rapid and chaotic movements of the green eyes, that the demented warp-hounds were either rambunctiously playing or viciously attacking, and based on Harvey's previous encounter with one, the former seemed highly improbable.

A feeling of déjà vu seeped out of his memory as he peered down into the canyon. He was certain that he had seen something similar to this before.

When Harvey was on Ecclon, he had looked down into Council Gorge, teeming with Flurn and warp-hounds. On that occasion, though, the purpose of the meeting was to discuss how to thwart evil, not to advance it. Harvey felt certain that the Flurn in the canyon below weren't in the habit of discussing and debating issues, but only in following the commands of their Vapid Lord.

"Bellock was right," said Sheef. "He's assembled an army to wage war, and by the looks of it, very soon. That horde of twisted Flurn and warp-hounds are marshalling for battle."

The color in Harvey's face blanched at Sheef's words and their implications. Once Nezraut's army took Ecclon, it would be easy for them to warp to every other dimension and planet. Soon it wouldn't just be Ecclon that would be dark.

"I've got to get back to Ecclon and warn Bellock. I don't know if there's anything he can do this late in the game to prepare for an attack from such a large army, but he has to know. Fromp will open a warp hole back to Ecclon for me, but he will need to recover before he can warp you into Nezraut's stronghold. If you wait until after sundown, Fromp should be rested enough for him to give you an accurate warp."

"You're going to leave me here alone?"

"Harvey, even if I stayed, you would be alone soon enough. The plan was always for you to fly solo. You know it's too dangerous for me to get close to Nezraut. He knows my vulnerabilities well, and if I were to go in there with you, there's a good chance that I would end up jeopardizing your safety."

"What do you mean?"

"You remember what happened to me the last time I tried to fight the enemy?"

"But, Sheef, you'd never turn on me."

"Tell that to Penpix."

Harvey had no response, stunned and struck silent by Sheef's comment.

Sheef continued, "Look, just warp in there, find the book or books, and get out as fast as you can."

"You make it sound so easy."

"Trust me. I know it will be anything but easy. My point is that you need to be about your business quickly. The longer you linger in enemy territory, the more you will be susceptible to deception. Lingering leads to becoming comfortable with your surroundings, and once you're comfortable with your surroundings, you'll lower your guard."

"But what makes you think that I will be any more successful against Nezraut than you were?"

“Three reasons. To begin with, you’re not going in with a cocky strut in your step like I did. Secondly, you’re extremely ‘quick on your think’. If this wasn’t the case, I would’ve fallen to my death. And lastly, you’re not going in alone. The Unseen is with you, and you’ll have the greatest warp-hound ever fighting by your side when things get messy.”

“But what do I do if I’m attacked by a mass of Insips like you were?”

“Raise your shields!”

“And what exactly does that mean?”

“It means, don’t give in to any negative thoughts. You can rest assured that once you’ve infiltrated Nezraut’s stronghold, any negative thinking will be from him or one of his minions. As soon as a negative thought appears, counter it with the opposite. If you let it hover in your mind, even for a few seconds, you will have given it enough time to germinate and spread, and when one of these thoughts takes root, it becomes much easier for others to find good soil.”

With those words, Sheef slowly stood to his feet, the pain in his leg having been replaced by a tender stiffness. He called to Fromp and thought a thought of returning to Ecclon. Within a minute, a warp hole opened and Sheef was gone. Harvey and Fromp remained. For the first time since his adventure began, Harvey was without a teacher and guide. The period of training was definitely over. His moment had finally arrived.

29

Once Sheef left, Harvey settled down behind the clump of bushes, doing his best to get comfortable by propping his back up against a small boulder. He estimated that the sun wouldn't even begin setting for another five or six hours. He wondered if the time would drag because he had nothing to occupy it, or if it would fly by because it led to something that he didn't particularly want to do.

Apparently, Fromp had no idea what he was about to step into, because he was curled up in a tight ball, contentedly snoring.

"If only you knew what was waiting for us at the other end of your next warp, you wouldn't find sleep so easily," Harvey remarked.

He briefly considered sending Fromp an image of them warping into a dimly lit subterranean cavern, filled from floor to ceiling with seething Insips, but quickly decided against it because of the cruel and unusual nature of such an act. If he had the choice of knowledge or ignorance about what was to occur, he would choose ignorance without hesitation.

With nothing but the white noise of a slumbering warp-hound in the background to distract him, Harvey became aware of a stinging sensation on his knuckles. He looked down and saw that the knuckles on both of his hands were bald, all of the skin having been abrasively rubbed away.

"When I was pulling up Fromp and Sheef, I must've grated my hands along the ground. I guess I was so juiced up with Kreen and adrenaline that I didn't feel the pain at the time."

In order to minimize the pain, he tried to restrict the movements of his fingers.

He whittled away the hours mentally rummaging through everything that had occurred since the unexpected visitation by Fromp. Eventually, a fog of sleepiness entered into his head through his eyes, and once the lids were closed and fastened, the fog hung heavily. Before long, he was sound asleep.

In his dream, he imagined that slugs were crawling across his knuckles, leaving a wake of slime, their movements creating contrasting sensations of pain and comfort. When the fog cleared and he awoke from his sleep-induced stupor, he saw that snails were not the cause of the strange and somewhat soothing sensations on his hands, but were the result of something just as slimy: Fromp's tongue. Apparently, he had woken up and discovered the bloody knuckles and tended to them in the manner that most dogs do when their owner is cut or scraped. He licked them moist and clean.

"Alright, alright, Fromp. That's enough, boy," Harvey said as he pulled his hands away from the nursing tongue. Even after the object of his licking was removed, Fromp's tongue continued to rhythmically extend and retract for another minute.

The sky to the west was stratified in blues, oranges, pinks, and reds as the sun lost its grip on the horizon and soon slipped away. It was time. Harvey scratched behind Fromp's ears, wincing a bit at the pain in his knuckles.

"Well, Fromp, it appears that the reason for you nabbing me from my backyard has finally arrived. Who in my neighborhood or school would ever believe that the future of Earth and all the other dimensional worlds, which they don't even know exist, rests on my shoulders."

Fromp tilted his head and donned a quizzical expression as if he was pondering the question as well. Up till this point, Harvey believed that warp- hounds were primarily capable of comprehending images sent from someone, but unable, with the exception of some basic commands, of understanding spoken languages, but the longer he was around Fromp, the less confident he was about this assumption.

"I'll tell you what, if I was the Unseen, I wouldn't have picked me. But I suppose he has different criteria for choosing than I do."

Fromp responded to Harvey's comment as if he had fully understood what he had said. The large hound pawed at his chest and licked his face.

"Fromp, it's bad enough that you glazed my knuckles with saliva, do you have to coat my face, too?"

His half-hearted protest, however, was in vain. Rather than reducing or ceasing his licking all together, the timing of his licks increased from half to quarter notes. Fromp seemed to be countering Harvey's last comment, encouraging him in the only tangible way he knew how. It was a good two minutes before his licker gave out, and Harvey was allowed to surface for a breath of air.

After using his hand as a wiper to clear away the residue of Fromp's affection, Harvey gently cupped the warp-hound's large head in his hands and peered into the eyes of the animal that he had come to love and said, "No use putting off the inevitable, boy."

Harvey stared intensely at Fromp and thought the thought that could very well alter the fate of every living creature in this world and beyond.

Harvey expected Fromp's expression to change to one of shock or dismay. Instead, a slight grin spread across his black gums, as if he had known all along what was coming and had anticipated its arrival.

The transmission of an image of a subterranean cave, which Sheef had described in detail to Harvey, was followed by Fromp hopping up and chasing his tail in the tight circular pattern that would initiate the opening of a warp hole. Within seconds, a portal emerged, spinning precariously on the narrow ledge of the canyon. Harvey glanced at Fromp and returned the hound's black-gummed grin. A moment later, he jumped and vanished into his destiny.

30

"Sweetie, wake up. Come on, Honey, it's almost time for dinner."

Harvey immediately recognized the familiar voice and groggily responded, "Mom, is that you?"

He opened his eyes, and there, right next to his rocking chair on the back porch of his house, stood his mother, with a beaming smile.

"Of course it's me. Why do you sound so surprised? You look as though you haven't seen me in weeks."

"But...? Where's the canyon? What happened to Fromp?"

"Who?"

"Fromp. I jumped into the warp hole to find the book and was about to face Nezraut and the Insips in the cave!" Harvey was becoming increasingly animated and loud.

"There are those words again. Sweetie, you've been uttering nonsense for the last ten minutes."

"Nonsense? No, it's not nonsense. I swear, Mom! I was on Ecclon with Bellock, and then back on Earth. Sheef trained me to fight!"

"On Ecclon? I don't know where that's supposed to be, but I can assure you, you haven't been anywhere but in your grandfather's rocking chair since you arrived home from school. I think someone's been having an extremely vivid dream again."

"A dream! No, it wasn't a dream. It was too real for that. I was there, Mom. I just know it. Fromp came to our backyard and warped me to another dimension and planet where I met Bellock. He said that I was going to help save everyone."

"Save everyone. Is that right?" She said with a giggle.

"Mom, I'm serious. The orb clouds on Ecclon are going dark because people are turning away from the thoughts of the Unseen, and there's this book that the enemy is using to..."

The rate of Harvey's explanation had gotten so fast that his mom placed her hand gently on his arm and interrupted him.

"Harvey, slow down. You're speaking nonsense again. Listen to me. You haven't left the rocking chair and gone anywhere. You fell into a deep sleep and obviously had a very imaginative, wild dream, which apparently was also quite adventurous."

"But, Mom, I'm telling you, I was there!"

"Sometimes dreams can be very, very realistic. I remember one I had when I was about your age. I dreamed that I was a trapeze artist in the circus and was in the middle of a very difficult performance. I had just let go of my trapeze in order to flip twice and then catch the hands of my partner, but when I reached out for him, he wasn't there. I fell all the way down to the net, where I bounced up and down at least a half dozen times. When I woke up, guess what I was doing? I was bouncing on my bed. Now, if you had asked me then if it was a dream, I would've sworn to you that it wasn't, and that I was a real trapeze artist."

She said all this with the most congenial, motherly tone, and all the while wearing the loveliest of smiles. And after she finished her dream anecdote, she bent over and lightly kissed her son on the cheek and tousled his hair.

"Come on, Sweetie, let's forget about this and get ready for dinner. I made your favorite tonight: fried chicken and homemade, cheesy mashed potatoes."

Harvey looked at his mother in astonishment. "Really? It sounds wonderful, but I don't ever remember you making that. I think Aunt Jean made it when she was here last year when you were in the hospital."

"Aunt Jean here? Harvey, Aunt Jean hasn't been here in three years, and I certainly haven't been in the hospital. I made this very dish last week after your soccer game."

"Mom, I don't play soccer. I've always wanted to, but because of your illness and Dad's work schedule, I never even asked."

"My illness? Harvey, I don't know what you're talking about. You must've bumped your head in that dream of yours. Look at me. Do I look sick?"

Harvey did look and had to admit that she appeared anything but sick. Her long, curly blonde hair framed a glowing countenance. She wore the boldest smile he had ever seen, and it merged with her vibrantly red cheeks. If anything, she looked too healthy, like a polished, airbrushed version of an already healthy woman.

"Why don't you wash up and then go get your father. I think he's in his office, probably still filing paperwork."

"Dad's not home. He's out of town this week on a sales call."

"Alright, young man, this had gone far enough. You know perfectly well that your father is a physician. Dr. George, family practitioner? His office is connected to the house. Your father is rarely ever gone. The whole reason he moved his office home was so that he could spend more time with you."

"What...? But..."

"No 'what' or 'but', just stand up and go get your father."

A bewildered Harvey rose from his rocking chair and warily followed his mother into the house. It was and it wasn't the same. The layout was unchanged, but the furnishings and floors were newer and nicer. He walked through the living room, but then stopped in the hallway leading to the bedrooms and garage.

"Harvey, what is it? You act like you're lost in your own house."

"Dad's office?"

"Please. Through the old garage, which as you very well know is the new waiting room, and then through the door labeled 'Dr. George M.D'."

Harvey nodded as if he had suddenly recalled something that he had known for his entire life, but actually, he hadn't a clue.

He began walking down the hallway but was halted by the opening of the door to the garage. It was his dad, but like his mom, a healthier, skinnier, and more vibrant version. He was carrying a soccer ball.

"There you are, Sport. I was just coming to look for you. How about we work on some dribbling drills, and then see if you can score on your old man again."

"That will have to wait you two," said a voice from the kitchen, "dinner's ready. I don't want Harvey's favorite fried chicken getting all soggy."

"Alright, Dear, we'll be right there."

"Dear? Since when did Dad call Mom that?" Harvey thought to himself. Everything was so pleasant, too pleasant, in fact. It seemed that his life had been doused with saccharine, artificially sweetening his home and family ad nauseam. Harvey always wanted a healthy and whole family, but this was like some strange caricature of what he had desired. He felt as though he was suffocating in the cloying atmosphere and wanted out. He thought that going outside might make him feel better.

"Uh, Mom, can Dad and I kick the ball around for a few minutes?"

"Okay, but just for a few minutes."

Harvey walked out onto the deck and then down the stairs to his backyard. His dad followed, bouncing the soccer ball on his knees as he walked. Mom came out also, saying how much she enjoyed watching her two boys play.

"Hey, Sport, let's pass the ball back and forth to each other five times, and after the fifth pass, you try and dribble around me and shoot for the goal between those two fence posts," his dad said while pointing to the right side of the backyard."

His dad kicked the ball, but Harvey, who was still trying to process everything, failed to react and let the ball roll unhindered between his legs.

"Son, what was that? Earth to Harvey. Harvey?"

"Sorry, Dad, I wasn't paying attention," he mumbled.

"Really. Here, kick the ball back to me and we'll try again."

Harvey's return kick broke left, away from his dad and went under the storage shed.

"Harvey, what's gotten into you? Are you not feeling well? Your mom can kick better than that."

“I heard that,” Harvey’s mom playfully said from the deck.

His dad retrieved the ball from under the shed and then kicked it back to Harvey. Being on the other side of the yard, his dad put a little more power into the kick, causing it to sail about three feet off the ground. Harvey’s reaction wasn’t any better this time; however, the ball didn’t have the opportunity to go through his legs, because it smacked him directly on the backside of his right hand.

“Ow!” Harvey shouted.

“What’s wrong, Son?”

“It’s nothing, Dad. It’s just that the ball hit me right on the knuckles and really hurt.”

Harvey reached down to pick up the ball but suddenly stopped. He stood erect and rubbed his left hand over his right knuckles. That stinging pain, he’d felt it before. He looked down at his knuckles expecting to observe some cuts or abrasions, but there was nothing. They appeared fine and unscathed. But when he rubbed his knuckles a second time, he experienced the same biting sting.

Clarity began to sharpen and define the blurry smudges. “No, this isn’t right. This is neither my life nor my family. This is all a LIE!” he shouted.

Looking down at his hands again, he observed the appearance of scaly, scab-encrusted knuckles. He knew then and there that everything he had experienced since waking up in the rocking chair was a ruse, a masterfully woven deception.

He raised his head to address whatever was posing as his father, but it wasn’t there. Turning to the deck, he saw both of his parents standing there smiling idiotically, the artifice of their expressions now no more believable than that of a mannequin's.

"I don't know what you are, but you are definitely not my parents! You're nothing but a twisted creation meant to immobilize me! I know the truth, and you're not in it!" He shouted all of this with an accusatory tone.

Suddenly, the congenial faces of the man and woman on the deck morphed into something sinister. The face of what he had once believed to be his mom lost its vibrancy. The lips turned grey and the radiant white teeth yellowed, then elongated into fangs. The face of the man changed in concert with the woman's, and before long, two snarling evil creatures were hovering above the deck. They both let out an eardrum-rending screech before flying headlong towards Harvey.

Throwing his arms up over his face, he dropped down on the grass. When he pulled his arms down and opened his eyes, he found himself in a dimly lit cave at the bottom of an enormous pile of slithering and seething Insips.

31

The weight of hundreds of wriggling Insips pressing down on his body was suffocating. As he gasped for breath, his mouth was filled with leathery wings and sharp talons. Though it would've been difficult to enunciate even the most basic monosyllabic words with a mouthful of jabbing Insip body parts, Harvey knew that the only way to extricate himself from the heap was to repel the creatures by declaring truth.

With muffled words he shouted, "I know where I am and who I am! I've aligned my life with the Unseen, and against Him you have no power! The only power you have is what I choose to give, and since I choose to give nothing, there's nothing you can bring against me! Now leave my presence and go spew your deceptions somewhere else!"

Though some of his words were garbled, and he didn't feel nearly as bold as they sounded, the Insips were forced to depart. Initially, they left by ones and twos, but by the time Harvey was uttering his last sentence, entire flocks were taking flight and disappearing into the darker recesses of the cave. When the last one had fluttered away, Harvey took a moment to locate his breath before staggering to his feet.

He was standing in the middle of the very cavern that Sheef had so accurately described to him. It was difficult to see, for the only light was coming from a single torch on the far side of the cave. Like a moth drawn to the flame, Harvey moved cautiously towards the light.

Even without the Kreen, Harvey's duller senses would have alerted him to the presence in the room. The thing was malevolent, like that of the Insips, but denser and more intricately woven. It was far too dark to see much of anything, but Harvey knew that he was being watched.

The floor was covered with small rocks, which rolled and slid with Harvey's every step, projecting out sound waves like pond ripples to the solid walls. They bounced off, echoed back through the still air of the cavern, and repeated the process on the opposite walls. This effect continued until the sound waves and their subsequent echo offspring began to merge together in a disorienting collision of noise.

The noise was soon deafening, but Harvey didn't know at the time whether it was really that loud, or if he was just overly sensitive to any sound because of his rising anxiety and the high levels of Kreen still present in his bloodstream.

His head started to ache. He ceased walking and began massaging his temples with his fingers. The noise had seeped into his head and was pounding against the inside of his skull. When it felt to Harvey that every bone in his body was about to be crushed, he knelt down on the ground and pressed both of his hands over his ears in a futile attempt to keep the sound and the pounding out.

"That unpleasant pounding, you know, is not really from any sound," said a crisp, melodious voice from the darkness. "Your small human feet scattering rocks could hardly have such a deleterious effect. If you want to know the actual cause, I would be more than happy to accommodate you, but I'm not sure that you will like the answer."

A chill went through Harvey's body. Even though he couldn't see who had spoken, there was no doubt in his mind who it was. His heart beat increased, and the fear erupted. But there was also something else, an assurance that he wasn't alone. He grabbed hold and hung on tightly to the feeling.

"I don't have to ask," Harvey gritted out, hands still over his ears. "I know what, or rather who, is causing it and why."

"Is that so, my young friend?"

"It is, and I'm certainly not your friend, Nezraut. You're trying to get control of and manipulate my thoughts!"

"My word, such audacity from someone so young. First you trespass in my home with that pet of yours, and then address me with such an unsociable tone. I just don't know what this world is coming to, Sköll."

At the name of "Sköll" two red eyes appeared in the darkness, and Harvey heard the unmistakable snarling of a very large creature. He was glad that the darkness masked the head and body attached to the two eyes. Nezraut's voice seemed to be coming from every direction, so when Harvey responded, he rotated in a slowly moving circle.

"I know what you want this world and all the others to come to. You're trying to destroy Earth, Ecclon, and every other place you can get your thoughts on through twisting and distorting thinking."

"Very well-articulated, Harvey, and you are mostly correct. The one area, however, where you are mistaken is in your usage of the word 'trying'. It is the second time you have used it in reference to me since your uninvited arrival, and I must say, I am a bit offended. You see," Nezraut said with a voice that was losing its pretense of amiability, 'trying' implies that there is the possibility that I may not succeed, and as you of all people already know, my control and rule of every world is all but a forgone conclusion. It would behoove you to remember that I do not ever 'try'."

With the utterance of his last sentence, the walls and ceiling of the cavern began to violently shake, and the intensity of the quaking continued to grow until they crumbled away into grains of sand. No longer enclosed by rock and stone, Harvey now stood in the open air. He was in the middle of a tropical beach, which was being lightly kissed by the gentle lapping of waves from a turquoise crystal-clear ocean.

"Now this is better. Is it not? I know you have always dreamed of traveling to a place such as this."

While he continued to speak, a figure emerged from a grove of palm trees. It was a middle-aged man with an attractive, charming face. He had thick, slicked- back brown hair, and was wearing rolled up khaki pants and a light, loosely fitting white cotton shirt.

Barefooted, he casually ambled over to Harvey. Seconds later, an enormous black panther emerged from the trees and plodded through the sand to the side of the one who was obviously his master.

Grinning at Harvey as if they were long lost friends, he said, "Now that we are face to face, let me formally introduce myself. I am Nezraut, the High Vapid."

Harvey looked at him with a stupefied expression.

"Not what you were expecting? I believe you thought that I would appear in a cloud of billowing black and grey smoke like the Vapid Lord you encountered in the city. I can change if you would prefer, but I thought that our time together would be more enjoyable if I appeared wearing something less threatening."

Nezraut's appearance and the beach setting had so surprised Harvey that he was unsure of how to react.

"No introduction from you? You really must work on your social etiquette, Harvey. Oh, I almost forgot to introduce you to my pet. This is Sköll, the leader of the Volkin Wolves, my improved version of Ecclon's warp-hounds. However, I believe that you have already met one of them. I decided to alter his appearance as well to make it more congruous with this environment."

The amiable face and tranquil surroundings had a calming effect on Harvey's nerves.

"You can change the appearance of things?"

"Yes and no. I am not actually altering the physical properties of anything, only influencing your thoughts. You see, this beach, the man you see, and even the black panther are all images that I borrowed from your memories. I believe the man that you see before you plays a character in one of your favorite classic, black and white films."

Ever since he walked onto the beach, Harvey had been racking his brain, trying to figure out where he had seen him before. He was surprised that he didn't realize it much sooner, but then again, who would have guessed that Nezraut would put on the face and body of an actor from an old movie.

"So that means that everything I'm seeing right now is not real. That we're not actually on a beach next to the ocean?"

"Correct. We are actually still deep in my cavernous home in the canyon, but what difference does that make?"

"The difference is that it's not true. This is not real at all."

"Harvey, young Harvey, what is real and true? Is it not what we perceive to be true with our minds? And if your mind tells you that you are on a picturesque beach, who are you to dispute it?"

"But it's nothing but an illusion: this beach, you, and that animal of yours!"

"Oh trust me, I am much more than a mere illusion, but I understand your point. Yes, what you see before you is an illusion, but is it not a wonderful illusion? Your own world is such a harsh and violent environment, filled with disappointment, strife, sickness, unfulfilled dreams, and broken promises. But here, Harvey, in what you refer to as an illusionary world, there is none of that, and if you desire, you can stay here for the rest of your life. You would never want for anything. All that you have ever desired could be found here, including a healthy family."

Nezraut raised his left arm and pointed to a large, open-air pavilion with a thatched roof under the palm trees. Harvey knew that seconds before, it had not existed. It was a casual restaurant, teeming with people of all ages, and sitting closest to the beach, were the perfect versions of his mother and father. When he looked over at them, they smiled and waved enthusiastically.

"That's not my mom and dad, and you know it!"

"I do not disagree with you at all. It certainly is not your mother and father. It is much better. It is the version of your parents you have always hoped for."

"But they're not real. You just made them up."

"There you go again, carrying on about what is real. What difference does it make? I assure you, all you have to do is choose to accept this world which you see before you, and in time, you will forget that it is an illusion. Think about what I am offering you, Harvey: a perfect world with loving parents who will always be with you. Is that not what you have always wanted?"

Harvey was still looking at his parents. Nezraut was right. This was the idealized life that he had always imagined late at night in his bed or sitting in the rocker on the back porch.

"Why not?" he thought to himself. "What would be so bad about letting go and falling into such a lovely life?"

Nezraut didn't need to read Harvey's thoughts to know that he was considering his offer, teetering on the edge. He felt that the slightest shove would topple him over and into his clutches forever.

"Tell me, Harvey, has Sheef, Bellock, or the one you call the Unseen, offered you a gift such as this? No, I think not. And what have they offered you instead? Nothing but pain and suffering. Do you think they care for you by sending you into battle with an opponent far superior to you in ability and power. They've sent you to your death!"

While circling Harvey, he continued speaking. "Think about it. What are the odds that a young teenager, who hardly has a hair on his chest, would ever be able to defeat the most formidable of the Vapid? They knew you never had a chance, and yet they sent you anyway. They simply found someone insignificant and expendable to do their dirty work. So now let me ask you, since you are so enamored with determining what is true, who is your true enemy?"

His head and heart clashed. Harvey's reason knew that giving in and embracing the deception would be wrong, but he couldn't remember exactly why. His emotions, however, were willing to sever the rope connecting his will to his moral and ethical convictions.

"Listen to me," said Nezraut, whose purring voice was now coiling around Harvey's head. "I am not your enemy. I never have been. You know now who the real enemies are. I am your friend, offering you that greatest gift any friend can give: life."

The strands of the rope were unraveling quickly. Harvey was already beginning to forget what had transpired in recent days. The young man who had been called to a monumental destiny was fading and disintegrating into the gratifying delusion before him.

"Let go, Harvey. You are almost there. The life you have always dreamed of is within reach."

Harvey began to repeat Nezraut's alluring and succulent words to himself, and as he did so, the color of the deception began to change until it was indistinguishable from the truth.

"Yes, within reach..." whispered Harvey.

From deep within Nezraut's deceptive stupor, Harvey heard a familiar bark. It was faint, as if he was at the bottom of a very deep well and the bark was coming from the distant surface. There it was again, but stronger and nearer. The animal continued to bark, and with each one, Harvey remembered. By the tenth bark, he had risen out of the well. He remembered who he was and to what he had been called.

"Fromp!" was his first word of liberation from the entanglements of the enemy. Having been so overwhelmed with the Insips' attack, followed by his disorienting encounter with Nezraut, Harvey hadn't even realized that Fromp was missing. But he was missing no more. Crashing through the tropical underbrush and bursting onto the beach was the beloved cosmic canine.

Nezraut's voice lost its pretense of civility. He snarled a command to his Volkin Wolf. "Sköll, take care of that mutt!"

The wolf in panther's clothing bolted in the direction of an oncoming Fromp. It was a furious collision of snapping jaws and lacerating nails. So much sand was kicked up in the fighting that it was impossible to see who was winning.

"Thank you for the offer, Nezraut," Harvey said with steel in his voice and eyes, "but I will have to refuse. You see, though your gift is tempting, it doesn't alter the fact that it's still a lie. And as such, like all lies, as soon as I give myself over to it, it will betray what it promised and destroy me. And only a fool would choose destruction instead of life."

"You cannot defy me!" Nezraut vented with growing rage. "Do you know how powerful I am and what I am capable of doing to you!"

Widening his stance and with even more defiance in his voice, Harvey replied, "I know that the only power you have over me is what I choose to give you, and today, I'm just not in a very giving mood. Now, why don't you stop playing games and show me who you really are."

Nezraut's entire body began to smolder, smoke rising from his head and arms. The once pleasant smile peeled back on itself, revealing a malevolent grimace. The skin of his body cracked, thin fissures spreading like spider webs in every direction. The cracking increased and the skin folded back as if it was burning. When his entire body resembled charred wood, his ash exterior crumbled away, carried off by the ocean breeze. And there before Harvey, stood the real Nezraut.

He was wearing a dark gray robe, at least that's what Harvey initially thought, but as he continued to stare at the strange being before him, whatever he was wearing appeared to shift, billowing out like a growing thunderhead. Then it seemed to change into a foggy mist before returning to what once again looked like human clothing. All of this made it difficult to determine whether Nezraut was composed of anything solid or was just a wispy apparition.

The face was even stranger. Harvey stared, trying to identify any recognizable facial features, such as a nose or a mouth, but it was nearly impossible. Streams of darkness were flowing from every direction to his head, where they swirled about his face, blurring whatever was buried underneath.

The only time Nezraut's facial features were distinguishable was when he spoke. The darkness would drain into both of his two thin-lipped mouths, one atop each other, allowing Harvey to see the skeletal face beneath. He had no nose. His eyes were deep set and glowing green, like those of the Volkin Wolves.

Harvey was simultaneously repulsed, frightened, and fascinated by his appearance.

"Is this more to your liking, my young friend?" Nezraut asked with biting sarcasm.

Flying in the face of all logic, the surge of fear he felt during Nezraut's transformation, suddenly drained out of his body as a living weightiness filled him to overflowing. Bellock and Sheef were right. The Unseen was with him.

Looking squarely into Nezraut's eyes, Harvey said, "Believe me when I tell you that there's absolutely nothing likeable about your appearance, but at least now they match, making it much more difficult for you to deceive me."

"I am sorry, young one, but I do not quite follow. What do you mean by 'they match'? "

"Your exterior and interior, your appearance and your motives. It's much easier to resist you when you look like...well, you know."

"Evil? Is that the word you're searching for?"

"Exactly."

"Well now, since dispensing with pretense provides you with so much pleasure, why not do away with all of it?"

Nezraut threw out both of his arms and spread his fingers wide. With this motion, the scene surrounding Harvey began to change. The palm trees bordering the beach turned charcoal, their fronds shriveling into thorn-crusted, gnarled branches. Dark Flurn.

Below the sand shone hundreds of eerie green lights. The nature of the lights was readily perceived when the sand of the beach fell away as if they were standing in an enormous hourglass. An army of snarling Volkin Wolves emerged, impatiently waiting for their master's word of release.

And to his left, Harvey heard what sounded like a train rushing towards him. A mammoth wave was building just off the beach. With each second it rose higher, until its shadow completely covered the shore. It broke over them, the edge of the wave crashing on the other side of the dark Flurn.

The entire beach was inside the tunnel of the breaking wave. The water, however, stopped moving, and its color darkened into that of earthen brown. The Flurn, Volkin Wolves, Nezraut, and Harvey were no longer inside a wave, but were standing in an enormous, underground cavern, exactly where they had been ever since Harvey arrived.

"Welcome to my fortress, Harvey," Nezraut charmingly said as a line of torches on the cavern's walls ignited.

32

The previously dimly lit cavern was now illuminated by flashes of red, yellow, and orange light dancing on the uneven texture of the walls and ceiling.

Harvey was standing on a raised platform of rock in the middle of the cavern. Moving outward from the platform, were concentric circles of quivering Volkin Wolves, thousands of green eyes focused on their desired prey. The wolves were standing in what appeared to be a military configuration: shoulder to shoulder and haunch to haunch. The outer rim of the last circle of wolves was flanked by dark Flurn, their branches intertwined with one another, making a latticework barrier of razor-sharp thorns.

Other than warping, there was no way out of the cavern, and at the moment, warping anywhere was out of the question. Fromp was pinned under the flesh-piercing claws of Sköll, who no longer resembled a black panther, but like his master, had been stripped of his artifice.

The Volkin Wolf was atop Fromp, his mouth agape and full of his victim's furry throat. He was awaiting Nezraut's command to finish the job. Not only was Harvey trapped, but even worse, his faithful friend and warrior was only one word away from death.

Nezraut, in all his hideousness, began speaking with his two mouths. "Here is everything 'matched' as you put it. You know you are a fool, Harvey. Your greatest desire - that of a loving and whole family living out their existence in a paradisiacal setting - was all yours for the believing. Alas, now you will die, and the last thought that passes through your mind before you draw your final breath will be that you failed. Ecclon and all the worlds will fall under my control because you and your mutt were unable to stop me. But please, do not blame yourself. As I said before, you really never had a chance of defeating me."

"You're wrong, Nezraut. You call me a fool for not embracing your deceit, but letting go to be entangled by your lies would've been the poorest of all decisions. I would've chosen to enter a self-imposed prison. The moment I embraced your counterfeit family and setting, I know that your so-called paradise would've evaporated, leaving me standing all alone, having forgotten who and where I was, and not even caring that I didn't remember. I know that once I crossed the line and severed my connection with the truth, a swarm of smaller lies and deceptions would've swept over my mind like a virus, rendering me your captive forever."

"Very good, Harvey. Bravo," Nezraut said condescendingly. "Perhaps you are not the fool I thought you were, but since you so decidedly refused my generous offer to be forever entangled in my web of deceit, you must accept the consolation prize."

"Consolation prize?"

"You will die, but I will let you decide whether you want to die by my hand or Sköll's teeth."

"You can't physically hurt me unless I give you something to work with."

For nearly two minutes Nezraut didn't say a word. He stood still, staring at Harvey with both of his mouths agape, displaying all of his serrated teeth. And then, for no particular reason that Harvey could see at the time, began speaking again.

"That is correct, Harvey, but when I told you that you were going to die, and I let you mull over those words, do you know what you handed over to me?" Nezraut paused. "No answer? Fear. You handed me a tremendous heaping of fear that I can now fashion into something very nasty to bring about your end."

"That's not true. I didn't give you anything. You're lying again, trying to get me to give you something."

"Am I? Oh, I do not think so. No, you are very afraid, and rightly so. I would be terrified myself if I were facing my own demise."

"I'm not denying that I haven't felt fear in your presence, but it's not anything you can use against me. You see, fear no longer frightens me. I know that sounds strange, but it's true. Before, when fear came upon me, I believed that the only way to combat it was to fight it myself, relying on my own strength and strategy. I guess you can get away with this if you are dealing with a manageable fear, but it really doesn't work so well when facing something terrifying like... well, you, for instance."

"I'm flattered," Nezraut replied coldly.

"But now it's different. I don't exactly know when or how it happened, but now, whenever I become fearful, I now know that He is with me, and because of that, there's really no reason to fear."

"He?"

"The Unseen."

Nezraut staggered backwards as if he had received a blow to his gut.

Harvey stood a little taller, feeling strength flow into him. "It's kind of ironic isn't it? You've been saying and doing things in order to frighten me so that I might give you something that you could use to physically harm me. Instead, your words and actions have put me in a place that is actually making me stronger. It appears that your plan has backfired."

Nezraut simultaneously bit both of the lower lips of his two mouths, leaving large gashes which released a foul smelling liquid. For a moment he lost his cool composure and looked unsure as what move to make next. Then his two mouths resumed their smarmy grins.

"Very clever. However, you seem to forget one thing. Even if I cannot hurt you physically, Sköll and the Volkin Wolves still can. They are made of the very same physical substances that you are, Harvey. I may not be able to kill you, but they certainly have the ability. But before I give the command for Sköll to snap Fromp's neck and for you to be attacked, I thought I would let you see the object that led you to my home in the first place."

"What object?"

"Please do not insult my intelligence," Nezraut snapped. "You warped here for the same reason that Sheef did, and unfortunately, it appears that he trained you too well, for like him, you have failed to destroy it."

Nezraut took two steps backwards. A square opening appeared in the floor of the platform, from which rose a rock podium. Resting on top was a large, leather-bound book.

"Is this not what you came for?" Nezraut queried as he picked up the book and walked over to Harvey where he held it out for him to take.

"Oh come now, take it. After so much trouble to get here, it would be a shame not to see what is written on the pages. I know your curiosity must be maddening."

It was maddening. Harvey was well beyond curious. What were the lies, thought and spoken by so many and so often, that they had actually taken on physical form by inscribing themselves on the pages of the book before him?

Harvey gazed down at the offered book. He heard music lifting from the book like butterflies lighting to flight. Airy and delicate. Crisp and sharp. Starlight cutting through a winter's night. Cool with the touch of enchantment, yet warm with the alluring scent of temptation.

An intoxicating melody unfolded and drenched his sense. The voice, young and innocent, pristine like an untouched mountain glade, but thick in the wisdom of time. It sang out, beckoning Harvey to drink it all in.

He took the book and opened it. Green letters outlined in gold were slowly pulsing like miniature human hearts. At first the language was foreign and incomprehensible, but as he continued to stare at the pages, the letters began to change into words which Harvey could recognize.

Before birth, after death, nothing,
Man standing stark and alone,
Only his wisdom for comfort and guidance,
Nothing before or beyond.

Desperate for meaning, searching for worth,
Absent of purpose and plan,
He builds and conquers by the sweat of his brow,
Perfection within the reach of his hands.

Harvey flipped the page only to find the same exact words. He flipped again. The same words. The third page was the same as the second, and the fourth the same as the third. He rifled through the pages from cover to cover, only to find that every single page was an exact copy of the first.

He averted his attention away from the book to the grinning mouths of Nezraut. "They're all the same," said a bewildered Harvey.

"Why yes. It is the oldest and most effective lie mankind has ever swallowed. We have used it for centuries to bend mankind's thinking away from the Unseen, but only recently have enough humans embraced it, allowing it to birth itself into the physical world and onto the pages you see before you. And when I and the other Vapid Lords read the lie back over the human race, it's deceptive power increases exponentially.

"So this is what millions of humans are thinking and saying every day?"

"Yes and no. What you read on the pages is not the precise wording. The words are merely created by a growing collective idea or feeling about man and his place on earth and in the universe. Can you understand how this lie is the foundation for every other deception that we use to darken human understanding?"

It was evident from Harvey's expression that he couldn't.

"Harvey, I thought you were brighter than this. It looks like I shall have to unravel it for you so that you might know the exact deception you were unable to stop. As should be obvious to every creature in this universe, the Unseen is the maker of all. Every inanimate and animate object was created by Him, making Him before, behind, above, and below all things. This is the ultimate truth that gives life to every other truth. It is the root which nurtures the rest of the tree, the foundation that provides stability for the house.

"Man's purpose, meaning, and value are all woven into to this conspicuous truth," Nezraut continued. "And so you must begin to understand that in order to be successful at turning man away from the thought energy of the Unseen, we do not simply attack the branches, but go much deeper, where we can destroy the root. It is really quite simple. Convince man that there is nothing beyond his senses. He is all alone in the vast and cold universe where he can only look to himself for meaning and purpose. Once man begins to focus all of his attention on himself and what he can accomplish, pride takes over, which soon renders him deaf and dumb to every other deception that is spun."

"And this is the lie that is causing Ecclon to grow dim?"

"It's the lie that leads to a host of other lies, but the cumulative effect eventually turns people away from the Unseen, causing Ecclon to lose her light."

"But why the same words on every page?"

"As this thought spreads and is reinforced by myself and the other Vapid Lords reciting it over the human race, more and more pages are filled. You didn't assume that there was only one book, did you?"

All along Harvey had hoped that there was only one, but since first hearing of Bellock's suspicions that there were more, he had a nagging sense that this was probably not the case.

"Well, I must say that I am surprised once again. You were hoping that there was only one copy, were you not? It looks like I will have to delay your permanent departure for some additional minutes."

Nezraut stepped off the platform and walked over to one of the cavern walls. He stopped, turned back to Harvey, and said, "Let me show you how many more. And Sköll, let go of the puppy for now. I will let you finish the job soon enough."

Sköll's delayed gratification caused him to emit a low growl. He let go of Fromp's throat, leaving the wounded warp-hound gasping for breath.

Harvey followed Nezraut. As they approached the side of the cavern, he noticed that there was a large iron door in the wall, previously hidden by the shadows of the fiery torches. Nezraut placed the long nails of his right hand into the lock of the door and twisted it a quarter turn. He swung the door wide, motioning for Harvey to enter.

He cautiously entered and found himself standing on the top flight of a long stairway carved into solid rock. A massive room opened up before him, so large in fact, that he was unable to see the other end. Parallel to one another, were rows and rows of bookshelves, rising forty or more feet in height. Every space on the shelves appeared to be filled with the same book.

Harvey descended the stairs and walked over to one of the shelves as if in a hypnotic trance. He knew what he would see when he opened any of the thousands of books before him, but felt that he still needed to see it with his own eyes. Slowly swinging back the cover of the first book he picked up, he read the same words as he had on the pages of the book from the podium.

Nezraut drifted up behind him and said, "Quite a collection is it not? It is true that most private libraries are collections of varied books, not duplications of the same as you will find in mine, but I doubt that any library in the world contains more books."

"How many are there?" asked Harvey, stunned and staggering in disbelief.

"I do not know the precise number, but it must be well into the hundreds of millions. And now it becomes clear does it not?"

"What becomes clear?"

"That you cannot stop me. Even if you were able to destroy the book on the podium and somehow escape, I would merely retrieve another copy from my vast store and resume my reading of the deceptions over mankind. If I let you stay in here night and day, and you did nothing but burn copies of the book, new ones would continually appear as mankind increasingly embraces and declares the lie.

"You see, Harvey, failure is the end of every scenario you can come up with to try and stop me. The only way to turn things around would be to turn vast numbers of people back to the thoughts of the Unseen, and my young friend, it is much too late for that," Nezraut concluded with a self-satisfied chuckle.

From the beginning, Harvey understood the daunting task before him, but there had always been hope, no matter how small. Now, however, it was as if the legs of hope had been kicked out from under him, bringing down any notion of halting Nezraut and saving Ecclon from going dark.

The deflating reality of the situation gasped its last breath when Sköll, who had once again latched onto Fromp and was dragging him by his throat, entered the library, followed by the pack of Volkin Wolves. Thousands of erratically flying Insips loudly flapped their wings, spreading out in the spacious room.

Within minutes, Harvey was again surrounded by green luminescent, hungry eyes. Above his head, a cloud of swirling Insips hovered.

"I know the wheels are spinning in your head, trying to figure a way out. The sad reality is that there is none. Even if a heavily armed human army were to rush in upon us, what would they see? Without the benefit of that Ecclonian fruit punch opening their eyes and ears, they would not be able to see the truth behind the curtain. They would merely happen upon a boy and his dog, dead in the middle of a large cavern filled with strange looking wolves. No Insips, Vapid, or books to be seen."

Nezraut was right. The wheels in his head were frantically spinning, searching for a plan of escape.

Nezraut interrupted his thoughts. "I must congratulate you, though, on making it this far and showing such fortitude. Most creatures that have ever had the misfortune of meeting me face to face have immediately collapsed in sheer panic. But you, a young man practically still wet behind his ears, faced me with courage. Perhaps it was more foolishness than anything, but nonetheless, still very impressive. Do you have any last words you would like to say?"

Harvey's mouth had gone so dry and his breath so shallow, that even if he had something to say, he wouldn't have been able to do so.

"Well, if that is the case, Harvey, it appears that our conversation has come to an end, and it is time for me to get on with more pressing issues. I have an invasion force to lead against Ecclon, which is both figuratively and literally, in the twilight of her existence."

Nezraut smiled at himself in the cleverness of his last remark.

"Harvey, I will bid you farewell with a question, though I doubt you will be able to answer it. Before, you told me that you were not afraid because the Unseen had given you strength when you felt weak and afraid. Where is the strength and fearlessness now, my friend?"

Harvey recalled what he had said only moments ago about his fear dissipating and being replaced by the Unseen's presence. If ever he needed an infusion of his presence, it was now. He thought a thought of desperation and flared it up to the Unseen.

The Volkin Wolves, with lowered backs and bristling fur, moved closer, while Sköll's grip on Fromp's throat tightened.

The Unseen responded. A thought flickered and glowed bright. In his mind's eye, Harvey saw Bellock speaking to him back on Ecclon, explaining the power of human thought.

"Think about it, Harvey, before any human paints, sculpts, composes, or builds, doesn't he or she first think of what is about to be created? Is the Unseen any different? Did He not first imagine all that He was about to create in His mind? And when

He was ready to bring them to life, what did He do? He expressed His thoughts in words. He created an entire world in a completely separate dimension. His thinking, expressed in spoken words, powerfully affected and altered life in another world. And if humans were created in His image, then is it not reasonable to conclude that humans might also have a similar impact with their thoughts?"

The image disappeared. "Thoughts altering reality," he whispered to himself. With no time to waste, he created a thought and fired it off to the two dozen Volkin Wolves close to Sköll.

Suddenly, the hatred and viciousness of the wolves, which had been directed at Harvey, turned and honed in on Sköll. The wolves collectively believed for some inexplicable reason that their leader was on the verge of attacking them. They made a preemptive strike. Seconds later, the shredded and bloody remains of Sköll were scattered on the floor. Fromp was dropped during the attack. He was badly wounded and unconscious, but miraculously, still alive.

Harvey formed another image in his mind. An enormous concussive wave, like that created by an exploding bomb, flashed out around him, knocking down everything in the library. He intensified the magnitude of this image as much as possible, and when it felt like his head would explode if he held the image any longer in his mind, he released it.

A deafening sucking sound filled the library. Harvey could feel energy being compressed all around him. It seemed that the entire atmosphere was being squeezed together in a thin space surrounding his body, and he feared that if it continued, he might soon hear the cracking of his own bones. The sound and sense of compressing air suddenly stopped, and for a brief moment there was nothing but silence.

An explosion of destructive energy shot out from Harvey. Volkin Wolves were picked up tossed like toys into the walls and bookshelves, wounding or killing them instantly.

The explosive power blasted Nezraut's face, shattering his serrated teeth. He screamed in a tone that he had only heard in his victims. Covering his mouths with each of his hands, he crumbled down to the ground and lay unconscious in a pool of Sköll's blood.

The concussion waves flipped bookshelves over and jettisoned them into the walls. The pages of the books were shredded into confetti- sized pieces of paper. The hovering Insips were knocked into the ceiling before falling back to the floor, where they hit it with the sound of smashing melons.

Within minutes, the only thing moving in the cavern were the tiny pieces of paper floating throughout the room. It looked like snow, serenely falling on a beautiful winter day.

Harvey hurried over to Fromp. He cradled the still unconscious hound in his arms and easily picked him up. The increased strength in his body from the Kreen was still present. A deep whine, intertwined with bubbling blood, dripped out of his mouth. Fromp was seriously hurt. The only way to save him was to somehow get him back to Ecclon, and soon.

A familiar voice echoed in the large cavern outside the library.

"Harvey, Harvey, are you in here? Harvey, can you hear me?"

It was Sheef. Sheef had made it back. Harvey, carrying Fromp in his arms, navigated his way around mounds of unconscious or dead Volkin Wolves. He burst out of the library and into Sheef, who was on the verge of walking through the doorway.

"Sheef!" Harvey screamed.

"Harvey, you're alive!"

Harvey set Fromp down on the ground and embraced Sheef, saturating his shirt with tears.

"Sheef, you have no idea how glad I am to see you."

"I'm just as glad to see you in one piece," Sheef said with the grin that Harvey had come to love so much.

"What happened here? Where's Nezraut and the book?"

"There's no time to explain. We have to get Fromp back to Ecclon. I don't think he can hang on much longer."

Sheef reached out and stroked his matted fur.

"I assumed that if you were alive, you probably need to warp out of here in a hurry. That's why I brought the girls."

Harvey looked behind Sheef at two beautiful silver warp-hounds.

"Let me introduce you to Joust and Jules. Joust got us here and Jules will get us out."

Sheef sent the thought to Jules, and soon she had opened a warp hole back to Ecclon. Harvey helped Sheef get Fromp into his arms.

"Here, take him and go. There's something I need to get."

"Well, whatever it is, get it quickly, this warp hole won't stay open for very long.

The weight of Fromp almost dropped Sheef to his knees. Unlike Harvey, his muscles were not imbued with Kreen nectar. Sheef recovered with a grimace, standing upright with the unconscious warp-hound in his arms. With Joust taking the lead, he stepped through.

Harvey ran over to the podium and picked up the book. He turned around and bolted for the warp hole. Seconds after he jumped through, it closed.

33

Sheef had Jules open a warp hole to Council Gorge. When he left Harvey on the ledge and warped back to Ecclon earlier that morning, he had informed Bellock and the Flurn leaders gathered at Council Gorge of the massive army marshalling for an invasion of Ecclon.

As soon as Harvey stepped out of the warp hole and onto the raised platform at Council Gorge, he frantically asked about Fromp.

"Relax, Harvey," Bellock consoled, pointing to a group of Flurns surrounding Fromp. "He is already being attended to. His injuries were substantial, and it will be quite some time before he is able to open a warp hole, but he is going to be just fine."

"Now, Harvey, tell us what happened? Did you destroy the book?"

"Not one book, but millions, but it makes little difference, more are being written as we speak. I think I bought us a little time to prepare for the invasion, but I don't know if there's any way to keep the orb clouds from going dark."

Harvey handed Bellock the book he had taken from the podium. Like Harvey had done, Bellock read the first page and then flipped through the rest of the book. He then passed the book to the other Flurn leaders.

"It makes perfect sense," said Bellock. "I do not know why I did not see it before. The one foundational lie that undergirds all others. It is a weed that has taken over human thinking, and it is now up to us to determine how to uproot it. Harvey, tell us every detail of what happened."

Harvey shared everything that occurred from the moment he and Fromp warped from the ledge to his return warp to Ecclon. Sheef was the first to speak after Harvey finished his narrative.

"You did what?"

"It's like I said. I sent the thought to the wolves to attack Sköll and then imaged an explosion."

"But the explosion thought...You didn't send it to another mind?"

"No, I just concentrated, trying to strengthen the image in my mind until I felt like I had to release it before my head exploded."

"Well, something certainly exploded, but I still can't believe how your thoughts were able to manipulate physical space."

"I don't get it either," said Harvey. "Maybe it was all the Kreen still in my system."

"I am confident Kreen was a factor," said Bellock, "but I also believe that the Unseen made no mistake when He chose you. He is with you in a unique way and has revealed the true power of human thought to you."

Just then, a warp-hound bounded up the stairs and bolted across the platform to a stout Flurn standing by Bellock. It was

Merum. The warp-hound dropped a cylindrical canister from his mouth. Merum retrieved it and examined its contents. Inside was a tightly rolled piece of yellowed paper. He quickly read the message inscribed upon it.

"Bellock, it is from the Flurn Watches on the borders of the Shellow Plains. They are reporting numerous sightings of large hound-like animals."

"Volkin Wolves," Harvey said.

Bellock responded, "They must be scouts, probing and doing reconnaissance for the coming invasion. Nezraut will quickly recover, and based on the numbers of dark Flurn and Volkin Wolves Sheef said were gathering on the canyon floor, he will still be able to field a very impressive invasion force, despite the number of wolves Harvey wounded or killed."

"Bellock," interjected Salix, "you know that there is only one option left. Now that we are aware of the invasion, we have time to prepare our own army, and we stand a reasonable chance of withstanding Nezraut's onslaught. Even if we do, however, the light of the orb clouds will soon be extinguished. We might win the battle, but we will lose the war. There remains only one way to save Ecclon. Harvey must go back."

"And what good would that do?" asked an exasperated Merum. "Harvey said new books are being created by the minute. Going back would be futile."

"I agree. That is why he must go further back."

"Bellock, what does he mean?" asked Sheef.

"He means that Harvey must not only go back to Earth, but to an earlier time."

"Back in time?"

"Salix is correct, Sheef. It is the only way. He must go back to the tipping point, when human thought, for whatever reason, began its departure from the thoughts of the Unseen."

"But how in the world will he know where or when to go?"

"I do not know, but there is one who might. Gnarl the Deep."

"Gnarl the Deep?" questioned Merum. "He's been dead for decades."

"Petrified, not dead, Merum," said Bellock calmly.

"Dead or petrified, what difference does it make when he is no longer alive?"

"He may no longer be alive, but his writings still are, and they should tell us when in Earth's time Harvey needs to go."

Bellock walked over to Harvey and placed one of his rootlet hands on his shoulder.

"Harvey," Bellock began, "I know we have asked much of you thus far, but you are the one who has been chosen for such a time as this. He has selected you, and if you do not go, there is no one else."

Harvey looked up into the empathetic eyes of the one whom he had begun this strange journey with and said, "Who am I to argue with the plans of the Unseen?"

Stepping deeper into his destiny, Harvey walked over to stand by Sheef and asked, "So when do we warp?"

ABOUT THE AUTHOR

R Duncan Williams has been in the education field for over twenty years as a speaker, trainer, and teacher. Along the way, he has crafted numerous stories for use in and out of the classroom. Williams currently resides in Austin, Texas, with his wife, two sons, a dog who thinks she's a human, and a cat who thinks he's a dog.

To learn more about R Duncan Williams, visit his website at www.rduncanwilliams.com